Sessha E

STRENGTH
OF
WILL

STRENGTH OF WILL

Copyright ©2013 by Sessha Batto

Print ISBN: 978-1482621198
Digital ISBN: 978-1-301705061

Cover by Sessha Batto

This is a work of fiction. Names, characters, places and incidents either are the product of the authors' imaginations or are used fictitiously and any resemblance to actual persons, living or dead, business establishments, events or locales is entirely coincidental.

All rights reserved. No part of this book may be used or reproduced or transmitted in any form or by any means, electronic or mechanical, including photocopying, recording, or by any information storage and retrieval system, without written permission from the copyright owner except in the case of brief quotations embodied in critical articles and reviews.

First electronic publication: February 2013
First print publication: February 2013

Published in the United States of America with international distribution.

DEDICATION

This book has been a long journey. Longer even than most, as this is its second publication. Along the way it has flitted from location to location, Japan, Scotland, Egypt and finally Italy in its original printing. Now it has come full circle, back to its origin in Japan. I have traveled along with it, from comfort, to adventure, confusion, discomfort and back to the safety of home. Along the perilous journey my family supported me unwaveringly, my first reader, Anzia, never lost faith in the story and my wise and talented editor Diane reminded me of its value. It is to them, my fellow wanderers on this convoluted path, that I dedicate this tale.

Prologue

The young man wandered deeper into the oldest part of the city, winding down narrow streets as he gradually worked his way toward the center of the maze. He lingered at times, stopping to sip from his water bottle and sketch whatever caught his eye. He'd been traveling aimlessly for well over an hour before realizing he had no idea where he was. *Guess I should figure out how to ask for directions.* He dialed up the appropriate section in the Japanese lessons currently residing on his mp3 player.

"Hosuteru no nixyuushu houhou ha?" he muttered over and over. *How do I get to the hostel.* "Eigo wo hanashi masu ka?" he continued hopefully. *Do you speak English? That's the one I really need.*

His attention was diverted, yet again, by a steep set of stairs tempting him to climb with a glimpse of the scarlet tori gate at the peak. When he finally passed underneath, a broad smile sketched across his face at the sight of the ancient shrine and the ornate statue at its heart. *So beautiful*, he thought, immediately reaching for his notebook to capture the image.

He slowly moved around the statue, carefully drawing various detailed views, before finally kneeling in front of the plaque at its base, squinting as he tried to make out the carving. Eventually inspiration struck, and he pulled out a piece of paper, laying it over the fading marks and rubbing with a stick of charcoal until the text could be clearly read. *Not that I understand what it means.*

Just then he was jerked from his perusal when something impacted his left side, knocking him to the ground and slamming the air from his lungs. "Watashi ha moushiwake naku omotte, watashi wo yurushi nasai," a smooth voice murmured, and he looked up into a pair of worried eyes.

"Eigo wo hanashi masu ka?" The hopeful look on the foreigner's face suddenly made sense.

"Hai … I mean, yes. Are you alright? I didn't see you there. What were you doing anyway?"

"I was trying to read this," came the mournful reply. "But it's in kanji."

"Oh, you're interested in our shrine. Are you an archeologist then, or a professor of history?"

"Oh no, nothing like that. I'm just an art student." Impenetrable dark eyes sharpened, studying him intently.

"Oh, I'm so sorry. I thought you were a lot older. It's your hair," the dark-eyed man finally stammered.

"I know. It's always been this color." The artist fingered his steely locks. "My name's Arthur, by the way, Arthur Farris."

"Yamada Shinosuke, but you can call me Shin. So, would you like me to tell you the story behind this monument?"

"Please," Arthur entreated. "It's so beautiful."

"It's supposedly a likeness of Fujiwara Aoshi, the first warlord to unite the warring daimyos," Shin began in a lilting voice. "It is said he was assassinated because of his humanitarian policies. As a result, slavery was abolished for a time." He carefully looked his audience up and down before continuing. "They say he did it because he fell in love with a slave. That's what this line says, *kare ha kare no saiai no hoka no gawa ni ari masu.* May he find his beloved on the other side." He warmed to the story, and his audience, and smiled. "Would you like to hear more?"

Chapter One

Ryuu watched his young charges fondly. In the five years he had been with this house he had seen two of the master's sons settled, one in the daimyo's court, another taking the robes at a Buddhist temple. Now, the third and final son was preparing to follow his older brother to court. Although the girls had studied along with their brothers, there were no plans for their future education. The family's need for a sensei ended today.

The young man pondered where he would end up after this. He had almost forgotten what he really was. The respect accorded to him as a sensei wouldn't extend beyond the compound walls. He sighed, realizing that tomorrow he would find himself back in the marketplace, waiting to be sold into a new home. He thanked the gods for his education, being able to read and write kept his price high. People were less likely to abuse an expensive piece of merchandise.

He stared blindly out the window, eyes resting on nothing while his mind wandered. The house was perched on the side of a mountain, and from here he could see the whole town spread out below. It was one of the things he was going to miss, vicariously experiencing so much activity.

The market under his window was a marvel. Traders from all over Japan made the journey here to barter their wares. Fine silks and porcelain rubbed elbows with food vendors and weapons dealers. Shinto and Buddhist shrines were scattered amongst food stalls and kimono makers in a chaotic jumble that stretched right up to the gates of the pleasure quarter.

Ryuu's eyes followed a young maiko as she picked her way through the crowd, until she finally crossed the bridge into the willow world and disappeared from his sight. With a heavy heart he tore himself away from the spectacle to prepare for what was to come.

He began to carefully pack his few belongings, neatly folding several worn but clean changes of clothes, adding a few scrolls his previous master had gifted him with and finishing with his most precious possession, a small painting of his mother.

Ryuu's mind wandered back to happier times, when he had been the favored son of a proud samurai family. All that had changed when his parents died in an earthquake. His new guardians were distant relatives, all too happy to take him in, or so it seemed. Once transferred to their care, however, he found they were actually all too happy to steal his inheritance and sell him into slavery.

He shuddered when he thought of it. The first days, especially, were a nightmare he preferred not to dwell on. The auctions were still frightening, even after all these years, but the terror he had felt at being torn from his life and dragged naked onto the stage to be eyed and poked by rough-fingered strangers still made his heart race.

As much as he hated it, he forced himself to examine the most painful memories, hoping to bolster himself for the ordeal to come. The noise was the thing that came back first. It had been deafening. He'd cowered in the corner, covering his ears and trying to avoid the press of unwashed bodies. *It's just a dream*, he kept telling himself, right up to the moment when a strong arm yanked him up in the air and carried him, kicking and flailing, onto the stage.

He had tried to cover himself with his hands but they were jerked up over his head, leaving him exposed to the eyes and hands of potential buyers. His muscles were felt, his mouth pried open and teeth counted, even his eyes examined, as if he were a prime piece of horseflesh rather than a human child.

The next part always replayed itself in slow motion. The man mounting the stage was, at first glance, not markedly different from those who had passed before him. His hair was pulled back into a low tail and his soft eyes and mild expression made him appear less daunting than the men who had gone before.

Ryuu winced as the memory continued, this was the part he hated himself for. Thinking this man seemed the best of a bad lot he stopped his struggling, hoping to show his desire to be chosen. *I asked for it, I asked for it all.* He remembered how shocked he had been when the man examined not his teeth or his eyes, but his genitals. He had frozen in shock when his penis was handled and his balls rolled, but what almost made him die from embarrassment was the finger that probed his ass, scraping roughly over his tender pucker.

When the bidding had started Ryuu wished he hadn't encouraged the groper, as he enthusiastically topped every offering. Then he found himself being led away by his new owner, his mind conjuring ever more horrible visions of what was to come.

Thank kami I hadn't the imagination to anticipate what was actually in store for me. Ryuu remembered his childish terrors, thoughts of beatings, hard labor and hunger the worst his boyhood mind could conjure.

Ten year old Ryuu's new master specialized in acquiring young, pretty boys and training them in the ways of sexual pleasure. Once they reached the age of twelve they were castrated to maintain their appearance and sold as pleasure slaves.

A tremor ran through his slender frame as the sensei remembered his first 'lesson'. As soon as they reached his master's home his clothes were roughly stripped from him. Large hands stroked and rubbed him wantonly, fueled by his weak struggles to free himself. Finally he was pushed to his knees, finding himself face to face with the master's erection. "Suck," he was told as the rigid length pushed against his lips. He had reluctantly opened his mouth when his nostrils were pinched shut. As soon as he did, it was filled.

Ryuu grimaced as he remembered his first taste of another man. *I may have gotten better at it,* he wryly concluded. *But I never learned to like it.* He did, however, become very adept at giving pleasure with his mouth and his hands. He and the other boys serviced the master and his guests in this way. The boys also learned to prepare themselves for sex, tonguing and fingering each other under master's watchful eye. The worst, however, was the stretching. Each night before going to sleep they lined up in front of their master, bending over so he could insert a carved ivory penis which they were to wear during the night. The size of these was gradually increased until even the smallest boy was able to endure penetration by the most well-endowed of men.

Actual penetration, thankfully, was the only forbidden act. The boys' value was highest if they were virgins at the time of purchase. Ryuu unconsciously traced the scar cutting across his face, the scar that had saved him. Two weeks before his twelfth birthday was Takeshi's. When the master came to take him for surgery the boy fought back. In the struggle Ryuu's face had been slashed, rendering him imperfect, and therefore unfit for his master's clientele.

So the almost twelve year old found himself back in the marketplace, drifting behind his master as he made the rounds, visiting buyers who supplied the brothels of the willow world, hoping to recoup his investment.

Listlessly waiting while his master talked, Ryuu overheard a man looking for slaves who could read and write. Hearing the jeering response of the trader he had taken a risk and spoke up, "I can read and write."

"Prove it."

Ryuu easily read the page put in front of him, gracefully mixing the ink and neatly writing out a reply. The next thing he knew he was leaving with his new master.

The old man had been kind, and Ryuu's duties as his scribe were not overly demanding. Under the guise of training him to do his job this new master continued his neglected education. When the master died, after eight years in his service, he had been sold into this house as a sensei. Ryuu had enjoyed the five years he'd spent there, living more as a family member than a slave, thriving under the freedom and intellectual stimulation. The children were like the siblings he never had, and he was sad to be leaving.

The next day dawned crisp and bright. Ryuu presented himself to the master of the house for the trip to the marketplace. The master thanked him for his service and sent him off with his retainer, giving instructions for the slave's sale.

Back again. Ryuu wished without hope for a day when he would be free from this humiliation. *Of course, it could be worse.* He glanced over at the pleasure slaves with a shudder before finding a place with a group of scribes. He composed himself and sat gracefully, purposefully refusing to engage in the conversations swirling around him, trying to set himself apart as a serious and sober man, one who could be trusted with the education of a family's treasured children.

He watched as people scurried out of the way of an oncoming group, samurai roughly clearing the way for the man who came behind. Ryuu found himself looking straight into the eyes of the one responsible for all the commotion. *He's very tall,* the teacher thought. *And that hair . . . I wonder how old he is?* The fascinating stranger, though tall and lean, was well muscled. His face was handsome—strong chin, defined cheekbones, and a long fall of raven hair streaked with white caught up in a high tail. When he turned Ryuu could clearly see a scar twisting its way from cheek to chin. He tried to imagine the battle that resulted in such a wound, eyes straying across the face to lock with eyes so dark and cold they appeared to have no iris at all. The effect of those eyes was paralyzing, he felt like a rabbit pinned under the gaze of a circling hawk.

* * *

Fujiwara Aoshi idly observed the group of slaves for sale as scribes. They were mostly older men with serious expressions who were passing the time debating each other in hopes of attracting buyers. *All in all an unimpressive lot*, he decided. *Still, anything is more interesting than that.* That being the group of pleasure slaves his men were currently examining.

The warlord was not a man who indulged in pleasure. He was a soldier, a formidable opponent who never wavered once he had set himself a goal. A man who, at the tender age of thirty, had built his reputation on the strength of his sword and his men's devotion.

His generals worried about his isolation. Believing they understood, he'd been pushed to purchase a pleasure slave. *What was I thinking when I agreed to this?* he chastised himself, imagining the groans of complaint after a day in the field. He studied the over-ripe odalisques and soft-skinned boys on display with disdain before turning again to the group of scholars.

This time, however, the crowd had shifted and his gaze locked with a slender young man sitting slightly apart. *Now he looks like a man who could handle the rigors of my lifestyle.* Aoshi's gaze roved over the bronze body before locking with sparkling chocolate eyes. *A scribe would be a useful thing to have. Besides, if he's educated he'll be more interesting to talk to.*

Decision made, the warlord merely pointed at the man he had been observing. "That one," he told his aide, turning to head back to camp.

"But, my lord," one of the generals protested. "He is a scribe, not a pleasure slave."

"A slave is a slave," the warlord replied. "He does his master's bidding, like it or not. I have made my choice. If you will excuse me, I have business to attend to. Leave the slave in my tent and I will deal with him when I have finished." With that he turned and strode away, his mind already drifting to more pressing matters.

Chapter Two

Ryuu found it hard to conceal his shock when the group of samurai began bargaining for him. What would warriors need with a teacher? He pushed his worries aside, he was grouped with the other educated slaves and his selling price was high. If they were purchasing him they must have need of his skills.

He gathered his possessions and joined the group, startled at the way they encircled him before heading out. After fifteen minutes he could stand it no longer. "Excuse me, but which one of you is my new master?"

The crowd of men laughed heartily, putting Ryuu off-balance. "I'm sorry," he tried again. "I was just concerned about my new duties. Am I to be used as a scribe or a sensei?"

One of the men took pity on him and answered his question. "What would one of us do with you? We could have gotten each of us a pleasure slave for the price we paid. You are the new toy of Fujiwara Aoshi," he concluded bluntly. "Though what he saw in you certainly escapes me."

Ryuu's breath froze in his lungs. *Pleasure slave,* his panicked mind echoed. He finally gathered a shaky breath. "There must be some mistake. I was supposed to be sold as a teacher or a scribe. They promised me."

"Promises are made to be broken." The samurai gave him a consoling pat on the back. "Besides, it could be worse. He's a jealous man. Not likely to share, if you know what I mean."

The young scribe paled even further at the thought of what 'sharing' could mean in a camp full of men. He was unable to contain the shiver that rippled through him at the next words, well intentioned though they were meant to be.

"I've fought alongside him since he was a child. He's a cold man, true, but loyal and fair. He rarely bothers with pleasure so he probably won't be too demanding, unless he tries to make up for lost time." The man continued to muse, not caring what effect his words might have. "Might be like a dam breaking."

Ryuu stopped, frozen by the memory of that predatory gaze from the market. *That's my new master, the warlord is my master.* He stumbled a bit in shock but quickly regained his composure and continued walking in silence, unwilling to let any of these men see just how disconcerted he was.

Before he knew it the group was entering an encampment on the outskirts of town. The warlord's aide startled Ryuu out of his thoughts. "He likes to stay with his men. Just wait here and make yourself comfortable. He'll be in when he finishes with the daily briefing." With that he parted the flaps on a large tent and ushered the sensei inside.

An oil lamp flared into life and Ryuu got his first look at what would be his home. A large worktable took up most of one side of the space. It was strewn with maps and scrolls, as well as some weapons and cleaning supplies. A battered shield leaned against one leg haphazardly, as if it had come to rest there after being tossed aside.

He shivered as he contemplated the armor on its display stand. The thought of the already intimidating warlord wrapped in it, fierce glare animating the grotesquely carved mask, scared him more than the vicious demons in the tales his mother told to keep him close to home.

On the other side were a couple of cushions and a large futon. A very large futon. Ryuu remembered just how tall the warlord had appeared across the marketplace. *He towered over those soldiers, and they towered over me.*

The sensei cast his eyes around the room, trying to formulate a plan to avoid being trapped under his new master. *At least for tonight. Let me ease into this if I have to do it.* He decided simplicity was best and discarded his clothes, freeing his hair and combing it to lie smoothly across his shoulders. Then he knelt by the door to wait.

* * *

Aoshi was tired, both in body and in mind. The strategy session had run much later than expected. News that his enemies were moving to the north and west had sparked heated debate on the best plan to oppose them. He grunted and flexed his shoulders, moving his head from side to side in hopes of working the kinks out. As he detoured to pick up his evening ration, the warlord stopped to talk with the men he passed, calling them by name and speaking easily about their families.

Genius of war he might be, however, it was not surprising that he had completely forgotten his impulsive decision to buy the young sensei. In truth, if he had remembered he would be chastising himself, desperately looking for a graceful way to get out of the situation.

Aoshi flung himself into his tent as usual. He kicked off his zori and dropped unceremoniously onto a cushion, reaching down to take off his tabi. He was shocked speechless when a soft voice said, "Let me get that for you, master."

The warlord looked down, and was met with the startling sight of a naked man unhooking his tabi and sliding them off. It was then he remembered his impulsive purchase. *What have I gotten myself into?*

Hoping to get his 'duties' over with as soon as possible, the scribe knelt between his new master's legs. He boldly unwrapped the intricate layers of fabric, fingers trembling only slightly as he removed Aoshi's fundoshi and placed a soft kiss on the head of his flaccid penis. Ryuu teased the length to full hardness, surprised that the taste was actually rather pleasant, not the cloying bitterness he remembered. *He's not as old as I thought, either*, the slave realized. *The white in his hair makes him look like an old man.* For the first time in his life the scribe wished he had paid more attention to the changing political climate. It would be nice if he knew more about this warlord.

Aoshi regained his voice when plump lips slid down his erection. He let out a long growling moan and threaded his hands in silky strands, urging the slave to pull back. Ryuu swirled his tongue under the rim before dipping it in the slit and sliding back down again. The scribe was on the verge of panic when the tip bumped the back of his throat, fighting memories of training he'd long tried to forget. He let out a small moan, and the vibrations caused the warlord to growl and urge the sensei to move still faster. Aoshi finally came with a startled shout, nearly drowning the slave with the strength of his ejaculation.

The warlord slumped in exhaustion, dazed in the aftermath of his orgasm, only vaguely noticing as the slave moved him to the bed and fetched a steaming basin of water. He groaned in pleasure as he was scrubbed and rinsed by deft hands before finding himself comfortably tucked in.

"Where do you wish me master?" Ryuu was pleased with his efforts to direct this first encounter. *Not bad at all*, he decided with a nod of his head. *I can do this.*

"Here," a deep silken voice replied. The sensei felt a shiver run through him, and realized this was the first time his new master had spoken in his presence. He gulped when the covers peeled back and a large hand patted the futon.

"What is your name?" his master continued. "I need to properly thank you for such a wonderful, though unexpected, welcome. I can see that our life together is going to be full of new experiences."

"My name is Ryuu, master, if you care to use it."

"What else would I use?"

"Whatever pleases you, master. I live to serve."

"What pleases me, Ryuu, is you here in this bed. Morning will come all too quickly and we can talk then." He reached out a long arm and snagged the sensei, pulling him clumsily into the bed and drawing the covers over them. The warlord murmured a soft "Good night," before drifting off to sleep, unable to keep his eyes open a moment longer.

Ryuu stayed awake for a long time, resting on his elbow and studying the face of the man who had made him what he had tried so hard to avoid. *Pleasure slave*, the words were bitter on his tongue. *Still, it wasn't so bad. I can do this. Besides it's not like I have a choice.*

Chapter Three

Tanaka Yuudai paced as the first rays of sunlight started to peek over the horizon. He had no idea what he should do. For as long as he could remember he had been roused, albeit unwillingly, well before dawn. The restless warlord was always eager to train before the seemingly unending stream of petty details that were the reality of his position demanded his full attention.

Over fifteen years, and he's never missed a single day. Should I wake him? The general shuddered at the thought of how this could end. *If I wake him and he doesn't want me to...* He gulped at the vision his brain supplied and hurried on to the next choice. *Okay, so I let him wake on his own. But then he's certain to miss something important.*

The heavily scarred man rubbed the back of his neck and tried to push down his rising panic. Today was not a good day to die, in his opinion. Just as he was debating the possible advantages of doing some long range reconnaissance he heard movement inside the tent. *Thank the gods,* he thought as he pulled the flap open and stepped inside. "Hey Ao..." He stopped dead, voice trailing off into a strangled squeak.

Oh gods, this is SO bad, was the only thought his brain could manage. The warlord Fujiwara was directly in front of him sprawled out on his futon, naked as the day he was born, strong arms holding an equally naked squirming body in his lap.

Shit, shit, shit, Yuudai's internal monologue continued. *I forgot about his new toy.*

"Morning, Tanaka," the familiar voice drawled before the general could organize his thoughts and flee. "What brings you here?"

"Um," the usually stoic man stuttered. "Uh, um, training?" His eyes flitted around the tent, pointedly not looking at the man he was speaking to. Yuudai had to admit his commander was attractive. And, while he'd never been excited by men, he found himself hardening at the picture the two made. *Great, just great.* He turned away and began thinking of every repulsive thing he could, desperate to quell his growing arousal before it was noticed. He had no idea how Aoshi would react, and he damn well didn't want to find out.

"—ing today." The warlord's voice broke through the fog that was his general's thoughts.

"Huh?" Yuudai responded, turning back to face his commander instinctively, thoughts derailed yet again when he realized the man had made no move to cover himself.

"I said, we'll have to skip training today. Ryuu and I were just getting ready to discuss his duties. Go grab some breakfast, I'll be along in a bit."

Yuudai, unfortunately, had once again zoned out at the mention of the slave's duties, his brain eagerly supplying him with a whole host of surprisingly erotic images. He gave a small whimper and fled as his arousal once again stirred to life.

"I wonder what his problem is?" Aoshi mused.

The sensei almost rolled his eyes. *Can he possibly be that naive? Certainly he must know how this looks.* "I believe he was embarrassed, master," Ryuu replied, still trying to free himself from the warlord's arms. "Unless it's usual for him to find you like this."

"No, I usually have to wake him for morning training." Aoshi continued pondering the general's behavior, still not seeing the reason for his sudden departure. He shook his head; it didn't matter in any event, he was just getting distracted. "Ah, yes, your duties. I must admit I hadn't really thought things through when I bought you. Some of my comrades were trying to convince me to get a pleasure slave, but they seemed like so much trouble. Then I saw you sitting with the scribes and you looked much more interesting."

Here the warlord stopped for a moment, grasping the slave's chin in his hand and gazing into his eyes, debating his next words. "I was thinking," he said with a rather distant look. "You could assist me with my correspondence. It is difficult for me. My education ended when my father fell in battle and I took his place. You will teach me what you know so that I will be able to lead men, not just soldiers."

"Certainly, master. It will be my pleasure to assist you in any way possible."

"About last night," Aoshi continued almost hesitantly. "Why did you..." He fumbled for words as he gestured towards his lap. "Not that it wasn't enjoyable. I've rarely bothered with such things and I was shocked by how much I liked it. But I never expected it from a scribe. Is it usual behavior among educated men?"

"I was told I was to be your new pleasure slave, master. I was merely trying to anticipate your desires and please you."

"Really." The warlord's voice was cold. "You think you know my mind, slave?"

"No ... no, master," the sensei stuttered. "I-I..." He was struck dumb by fear, trying to figure out the correct answer to avoid punishment and panicking at how quickly the atmosphere in the tent had turned deadly.

Ryuu opened his mouth to say something, anything, but all that came out was a strangled squeak as his fear overwhelmed him and the dam broke. "I'm not a pleasure slave, I'm not. I've worked so hard to avoid it, and they promised I would be sold as a scribe or a sensei. When he said I was to be your toy I tried to think of the easiest way out, before you had a chance to make me do something worse." He tried to stifle a sob, a few tears trailing down his cheeks.

He nearly jumped out of his skin when that strong hand grasped his chin again, forcing his head up to meet Aoshi's gaze. A shudder ran down his spine at the unreadable look in those sharply focused eyes. "You manipulated me, didn't you, Ryuu?" The deep voice practically sparkled with mirth and moments later the imposing warlord doubled over in laughter, frightening the slave still trapped on his lap even further.

"You have spirit. I like that. I also liked what we did last night. I'd like to do it again, but I will not force you. Now," he said as he rose and set the sensei on his feet, "it is far past time to begin the day. Dress and we will get something to eat." The warlord turned and began pulling on his clothes. "By the way, who was it that called you my toy?"

"I do not know his name, it was one of the men that purchased me. He was tall. You're all very tall," Ryuu muttered.

"Anything else?" Aoshi asked, thoroughly enjoying the play of emotions on the slave's face.

"He was bald, and he had a scar here." The sensei traced a

crooked path down the side of his face.

"Aaaa," was the enigmatic response.

The slave turned to see his master fully dressed and ready for the day, his expression unreadable. "Come, Ryuu." Aoshi threw the flap open and strode out of the tent, the slave scrambling to keep up.

As they passed through the compound, Ryuu was impressed to see the deference shown to his master, and pleased to see that he knew his men and greeted them familiarly. He was looking forward to instructing this man. At the same time he had a running monologue going in his head, chastising himself for his actions the night before. *He never even thought of it*, he berated himself. *What kind of idiot makes someone think about the one thing they're trying to avoid?*

Ryuu was so engrossed he missed the pointed looks directed at him. When they reached the mess, however, the looks turned to yells and catcalls, which were impossible to ignore.

"Hey, Fujiwara-sama," one of the men called. "Have a good night?"

"It was surprisingly pleasant," was the dry reply.

"Aw, come on, give us details. Is his ass still nice and tight?" another man called out, making those sitting at his table laugh.

The laughter stopped abruptly when a large hand grabbed the speaker by the throat and lifted him to hang in the warlord's grasp, those unreadable eyes sparking with anger. "Mine." Aoshi's voice was icy. "My property, my business. Understood?" Then the hand retracted, leaving the soldier to tumble to the floor, coughing and gasping.

"Do you all understand?" he continued, casting his hawk-like gaze around the room.

Finally, a timid "Hai," rang out from the back. At that the warlord turned on his heel and left the tent, all thoughts of breakfast forgotten, Ryuu hurrying to keep up with his long strides.

Chapter Four

As the days passed they fell into a routine. They would rise early and Aoshi would train while Ryuu organized his correspondence and prepared for the day. On his way back from training the warlord would stop for breakfast and draw the sensei's ration before heading to his tent. They would spend the next hour conversing about politics, geography, religion, philosophy, any subject the commander thought would help him rule both wisely and fairly. Surprisingly, for someone who had made their fortune at the game of war, he longed for a time of peace and prosperity. He had enough blood on his hands.

While the warlord was off reviewing the troops and commanding engagements in the field, the sensei confined himself to the tent. Many of the men eyed him like a piece of meat. While his owner would be free to seek whatever retribution he wished, or none at all, should someone molest him, Ryuu would not be able to fight back. Resistance from a slave could be instantly punished by death with no real repercussions, other than, perhaps, reimbursement to the owner for the price he had paid.

Their evenings were spent in conversation, Ryuu helping his master with any paperwork he needed to complete. At night they slept together in the warlord's remarkably comfortable bed. Aoshi kept his word and had not even mentioned more intimate activities.

This night had, so far, followed the same pattern. Just before snuffing out the lamp the warlord propped himself up on one elbow, eyes intently studying the man next to him. "Ryuu, I'm leaving in the morning for the northern outpost. I'll be gone for about a week. Will you be alright here?"

"Of course, master. Is there something you wish from me in your absence?"

"Just try and keep up with the blasted paperwork." He hesitated before continuing. "I'll miss you. It's been too long since I've had a companion." Aoshi quickly extinguished the flame and flopped down on his back, glad the dark hid the heat he could feel in his cheeks.

Ryuu felt his heart swell at being referred to as the companion of this remarkable man. Forgetting his status he leaned over and placed a soft kiss on the twisted scar below the warlord's eye. Aoshi instantly grew rigid, hands clenching into fists at his sides.

"Master, did I do something wrong?"

"It makes me feel funny," was the rather bemused reply. "I don't think anyone's kissed me since my mother died. I was four, I think. You surprised me. You do that a lot."

"It was the nicest thing anyone's said to me since I became a slave. I wanted to thank you for making me feel normal." Ryuu paused, considering his options. The warlord had stayed true to his word and hadn't initiated any physical contact. At the same time the scribe knew Aoshi had enjoyed their intimacy the first night. He weighed his options and made a quick decision.

Ryuu slid under the covers, nipping and licking his way down defined abs, stopping to thrust his tongue into the naval as he passed, before continuing down to Aoshi's burgeoning erection. He nibbled the thick vein before taking just the head into his mouth, running his tongue around the rim and flicking the slit, making the normally controlled samurai let out a long groan. "Gods, Ryuu," he muttered huskily before arching further into the inviting heat. The scribe relaxed his throat, engulfing the rigid length to the base.

He slid up to the tip, twisting his tongue as he withdrew. As he slid back down he began to hum and the warlord's control broke. He fisted his hands in the sensei's hair to hold him in place and began to thrust his hips, moaning and growling as the sensations overwhelmed him. It wasn't long before his thrusts became erratic and he came with a roar, pumping his seed down his slave's throat.

Ryuu emerged from under the covers, licking his lips. He stopped, totally captivated by the blissful expression visible on the usually closed face and the hazy lust glowing in often cold eyes.

"Can I…" The warlord hesitated. "Can I do that to you?"

The sensei's mouth almost dropped open in shock. "You don't need to worry about me, master. I'm your slave. A slave's pleasure is of no importance."

"You are my companion, Ryuu," Aoshi replied. "I thought I made it clear that any intimacy was outside of your duties." He stopped for a moment, considering. "Has anyone ever done that for you?"

"Of course not, I'm a slave," he snapped, thinking back to his days with his first master. Ryuu was certain his pleasure had never been considered, or he wouldn't have been there in the first place.

"Well then, it's high time you experienced it." Aoshi knelt over the sensei, bending to tentatively touch the tip of his tongue to one of the pearly drops now steadily collecting at the tip of his erection. The warlord cocked his head, seeming to consider the taste before swooping back in for another lick, eagerly running his tongue around the head and dipping into the slit.

"You taste good," he concluded before he took the head into his mouth. He tried to emulate Ryuu's smooth slide, but almost choked when the scribe's cock hit the back of his throat. He pulled back, sputtering, and the slave attempted to stop him.

"It's alright, master, really." He pulled on the broad shoulders, trying to maneuver the warlord to lie down. Instead, he was shaken off and pressed flat by muscular arms.

"No, it's not," was the curt reply before his erection was once again swallowed. This time Aoshi knew what to expect and made sure not to go too fast. Slowly he slid until his nose was nestled in raven curls. He breathed deeply, liking the musky, comfortable scent.

He retreated just as slowly, feeling immensely powerful when the sensei arched into his mouth and moaned. He gradually sped up the pace as he became more comfortable, until he was bobbing up and down, and Ryuu scrabbled for something to hold on to.

With a loud wail the scribe thrust up into that heavenly wet heat and came. When Ryuu opened his eyes he was being watched intently, bottomless eyes searching his face for signs of displeasure. "How was it?"

The dazed slave wet his lips and tried to express just how wonderful it was. "Amazing," was the single word he managed to form.

"Alright then, sleep." The warlord gathered the spent figure into his arms and arranged them comfortably, tentatively carding his fingers through smooth locks as the sensei drifted off to sleep before succumbing himself, hand still tangled in Ryuu's hair.

Chapter Five

I don't care how late it is, Yuudai decided as he paced outside the warlord's tent. *There is no way I'm walking in on them again. But, if we don't get going soon we won't make it before dark.* He continued to fret, pacing back and forth, not even noticing when the warlord stepped from the tent and stopped behind him.

"Ready?" Aoshi startled the general out of his thoughts.

"Hmm ... oh, sure. Where's your slave?" He peered around the warlord in search of Ryuu. "He needs to hurry up or we'll be late."

"Ryuu's not coming. The border's dangerous and he's no fighter. Besides," Aoshi continued as he bent to adjust his sandal, "he's still asleep." A self-satisfied smirk etched across his face as he muttered half to himself. "He liked the way I sucked his cock." His grin faded as he pondered his last statement. *He didn't actually say that, but he said it was amazing. Is that always good?* Aoshi cocked his head to the side, contemplating his next words. "Hey, Yuudai, can I ask you something?"

The general vaguely wondered what he had done to deserve this torment. His mind was stuck on an image of his commander, his friend, devouring his pretty slave's cock, and damn if it wasn't turning him on. He squirmed uncomfortably, hoping to hide his growing arousal from the warlord's too sharp gaze.

"Hmm," he grunted, startled out of his thoughts by Aoshi's voice.

"Can I ask you something?" the warlord repeated. "I need some guidance. You're older and you've lived a more normal life than I have. You know things I don't."

Yuudai was sure he did not want to have this conversation. But he swallowed his reservations. If his commander needed his advice he would give it, to the best of his ability. "Of course, Aoshi. I'll always do my best to help you."

"Let's head out, we'll talk as we ride." The warlord swung himself onto his waiting mount, wheeling to face the general before they set off at a gallop, eager to regain some lost time.

A tall figure stood from the nearby bushes, still in shock at what he had overheard. The mighty warlord Fujiwara sucking the cock of a slave. He shook his head, despairing at the thought of such a man stooping so low, even as he pondered how to turn it to his advantage.

I think there's a slave who needs to learn his place. His grin twisted to a nasty smirk. *We need to make sure the overpriced whore never dares to corrupt the commander again.* Rubbing his hands together he slipped away to prepare.

* * *

Ryuu woke with a smile on his face. He turned to greet the man who'd made him feel that way, only to remember the warlord had gone to the outposts. He sighed, then shook his head. *Don't get too attached*, he reminded himself. *It's bad enough being sold without having your heart broken as well.* He wanted to believe Aoshi was different, but nothing in his life gave him any reason to believe it would be true. *Just enjoy it while you have it. It's already more than you ever dared hope for.*

With that thought buoying him, he quickly rose and dressed. He set off for the mess at a brisk pace, eager to draw his ration and get to work. Even though Ryuu had been in camp for weeks, this was the first time he'd been seen without his master. Hungry eyes followed his progress, some almost licking their lips at the thought of catching the slave alone.

When he entered the mess it grew strangely quiet. The scribe hurried to draw his ration, wanting to return to the safety of the warlord's tent as quickly as possible. He closed his ears to the jeers and catcalls; however, he couldn't help but jerk when his ass was roughly groped. "What's the matter pretty boy? Too high and mighty to associate with common soldiers?" a rough voice jeered as its owner leaned in to nip the sensei's ear.

"I'm afraid you are mistaken," Ryuu responded rather shakily. "I am the warlord's scribe, nothing more." Keeping his eyes on the ground he grabbed the rations being held out to him and fled the tent, deftly avoiding a few clutching hands.

As soon as he'd scurried outside, Ito Benjirou rose and cast a hard eye on the men around him. "That's not true. I heard the commander himself say that slave convinced him do things, disgusting things."

Immediately a babble of excited voices rose, drowning each other out in their excitement. "You're kidding." "No way." "He would never." The words were different, but the sentiment was the same, the men were outraged at the thought of their commander submitting to anyone, especially a slave.

"So," Benjirou continued. "What are we going to do about it?"

"Teach him a lesson," they roared.

"Alright, this is the plan." Benjirou began to outline what he had in mind.

* * *

Ryuu was happy when he regained the safety of Aoshi's tent. He was sure no one would bother him there. Tomorrow he'd rise early and collect his ration before the men started to gather. He nodded to himself as he bustled about, making the bed and straightening the tent before moving to the worktable and beginning to draft responses to the correspondence they had reviewed the day before.

He didn't hear the tent flap being pulled back or the men creeping in behind him. He looked up, startled, when a gruff voice rang out. "I think you need to learn a few lessons, slave." The men ringing the tent called out in agreement.

Darting his eyes from side to side the scribe looked for a way to escape, but there were too many men, too close. He was sure to be caught, and once caught, punished. "I'm the warlord's personal slave, he won't be happy about this," he declared, hoping fear of Aoshi's wrath would deter them.

"I've been with him for years," was the amused reply. "Do you actually think he'd take a slave's word over mine?" The cruel laugh that followed killed Ryuu's last hopes. He slumped in defeat and sat very still. The frightened scribe desperately tried to clamp down on his urge to resist, hoping to survive this encounter.

The ringleader's large fist caught his ponytail and yanked, jerking the sensei from his cushion and onto the floor at his feet. "I hear you like to have your cock sucked. Time for you to return the favor." And with that his mouth was filled with Benjirou's erection.

The scribe quailed at the sour unwashed taste, forcing back the urge to vomit and trying to recall the pleasant taste of Aoshi. Suddenly the suffocating length withdrew and Ryuu gasped for oxygen, too weak to fight back when his head was roughly forced to the floor and pinned. Large calloused hands grasped his hips as the voice of his tormentor rang out. "Hold him down boys, you'll all get your turn."

Before he even had a chance to resist, his captor thrust into his unprepared entrance. The pain was bad enough, but even worse was the loss of something Ryuu had held dear, his virginity. He had hoped against hope that he would be able to make the choice to share himself this way. He knew it was foolish for a slave to care about such a thing, but most other choices had already been taken out of his hands.

The hands holding his arms pulled his upper body up and his mouth was filled with yet another hard cock, as Benjirou continued to pound into him from behind. With a final brutal thrust the bald man came with a triumphant roar, spitting on the limp slave before pulling out. "You sure are a shitty lay for being so expensive, but at least you're not a total waste," He turned to the waiting soldiers with a leer. "Who's next? Step right up and take your turn."

As one man finished another took his place, until Ryuu succumbed to the pain and lost consciousness. The men continued to pound into him until they had all been satisfied. When they were done they left the slave where he lay, crumpled on the floor in a puddle of blood and semen.

No one noticed when he failed to collect his ration the next morning, or the one after that. The men who knew what had happened certainly weren't going to bring it up, and since no one was used to seeing him around camp his absence went unnoticed. In fact, the sensei might well have laid where he was until Aoshi returned had a courier not stopped to pick up messages intended for the commander.

Suzuki Akemi had been a soldier for a long time. He thought he'd seen man's inhumanity on the battlefield, but the sight that met his eyes when he entered the warlord's tent was enough to bring even his cynical heart to tears.

At least he's still breathing. Akemi carefully rolled the slave onto his back, gently patting his face and trying to rouse him. When he got no response he scooped the limp body up in his arms and raced for the healer's tent, hoping that it wasn't already too late.

After leaving Ryuu with the healers, along with stern warnings about caring for the warlord's very valuable property, Akemi grabbed a fresh mount and headed back to the outpost to let Aoshi know what had happened. *Hopefully from horseback, across a field,* he plotted, not wanting to die at the man's hands for delivering bad news.

Chapter Six

Once they were a few miles outside of camp Aoshi pulled his horse up and slowed to a walk, the general reining in his mount to pace him. "So, Yuudai," the warlord began. "It's about Ryuu. Before him I never thought about sex. I mean, I grew up among soldiers and I heard the talk, but it never connected with me. Of course, I've visited the willow world, we all need the occasional release. But I certainly didn't want or need that on a regular basis. Everyone was urging me to get a pleasure slave, but I just didn't see the attraction. They all seemed so weak and soft and useless. So I bought a scribe. My education's not the best and he helps with the correspondence."

The warlord stopped for a moment and tugged at his hair in frustration. "That first night, I had forgotten I'd bought him. I came in and sat down, I didn't even have the energy to get undressed and, all of a sudden, there he was all soft and gentle. He rubbed my feet and then he sucked my cock and, kami, I had no idea anything could ever feel that good. But he only did it because he thought he had to."

"Well, he is a slave," the general pointed out. "It's not like he has much choice in anything."

"But it just didn't seem right like that. I told him he didn't have to unless he wanted to." Aoshi's face twisted into a frown. "So, until last night we didn't. But then he did it again, and it was so good. You have no idea." The general's face was practically glowing with embarrassment at this point and he wondered if he'd make it through this conversation without either having a stroke or coming in his pants.

"I wanted him to like it, to want to do it again. So I did it to him and I think he liked it, but I'm not sure. How do you know if you've pleased someone?" Aoshi suddenly appeared very young and ill at ease, definitely a new look for the stoic soldier.

"I don't know what to tell you. I mean, he's a slave. If it's what you want, just do it. Why does it matter?"

"I don't think of him that way, like an object. I can't. He's my companion and I like it when he's happy."

"Oh Aoshi, that's ... you can't ... if you want someone to be close to I'm sure there are lots of people who'd be interested." *Like me*, Yuudai thought, hit with the sudden realization and stopping dead, seriously considering his next words. "Like me. I mean, you're very attractive, very sexy. Hell, anyone would be better than a slave."

The warlord pointedly decided to nip the declaration of interest in the bud. "Yuudai, I like you, you're my right arm. I depend on your strength and your guidance, but I just can't see you like that. I've never been able to see anyone like that before Ryuu. What's wrong with him anyway? He's smart and he helps me. He likes me and I like him. I don't get it." Aoshi sighed, grasping his head in his hands as if to squeeze the offending thoughts out.

"He's a slave," the general said bluntly. "And as long as he's a slave, he isn't worthy of those feelings. If you honestly want him as a companion you have to set him free. Even then there aren't many who'll accept two men in a relationship. I mean sex is one thing, but what you're talking about, it's not natural."

"But what if I set him free and he leaves me? What would I do then?" The warlord worried his lower lip between his teeth. "Would you stay?"

The general wiped his brow with the back of his hand; this was definitely the most awkward conversation he'd ever had. "Yes, I would stay, but that doesn't mean he would. There's no way to predict these things. If you're serious you need to talk to him about it, see if you can figure out some answers to your questions. But in the end, no matter how you try to analyze it, it's a risk."

Aoshi frowned and the general could practically see the wall falling back down between the warlord and the rest of the world. He urged his horse to a gallop and headed toward the outpost, now anxious to complete his journey and return to camp.

Upon their arrival the warlord met with the outpost commanders, assessing the situation and laying out a strategy to overcome any incursions into their territory. Several hours later the general was convinced that, at least, Aoshi's madness didn't affect his tactical skills.

The warlord slept fitfully, partly because his mind kept turning his questions and Yuudai's answers over and over, examining them from every angle, and partly because he missed having the sensei's warm body in his bed. He snorted in disgust at how quickly he had become used to the pleasure of human contact.

The next day dawned raw and grey. Aoshi had risen even earlier than usual and trained in a frenzy, skipping breakfast to walk the camp, his face cold and stoic. Now he was impatiently waiting for the rest of his party to assemble so they could tour the border. The sooner they left, they sooner they'd return.

He stayed wrapped in his own thoughts for most of the day, only losing his haunted look when they stopped for the evening and began to prepare something to eat. Then he appeared to be his usual self, talking easily with the men as they lounged around the fire.

Aoshi relaxed for the first time all day. He had finally decided on a plan to convince Ryuu to stay with him, and once he was sure of the outcome he'd free the scribe and they could be companions. *That's what I want,* he told himself firmly. *And I always get what I want.* With a smile he joined in the banter as the embers crackled, at peace with the world for the moment.

They finally arrived back at the outpost late the next afternoon. All Aoshi and Yuudai wanted to do was bathe and sleep, and since there were no bathing facilities it narrowed down to sleep, neither man bothering to undress.

* * *

The warlord woke instantly and silently at the call of his name. "Commander, Commander, Fujiwara-sama, you need to wake up."

He sat up and blinked. "Ah, Akemi." He finally recognized the man next to his futon. "Just leave the dispatches and I'll look at them in a bit."

Immediately the courier backed up until he was hovering in the door of the tent.

"There's something you need to know, sir. It's about your slave."

"Ryuu, what about him?" the warlord asked with a yawn, scrubbing his eyes with his hand as he tried to focus on the man speaking to him. "And why are you way over there?"

"I found him when I went to pick up the messages," Akemi hedged. "He'd been attacked."

"What do you mean, attacked?" Aoshi's voice rose as he stood and advanced on the now frightened courier. "What exactly happened? Is he alright?" he demanded, now nose to nose with a visibly shaking Akemi.

"He'd ... he'd ... could you back up a little, you're making it hard for me to think," the courier squeaked, trying to ease away from the angry warrior now towering over him.

"Tell. Me. Now." The warlord fisted his hand in the front of Akemi's shirt and lifted him until he was pinned under that fierce glare.

"He'd been raped. He was laying there in a pool of..." The courier's answer was cut off when the support holding him in the air suddenly disappeared. He hit the ground hard as the warlord strode out of the tent.

"Yuudai, we're leaving, now." Aoshi signaled for his mount and swung into the saddle with practiced ease. By the time the general stuck his head out of the tent all he could see was the cloud of dust left in his wake.

He spotted the courier staggering out of the warlord's tent, looking shell-shocked. "Oi, Akemi, what's going on? Was there an invasion? Quick, give me the news while I grab my stuff, I have to hurry or I won't catch him."

"His slave was raped. I found him and got him to the healers, but it didn't look good. I thought he was going to kill me." Akemi shuddered when he remembered the look in the warlord's eyes. "I would not want to be the one who damaged his property. If he gets that angry over a slave, I can't imagine what he'd be like if he was really upset."

Yuudai contemplated this turn of events. Aoshi was going to kill someone over a slave if he wasn't stopped. Quickly grabbing the rest of his things he saddled up and took off after the warlord, hoping to catch him before things got out of control.

Chapter Seven

This is all my fault, I should never have left him alone, Aoshi berated himself as he tore across the landscape in a daze, ever more terrifying visions of Ryuu broken, bleeding, and dying parading across his mind. *He's so small*, was the warlord's last coherent thought before he allowed himself to be swept up in his rage, roaring his anger to the world as the miles sped by.

It was evening by the time he arrived, his horse spent and his rage congealed into a cold shard.

The warlord dismounted in front of the healer's tent and turned his glare on the small group of men standing nearby. "Not me, not me, not me," they all muttered to themselves, the blood lust rolling off the man in front of them sparking their flight responses.

"Someone," Aoshi began coldly, in a voice just loud enough to be heard, "touched what was mine. I want to know who." At that the men scattered, frantic to find someone, anyone, else for their commander to focus his anger on.

The warlord turned on his heel, lifted the flap to the healer's tent, and stepped inside, squinting as his eyes adjusted. He spotted the scribe on the floor and was instantly at his side, dropping to his knees and examining him closely.

"Healer, why is this man lying on the floor when there are beds empty? Has he been tended to at all?"

"He's someone's pleasure slave. He'll survive, probably, just had a bit too much fun," the clueless healer chuckled. "He's pretty enough. I'm sorry I missed the party."

In the blink of an eye he found himself pinned by a hard forearm, inches from the intimidating face of Fujiwara Aoshi. "He is *not* a pleasure slave. He's my scribe, mine, and extremely valuable. You should thank the gods you weren't at the 'party'. I never share what's mine."

He pulled away, leaving the healer gasping for air, and returned to Ryuu's side, carefully picking him up and heading out the door, back to the relative comfort and privacy of his own quarters. Every eye followed his progress as he strode through the camp with the small limp figure in his arms, collectively breathing a sigh of relief when they finally disappeared into the warlord's tent.

Aoshi faltered when he entered; the worktable had been overturned and scrolls and maps were scattered everywhere. The odors of sex and blood hung heavy in the air, and a few flies buzzed lazily around some still sticky puddles of fluid. Gathering his composure, he continued to the futon, tenderly placing Ryuu on it and smoothing back the matted hair from his forehead.

He lit the fire and set a couple pails of water to boil before moving to air out the tent and begin straightening the mess, righting the table and gathering the scattered papers. Once the water was warm he took one of the pails and a soft rag and carefully began cleaning the unconscious scribe, tenderly washing the residue of his ordeal away, all the while murmuring a constant stream of apologies. He even clumsily washed raven locks, patiently combing out the tangles until they lay smooth.

By the time Yuudai caught up with him he was slumped in a chair beside the bed, stroking a thumb over the back of the small hand clasped in his large, calloused one. "They almost killed him. It's my fault. I should never have left him alone." The warlord turned pain-filled eyes on his friend. "He'll never forgive me for this. How could he? I've ruined everything." Aoshi dropped his head, unable to look the general in the eye.

"Aoshi, look at me," the general commanded. When the warlord finally raised his face he continued. "You've done nothing wrong. You failed to anticipate this situation, true, but you couldn't have expected it. You need to calm down and take care of Ryuu, he needs you right now. I'll see what I can find out about what happened." Yuudai nodded, pleased with his solution. At least this way he wouldn't have to clean up a bloodbath.

"I warned them," a very cold voice broke into his pleased assessment. "I made it very clear on day one he was my property, my business. Someone thought they could do this, in my tent no less, and get away with it. I want to know who it was. There are some people in this camp who need to learn a lesson about loyalty and respect. I'm more than ready to give them some one-on-one attention, make sure it sinks home with everyone."

The general shuddered at the look in Aoshi's eye. The last time he'd seen it had been in battle; over a hundred men had fallen under the warlord's blade that day. "Look, let me see what I can find out. I'll stop and get you something to eat on my way back." With that he left. He needed some answers, and soon. He refused to even think about what would happen if the scribe didn't recover.

Yuudai headed for the mess as it was the best place to hear the latest gossip, and someone had to be talking about this. He was met with the raucous din to be expected from several hundred men. He grabbed some food and headed for a likely table, plunking himself down and greeting his neighbor. "Oi, what's the news. I've just gotten back from the front."

The men were quick to chime in with various stories from the past several days, none of which involved the warlord or his scribe. The general did notice that one man was conspicuously silent. Inoue Goro poked listlessly at his food, never meeting anyone's eyes, and soon rose and shuffled out of the mess. Yuudai was quick to follow.

"Inoue-san, hold up a minute," the general called. Goro stopped, fists clenching at his sides. "What's wrong? And don't tell me nothing."

"I did something I shouldn't have, I feel bad about it but I can't undo it," Goro ground out, then he paused for a moment before continuing. "I don't even know how to begin to fix it and it's eating me up inside."

Yuudai steered him to his tent where they'd have some privacy. "Okay, just you and me. What did you do?" The other man merely stared at the ground. "If you don't tell me I can't help."

"It was Benjirou's idea," Goro said. "He told us the slave had disrespected Fujiwara-sama and needed to learn a lesson. We'd be doing the commander a favor. He made it sound reasonable, so I went along. But it went so much further than I thought. The slave was bleeding and I wanted to stop it but I didn't know how. Then I just left him there, like everyone else. I left him to die and it's killing me." He looked up and Yuudai was shocked to see tears running down the hardened soldier's face.

"Goro," he began tentatively.

"No," he was cut off firmly. "You don't understand. I was enjoying it until… I'm no better than an animal."

Yuudai felt for the man in front of him. But his loyalties were clear. "Come with me." He grasped the man firmly by one arm and pulled him up and out the door.

When they reached the warlord's tent, Goro panicked and tried to pull back but the general kept his firm grip. "You want to make it right, this is where you start," he said firmly as he dragged the terrified man inside. "Aoshi, come here a moment."

The warlord looked up and pinned Inoue with a cold gaze. "Is this the source of my problems, Yuudai?"

"Not exactly. Just listen to what he has to say."

Goro haltingly told his story, flinching a few times under Aoshi's hard stare. When he finished he stared at the ground, waiting for the death blow he was sure would follow.

The warlord clenched his fists. He wanted to kill the man in front of him for hurting Ryuu, but he did honestly seem to regret his actions. Besides, he had confessed and thrown himself on Aoshi's mercy. Leadership had a heavy price. This time the right decision was at odds with what his heart clamored for. "Inoue-san, what you did was horrible, but I believe you are truly remorseful. I appreciate your loyalty in telling me this, it could not have been easy. You are dismissed."

Goro couldn't believe his ears. "Thank you, Commander." He bowed low then dashed from the tent before the warlord could change his mind.

"Yuudai, I will deal with the others involved in this little incident in the morning. At muster." The general bowed and left the tent, grabbing some guards to help him round up the men Aoshi wanted to see. He wasn't taking any chances on the perpetrators being tipped off and bolting.

The warlord returned to his vigil by the bed, gently squeezing a limp hand. "I'm back, Ryuu, I'm right here. Please wake up and talk to me. I need your guidance." He fell silent, holding onto the small hand like a lifeline as he fell to deciding the fate of the men who had destroyed his fledgling happiness.

Chapter Eight

It's raining, was Ryuu's first thought as he regained consciousness. *But I'm indoors.* Another drop fell on his cheek, causing him to slowly crack open his eyes.

At the first hesitant flutter the warlord began to whisper encouragement. "That's it, Ryuu, open your eyes for me. Please come back, I need your help. Open your eyes for me."

"Master?" the scribe croaked. "Why are you crying?" He reached out a shaky hand to wipe tears from a scarred cheek.

"What do you remember?"

The scribe obediently searched his recent memories. "You went to the outposts. I went to the mess and came back here to work." He lifted hazy eyes to meet the warlord's worried gaze. "I must have fallen asleep. Why are you back? Did something happen? Were we invaded?"

"You were attacked," Aoshi began in a soft voice, deciding not to give the scribe any details for fear of upsetting him. "Akemi found you unconscious and took you to the healers before fetching me. You've been unconscious for several days. But now you're back. I was so worried." He hesitated before reaching out a hand to stroke Ryuu's cheek. "I'm so, so sorry. This is all my fault. I should never have left you alone."

"I'm a slave, master. It's not right that you worry about me."

"You are my companion," the warlord corrected him with a small smile. "And I couldn't stop worrying if I tried. I was afraid I was going to lose you. You have become," he hesitated for a moment, searching for the right word, "precious to me. I have grown to depend on your counsel. You're really very wise."

Ryuu was stunned. This was more than he could process right now. A part of him was jumping with joy at the declaration, but another part reminded him that all he'd have, in the end, was a broken heart.

"I hate to do this, but I need your help. I have to punish the men who hurt you. I want to kill them, slowly." Aoshi clenched his fist and Ryuu recoiled from the hatred in his eyes. "But I can't afford to alienate the troops. Will you be very disappointed in me if I let them live? I promise, they will suffer."

"Master, you can't punish free men for injuring a slave." Ryuu attempted to push himself up in the bed, only to fall back, wincing at the pain. "It doesn't matter how badly they hurt me. Your men won't stand for it."

"Fine," the warlord bit out. "Then I'll punish them for their disloyalty to me, but, make no mistake, they will be punished." His mouth was set in a hard line and his eyes seemed to be focused miles away. "Now, do you think you could eat or drink something?"

Ryuu managed a few spoons of miso broth, and it lifted Aoshi's spirits. The warlord carefully tucked the scribe in, murmuring words of comfort as he gently stroked his tense back, finally falling into an exhausted slumber himself.

* * *

Yuudai's expression was grim. No matter how it turned out, this was a bad business and he couldn't wait until it was settled. He had already managed to round up half the men he was looking for, and he had a feeling he'd find most of the rest of them gambling behind the mess tent.

He smiled when they rounded the corner and spotted four of the five men he was looking for, including Benjirou. The general cleared his throat to gain the players' attention. "Good evening, men," he began conversationally, giving the guards time to move into position behind those being arrested. "How's your luck this evening?"

"Join us and find out," one of them urged.

"I'd love to, but I can't. I'm here on business." At that the guards took hold of the four men, forcing them to rise and face the general. "You four are under arrest for treason. You performed acts of disloyalty against our commander and dishonored him. He will pass judgment in the morning at muster."

Three of the men stayed silent, knowing it was pointless to argue. Benjirou, however, was incensed. "What do you mean, treason?" he growled. "I have always been loyal to Fujiwara, I've served with him for years."

Yuudai's reply was short and to the point. "Oh, so you define loyalty by rape? I haven't heard that before."

"Rape? All I did was put an uppity slave in his place. Besides, it's his word against mine."

"In the first place," the general ground out through clenched teeth, "that slave is the very expensive property of the commander. He is a trained scribe and cost more than you make in five years. Even if he was a pleasure slave, the commander does not share his personal property. And it's not his word against yours; unfortunately for you he has yet to regain consciousness. One of your little party decided to come clean and confessed. Since he had everything to lose, yes, his word does carry more weight than yours. In any event, it is out of my hands. Fujiwara-sama will deal with you in the morning. If I were you, I'd pray that his slave wakes up before then."

With that Yuudai turned and left in search of the last man, leaving the guards to escort the prisoners to the makeshift jail.

Once all the men were under guard, Yuudai headed to the warlord's tent to let him know. He thought nothing of pulling the flap back and striding in, sure that, this time at least, he wasn't going to be interrupting any intimate activities. What he found was, in his opinion, even worse. The warlord was tenderly clutching the slave to his chest as he slept, one hand woven in the scribe's long locks, the other on his lower back.

Yuudai stared at the pair soberly for a long time. *This is what Aoshi was talking about*, and he still found it profoundly disturbing. His friend had lived a hard, lonely life and he didn't begrudge him companionship; but this was a weakness, and a warlord could not afford to be weak. *I'll mention it to him again, but I won't push the matter. We need to get through the morning first.*

"Oi, Aoshi," he whispered as he shook his shoulder. "It's Yuudai."

The warlord opened his eyes and fixed his gaze on the general. "Is my problem taken care of?"

"They're all under guard. Only Benjirou gave me a hard time. May I ask what you intend to do to them?"

"Everyone except the instigator will lose rank and get ten lashes, public lashes, all to attend, no excuses. As for Benjirou, you'll find out tomorrow with everyone else." His eyes softened as he looked down at the man sleeping on his chest. "He doesn't remember, Yuudai, and I don't want him to find out. Tomorrow morning send Akemi here to stay with him during muster. He doesn't need to know about that either, at least, not yet."

"As you wish," the general replied curtly before turning to leave.

"Yuudai." A steely voice stopped him in his tracks. "You have a problem with something?" The threat was clear, but the general could no longer hold his tongue.

"Yes, I damn well do. I have a problem with this." He waved his hand at the picture the warlord and his slave made. "It's going to lead to grief. You need it stop it, now."

Aoshi merely shook his head, loose locks shading overly bright eyes from view. His voice was husky when he finally replied. "I couldn't even if I wanted to, and I don't. I will not discuss this again." The general merely nodded, tight lipped, before wheeling and exiting the tent.

* * *

Morning dawned grey and raw. The warlord had been up pacing for hours, readying himself for the task facing him. All too soon Akemi was waiting outside. "I need you to keep an eye on my scribe this morning, make sure he doesn't leave the tent," Aoshi ordered. With that he strode off, heading for the training grounds.

The men assembled hurriedly. Morning muster was something best put behind you for the comfort of the morning mess, so there were rarely any stragglers. Once they assembled, eleven men were brought out to face them, hands tied behind their backs.

"Wait," called a voice from the ranks, and Inoue Goro moved forward to join them.

"Inoue-san?" the warlord asked. "What are you doing?"

"I am as guilty as they are, I will take my punishment with them." He lowered his head in shame. "Perhaps it will help me accept what I did."

Aoshi merely nodded his acquiescence and turned to face the ranks. "These men stand accused of treason. They brutally assaulted my scribe in my tent and left him for dead. Not only are they guilty of damaging my property, but of endangering our campaigns as well. The scribe's abilities are vital to our continued correspondence with the borders and beyond."

Here the warlord stopped and swept his gaze over the assembled men, all of whom quailed at the hardness in his eyes. "I have been told this attack occurred out of some misguided loyalty to me on the part of most of these men. Although, to set the record straight, my slave has never been anything but obedient and subservient, as he should be. Even if that were not the case, I am more than capable of disciplining a slave myself should the need arise. Do I make myself clear?"

The men held their collective breaths, they had never seen their commander this serious outside of battle. "I hope so," Aoshi continued. "I would not like a repeat of this incident. Punishment for a second offense would be far more severe."

The warlord began to list the names of eleven of the prisoners, ending with Goro. "You shall lose one grade in rank, loss of leave for one month and ten lashes, to be administered now." One by one they were stripped of their upper garments and tied to a large post. As each man took his turn Aoshi stood, tight lipped and hard eyed. He, himself, wielded the lash, making sure the tip wrapped around to tear at the soft flesh of their chests even as the skin on their backs split and bled.

When he was done he waited for the last of the men to be taken away and tended to before turning to Ito Benjirou. "You, Ito-san, are an entirely different problem," the warlord admitted. "I believe you have aspirations to replace me."

Benjirou said nothing, but the side of his mouth quirked up in a smirk and his eyes glittered with mirth.

"Since you say nothing in your defense you are found guilty of high treason, punishable by death. May the gods have mercy on you because I will not." The warlord pulled out a tanto, thumbing off the sheath and letting it fall. With that Aoshi grabbed Benjirou around the throat, lifting him to dangle in front of him. The blade of the tanto glinted in the weak morning sun as he slashed the traitor's chest open, cutting out his still beating heart. Holding it in the air, he dropped the carcass and turned to the dumbstruck ranks. "Does anyone else wish to challenge my leadership?" When no sound was forthcoming he continued, "I thought not. Dismissed." He walked away, heading back to his tent and Ryuu, leaving his trusted generals to shake their heads and wonder what would come of this day.

Chapter Nine

Ryuu woke to an empty bed. He levered himself up on one elbow with a groan and looked around, spotting Akemi lounging in a chair near the door.

"Good morning," the courier said when he realized he was being watched. "I hope you're feeling better. The commander's gone to morning muster. He'll be back soon. Do you need anything?"

"Water," Ryuu croaked hoarsely as he attempted to slide out of bed.

"Whoa, where do you think you're going?" Akemi intercepted him, ushering him back in bed before handing him a cup.

"I have to stop him. He's going to ruin his life. He can't punish those men for attacking a slave."

"Well, you may be a slave but you're also a human being. You didn't deserve what was done to you, and you couldn't fight back. Trust the commander to make the right decision, he usually does. Now you," he said as he tucked the scribe back in, "are supposed to be resting. Can you eat something?"

"I can try." Ryuu dropped his head to stare silently at the covers while the courier heated some broth. He sipped at it listlessly, but finished before curling up on his side under the covers, falling into a restless sleep.

* * *

The warlord strode into the tent after muster, eyes blank and hands covered in blood. "Dismissed." Akemi took no time vacating the premises; whatever happened, he didn't want to be involved. Treason was dirty business and it had a way of rubbing off on people.

Aoshi sighed as he stripped off his soiled garments. *I shouldn't have lost my temper*, he berated himself. *Now it will be much harder to figure out who instigated this.* He knew he had overreacted, but the thought of someone sneaking around and spying on him made his blood boil. He knew Benjirou wasn't smart or well-liked enough to swing a power shift on his own. Someone was supporting him, whispering in his ear about how much more worthy he was. *One of the noble families perhaps? It would make sense, they have lost power under my rule. Now, how to find out which one dares to aspire to my position.*

Lost in contemplation, he didn't hear the scribe entering the room behind him. "Master." He placed a hand on the warlord's shoulder, startling him out of his thoughts. "What did you do?"

Aoshi didn't answer right away, but when he did his voice was barely audible. "I upheld my rule, I punished a traitor. I killed a man I thought I knew." He looked the scribe in the eyes. "Have I disappointed you?"

"It's not my place to judge you. You are a fair and wise man, a good ruler, much loved by your men. Why does the opinion of a slave matter?"

"I've said it before, you are not just my slave, you're my companion. Your opinion is the only one that does matter. I trust you to tell me the truth, regardless of whether it angers me." The warlord paused for a long moment. "Do I need to free you to prove it? Will you stay with me if I do, or will you leave me like everyone else?"

"Master, you need to relax." Ryuu coaxed the warlord to sit, reaching for a cloth to begin scrubbing off the blood.

"You didn't answer my question. I need to know. Would you stay with me?" Aoshi turned his piercing gaze on the scribe, patiently waiting for his answer, even as he feared it.

"The truth is, I don't know. You are good to me but, it's been so long since I've been free. Would I be truly free if I stayed? I won't lie to make you happy. I'm just not sure. I do know you've done more for me than anyone since my parents died. I enjoy being with you and I love it when I make you smile. You don't smile enough." The scribe bent to kiss the scar below the warlord's eye. "I'm here now, so just lean back and relax for me."

Aoshi shook his head. "I've called for a tub and I want you get in with me, a soak will do you good."

A few minutes later three men wrestled a massive bronze tub into the tent, filling it with steaming water before bowing and retreating. The warlord gratefully stripped and slid into the water with a sigh. Ryuu dropped his robe and climbed in, settling himself between long legs. He found himself wrapped in strong arms and pulled back to rest against a broad chest. The warlord nuzzled his slave's nape, allowing himself to truly relax for the first time since he'd gotten word of the attack.

Ryuu squirmed when he felt the warlord's erection rubbing the cleft of his ass, making Aoshi moan and clutch him tighter. The scribe squeaked in surprise when a strong hand wrapped around his erection and began to stroke, making him arch into the touch.

"Relax, let me make you feel good, let me watch your face while I pleasure you. I promise I won't hurt you." The scribe moaned and squirmed, his head falling to rest on a strong shoulder, the husky whisper making him harden even more.

Soon the two were writhing together, Ryuu's movements driving the warlord mad, his erection sliding between firm bronze cheeks. Finally the scribe came with a strangled shriek, spilling his seed over a calloused hand. His shudders of completion drove Aoshi to thrust against him several times before releasing, dropping his head to pant against the scribe's shoulder.

The two sat slumped in the now cooling water, too sated to even consider moving. Eventually the warlord stood, scooping the scribe up in his arms and striding to the bed, sliding him between the covers before turning to dress.

"Stay with me?" Ryuu asked, pulling back the cover and patting the bed, much as the warlord had done their first night together.

"As much as I would love that, I need to know what people are saying about this morning. But, don't worry, I'll post a guard outside, you can sleep in peace. I need you back on your feet. I'll be back for supper, rest now and heal." Aoshi laid his hand against Ryuu's face for a moment before turning and heading out.

The scribe lay quietly for a long time, pondering what Aoshi had asked earlier. Although he hadn't admitted it, Ryuu was afraid it was already too late for him to consider leaving the warlord, no matter how wrong such thoughts were. He had to hope his answer would prevent him from being freed. The commander might not see the problems inherent in what he wished for, but his slave did. Even free their relationship would always have started like this, and would never be accepted.

The warlord headed for Yuudai's tent, he needed to know how his punishment had been accepted by the men, and he counted on his general to have the information. "Yuudai, are you here?" he called as he stepped into the tent. He stopped to consider the sight that met his eyes. His courier, Akemi, was bent over, naked from the waist down, with the general pounding into him.

Yuudai looked up at the call of his name and met the eyes of the man who had first caught his interest. Their gazes locked and he came hard, biting his lip to keep from screaming the commander's name. "When you have a chance," Aoshi said before turning and striding out.

The general ran a hand over his face, and shook his head. It seemed he was fated to continually embarrass himself in front of the warlord. He petted the smooth back in front of him absently as he pulled out. "Sorry about that," he whispered. "I'll be back in a few minutes." He pressed a rough kiss to the nape of Akemi's neck before yanking on a yukata and heading outside. He hoped Aoshi would let what he'd just seen lie and concentrate on more pressing matters, but being practical he steeled himself for yet another awkward conversation.

Chapter Ten

"About this morning," Aoshi began once the general joined him. "What was the reaction? Any hints of who might have been behind Benjirou?"

Yuudai sighed in relief, as bad as this topic was it certainly beat talking about what the warlord had just witnessed. "Most of the men seem to be firmly behind you. Of course, they were even before your little temper tantrum this morning."

"Temper tantrum? You have no idea how much restraint I showed." Aoshi's eyes flashed as he gripped the general's robe. "Do you think I should have left Ito-san's plot to simmer?"

"No, of course not." Yuudai pulled himself free from the warlord's grasp. "I just wish it wasn't tied to the attack on your slave."

"He has a name, Yuudai, I wish you'd use it. Or do you think he's less than human because he had the bad luck to end up a slave?" Aoshi asked soberly, crossing his arms and waiting patiently for an answer.

"Of course not, but slavery is a fact of life. Like it or not, slaves are property, they have no rights. Would you have doled out the same punishment if they had tortured your dog?"

"Perhaps I shall have to abolish it then. If Ryuu's any example, slaves should have the same rights we do. No one should ever be hurt like that, or be ignored when they need a healer's treatment, simply because they've been forced into servitude. Or do you know of someone who volunteered for slavery? What if it was you or I captured and turned into slaves, would you still think it was right?"

Yuudai shook his head and ran a hand across his face. "Look, I see what you're saying, but don't you have enough problems right now without garnering the hatred of every slave owner you govern?

You can't handle that and the border incursions at the same time. I'm sorry, but you have to be practical."

"No," the warlord retorted. "What I have to be is fair, that's most important."

"I'll support you no matter what you do, you know that. But my opinion is, you need to let it go. Now, if we're finished?"

"Just one more question. What exactly were you doing with Akemi just now?"

The general flushed dark red. He took a deep calming breath before answering. "I think it was fairly obvious."

"Enlighten me."

"We were having sex, happy? Now, if you're done with your little inquisition…" Yuudai turned to go back into his tent.

"What's sex with a man like?" Aoshi pressed.

"Look, if you're so interested why don't you go ask your precious Ryuu instead of bugging me. I'm sure he could tell you all about it. And, by the way, next time why don't you give me some warning before you come storming in. Now, if you'll excuse me, I have someone waiting." The general turned on his heel and disappeared back into his tent, leaving the warlord to watch his retreat with narrowed eyes.

"Shit, I'm so sorry about that." Yuudai reentered the tent, gulping when he caught sight of Akemi, now completely naked and stretched out on his bed.

"Why don't you make it up to me?" the courier whispered huskily and Yuudai felt himself harden all over again. He made quick work of his clothes and crawled onto the bed, hovering over Akemi before capturing his lips. Their hard cocks rubbed together as they kissed, driving them to break apart with a moan. The general wrapped a large hand around both their erections, giving them a rough squeeze and a pull before diving back in for another hard, sloppy kiss.

The courier moaned wantonly when he felt the head of Yuudai's cock poised at his entrance. The general lifted muscular legs to wrap around his waist as he slowly slid in, pausing only when his balls pressed against the soft flesh of Akemi's ass. He took a deep breath before he slowly pulled out, waiting until the man below him was writhing and whining before pushing back in. His eyes slid shut and the pace increased as his mind fed him images of doing this with someone very different. His breathing became ragged as he pictured the warlord's head thrown back in passion. His eyes snapped open as the man beneath him cried out and came hard between them. The convulsions of Akemi's passage pulled him over the edge after a few thrusts, and the general sprayed his seed deep inside the courier.

He collapsed to the side, his mind awhirl with confused thoughts of just how bad an idea this might have been. Akemi rolled to face him, laying a kiss on the side of his face. "Mmm, that was very nice, we'll have to do it again, soon."

* * *

Aoshi strode back into his tent, his mind examining all he had just learned. Once inside he visibly relaxed, slipping off his shoes and padding over to sit on the edge of the bed. "How are you feeling?" he asked when sleepy brown eyes blinked open.

"Sore, but otherwise alright. Do you need something master?" Ryuu sat up and prepared to get out of bed.

"Just to talk to you, lay back and relax." The warlord pushed him back down with a firm yet gentle hand. "I want to ask you some questions, if you don't mind."

"I live to serve you," the scribe replied, eyes flicking down to study the bed covers. "I will answer to the best of my ability."

A strong hand turned Ryuu's face to meet the warlord's serious eyes. "Please don't look away from me. I won't hurt you. I want to know more about you. I'm not going to judge you, I promise."

The scribe merely nodded, eyes locked with Aoshi's. "I'll do my best."

"How did you get to be a slave? You obviously weren't born into it."

Haltingly Ryuu began to tell the story, shivering a little as he lost himself in the memories. He jumped when arms wrapped around him and pulled him against a broad chest, relaxing in the safety promised by the steady heartbeat beneath his ear.

When it came time to recount his experiences with his first master, Oki, the scribe was sure he'd be pushed away for being so tainted. The warlord's husky voice instead whispered words of comfort, promising to protect him.

Aoshi's lips thinned in anger as Ryuu recounted his brothel training. The thought of those things being done to children made him sick, and he understood the scribe's desperation not to become a pleasure slave. His heart filled with tenderness for this resilient man who had suffered so much and still retained his sweet nature. Unable to restrain himself he dipped his head and clumsily sealed their lips together in his first real kiss.

One taste and the warlord was addicted. Ryuu's mouth was a treasure he wanted to devour for the rest of his life. They relaxed into the kiss, mouths opening and tongues coming out to dance. Aoshi gently laid the scribe down, hovering over him before diving back in for another of those delectable kisses.

Eventually they broke apart for air, the warlord retreating from the bed to strip off his clothes before sliding back in next to the scribe, pulling him close and raining kisses over his nose and cheeks, tracing the jagged path of the scar across his face before once again capturing kiss swollen lips.

Their hard cocks were trapped between them, sliding on sweat-slicked flesh, occasionally rubbing against each other, sending electric shocks through the pair and making Ryuu break the kiss to cry out.

"Are you okay?" the warlord asked nervously.

"Do that again." Aoshi was happy to comply. The sight of the scribe spread out below him, wanton and writhing, was rapidly becoming more than he could handle.

"I'm close, Ryuu."

"Touch me." The scribe guided a calloused hand to his neglected cock. A few strokes was all it took and Ryuu was spraying his release between them. Aoshi followed immediately after. The warlord dove in for more breathless kisses as they shuddered through the aftershocks, eventually lying still, enjoying the feeling of being so intimately entwined as they succumbed to the call of sleep.

Chapter Eleven

Yuudai finally woke early in the evening. He groaned when he remembered how badly his talk with Aoshi had gone. *Talk hell, it was a confrontation. If I'm not careful I'll alienate him completely. I've got to get over this obsession. He's not interested.* He tugged his hair in frustration. *Face it, you're jealous of a slave, and you are being ridiculous.*

As the general rolled over to heave himself out of bed he noticed a piece of paper lying on the covers.

- That was fun! Look me up when you need some more stress relief -

Now that's not a bad idea, he decided and he rolled off the bed to dress and head to the mess, intent on eating and then tracking down the courier. Stress relief indeed, that was exactly what he needed more of.

* * *

Aoshi woke with a smile on his face and breathed in the comforting scent of the man in his arms. *That was . . . well, I don't know exactly how to describe it, but I definitely want to do it again. I can't remember ever feeling this relaxed, or happy.* He tried to recall the last time he'd felt that way. *My sixth birthday,* he pondered, cocking his head to the side. *My father gave me a sword. I was happy to be all grown up.* He frowned at the memory of his younger self, always so old even then.

I've never felt like this, his last thought before he was distracted by the figure beginning to stir in his arms. "Good morning, Ryuu, how are you feeling?" Aoshi smiled as sleepy eyes blinked open, before leaning in and capturing his slave's mouth in a deep possessive kiss.

"Ahhhh," was all the scribe managed when the kiss finally broke. "I feel good." He let out a groan when their cocks brushed. "Really good." Ryuu winced when he shifted to sit up. "But really really sore. I think I need to heal some more before we try that again. You're surprisingly heavy."

The warlord frowned, "I'm sorry I hurt you. We don't have to do it again if it hurts."

"Oh, no," the scribe said, blushing brightly. "I just haven't healed yet, then it will be fine. If you want to, I mean."

"How could I not?" Aoshi kissed the scribe tenderly, deepening it as he reveled in the sweetness that was Ryuu. The warlord spent a long time committing the taste, the smell, the feel—everything that was the man in his arms—to his memory. When they broke for air he whispered huskily, "We could do it another way, with you inside me, couldn't we?" The warlord smiled at the dumbstruck look he was graced with. "I want to try, I trust you to make it good. Don't you want me, Ryuu?"

"Master, it wouldn't be right."

"Stop it. It's right if I say it is. And here, like this, you will not call me master. I have a name, use it. I use yours."

"If you're sure, Ma— Aoshi," the scribe said slowly, tilting the warlord's head to gaze into lust-filled eyes.

"More than sure. Where do you want me, Ryuu?"

The scribe almost came just picturing the warlord spread out underneath him. "Come here." He gathered the tall man in his arms and kissed him deeply, breaking away to nibble at the column of his neck before sucking on a tempting collarbone.

Ryuu maneuvered them so he was hovering over his master, moving to suckle a tempting pink nub while his hands stroked over all the skin they could reach. He broke away to continue his ministrations on the other nipple, teasing it to a taut peak before nipping and sucking the thick scar running just above it, making the warlord give a breathy cry.

His hot tongue danced down hard abs, soothing hard nips with soft licks before diving into a perfect naval, swirling and sucking, making the man beneath him twitch and groan. He followed the faint smoky path downward to settle between muscular thighs, nuzzling and nipping, coaxing them to spread wider to admit him. He licked his lips as he bent to greedily lick up the pearls welling from the slit of the erection bobbing desperately in front of him. Aoshi shifted his hips, aching for more contact, but a firm hand held him in place. "Ryuu, please," he moaned wantonly. The scribe relented, circling the head with his tongue before tracing the thick vein, finally taking the tip in his mouth and sucking gently while his tongue swirled in the slit, making the warlord give a sharp cry.

Ryuu finally relented and took the length into his mouth to the base, humming as he swallowed, then retreating to tease the tip again. He moved lower to nuzzle the warlord's sac, taking it into his mouth and rolling and sucking the wrinkled flesh, reveling in the taste that he was rapidly becoming addicted to.

He lifted lean hips and spread muscular cheeks, swiping his tongue across the pink pucker. Aoshi gave a guttural moan that ran through the scribe like lightning, sending an electric pulse to his groin that almost had him coming right there. Ryuu lapped and sucked at the ring of muscle, slicking and loosening it until his tongue could dart inside, stroking and swirling as it plunged in and out.

An oil-slick finger joined the play, sliding deep, before retreating, gently easing the passage open. One finger became two and they spread his ring wide, allowing that wicked tongue to delve even deeper. "Ahhh, Ryuu, more," Aoshi moaned as shudders of pleasure raced through him. "Want you now." He writhed and whimpered, biting his lip in an attempt to gain control. "Hurry, please."

The scribe had to reach down and squeeze himself hard to keep from coming at the sound of that deep commanding voice begging for him. He rapidly oiled his cock and positioned himself carefully, lifting long legs to rest on his shoulders. He could feel the warlord's hot entrance quiver as he rested the tip of his erection against the softened pucker.

Alert for even the slightest sign that the man beneath him had changed his mind, Ryuu ever so slowly began to push forward, gradually easing inside with a gentle rocking motion until he was fully seated, his balls pressed up against the curve of the warlord's ass. He gently stroked Aoshi's chest. "Relax. That's it, just relax and it will feel good, I promise."

Finally, Aoshi began to rock his hips. "Move." The scribe was happy to comply, pulling out smoothly and then pausing before suddenly sliding in to the hilt, striking the warlord's prostate, making him cry out. He continued thrusting deeply and erratically until the body below him was writhing with pleasure. He grasped the commander's neglected member, stroking it in counterpoint to his thrusts and rubbing his thumb across the head.

Aoshi was so close, his balls tightened further with each stroke across his prostate. A calloused thumb dipped into his slit as his prostate was struck and the warlord exploded with a loud cry of his slave's name, shooting burst after burst of hot cum between them. Ryuu, overcome by the sight of Aoshi in the throes of pleasure, captured his mouth in a sloppy kiss as he let go, coming hard deep inside his master's welcoming body.

They stayed like that, tangled together, as twilight fell and the world continued on without them, deaf and blind to everything beyond their thundering heartbeats and sweet sated kisses, happy to remain in their private world.

Chapter Twelve

The pair lay there for a long time before Aoshi finally murmured, "Can we do that again?"

"Whatever you want. Anything for you." Ryuu hungrily captured kiss swollen lips, surprised to feel himself hardening again.

"Now?" the warlord asked when they broke apart for air. "I want you inside me again."

The scribe shuddered at the heat in the sultry voice. He manipulated the taller body until the warlord was on his knees in front of him, face pressed to the futon and that perfect ass raised high. He smoothed a soft hand over the perfect cheeks, squeezing and caressing before delivering a sharp slap, watching in fascination as red bloomed on the pale flesh and Aoshi squirmed wantonly.

Several more slaps saw the proud warrior begging for Ryuu to take him, making a surge of pride rise in the scribe as the warlord was reduced to lustful pleas. He pushed inside with one smooth motion, swirling his hips as he slowly retreated, only to thrust back inside. He pulled the lanky body into his lap, biting and sucking on the column of his neck as he rocked up into the clutching heat, the change in angle allowing him to stroke over Aoshi's prostate with each thrust.

The scribe wrapped a surprisingly strong arm around the writhing figure in his lap before grasping Aoshi's bobbing erection with his free hand, rubbing and stroking, the slippery precum lubricating the hard shaft. The warlord leaned forward and placed his hands on the bed, using the leverage to work his hips against the thrusts, letting out a warbling cry at the heightened stimulation.

The combined sensations were rapidly making Aoshi lose his mind. All he knew was the hard cock piercing him, sending shivery bolts of pleasure rocketing through his frame, and the hand stroking him to madness. After what seemed like an eternity, and yet all too soon, he could hold out no longer. He sprayed his release across the bedding, loving the feeling of the hard length still pistoning in and out of him.

* * *

Yuudai searched the camp for Akemi, but came up empty handed. He realized he would be spending the night alone, and tried to come up with something to do to kill some time. He reluctantly decided it would behoove him to patch things up with Aoshi; it wouldn't do to let their disagreement fester. That decided he changed course, heading for the warlord's tent, whistling aimlessly as he walked.

He strolled inside without announcing himself, a petty part of his brain hoping he'd interrupt something and get some revenge for the warlord walking in on him earlier. He never expected the sight that met his eyes. There was Aoshi, writhing on his hands and knees as Ryuu pounded into him.

Oh hell, no. He reacted automatically, wrenching the slave away and tossing him to the floor. When he reflected on the incident later, Yuudai decided he must have gone temporarily insane. There was no other explanation for what he did next. Faced with the sight that had haunted his dreams he pulled out his cock and fisted it roughly. "You want to know what it feels like? I'll show you how a real man fucks." With that he roughly thrust inside his commander, groaning at the tight heat.

He paused for a moment when he was fully seated, and the warlord took the opportunity to turn the tables, bucking the general off and grabbing his sword. "You dare," he hissed, drawing himself up to his full height. Yuudai drew his sword, but couldn't seem to focus, the sight before him sending his mind reeling as he recalled the velvety heat he had been so briefly sheathed in.

The general parried weakly, barely fending off the frenzied onslaught. "I should kill you," the warlord muttered as he forced Yuudai against the wall, the entire tent groaning at the force. "Or perhaps I should just castrate you." He pondered his choices as he shifted his blade into position.

Yuudai gulped as cold steel kissed the side of his now limp member. Reality was crashing down around him and he frantically searched for a way out of the mess he'd created. He dropped his blade and shut his eyes, tilting his head back to expose his vulnerable throat, forcing the tension out of his body. He relaxed when the blade retreated a bit and dropped his eyes to the floor, unable to look the warlord in the eye now that he had dishonored him so completely.

"I don't know what came over me," the general said in a soft trembling voice. "You should kill me." He was surprised when a few tears slipped out to trail down his scarred cheek. "You must hate me."

Aoshi leaned in close and whispered in the general's ear. "I depend on you, Yuudai, and I don't hate you, but right now you need to get out of my sight before I do something I'll regret. We will discuss this when we've calmed down."

Yuudai thanked all the gods for the warlord's mercy. He grasped his friend by the shoulders, pressing a rough, hard kiss to his lips before breaking away and literally running from the tent.

Halfway through his panicked dash he ran into Akemi. "What the hell happened to you?" the courier asked, taking in the pale complexion and the slight tremor in the general's hands.

"I-I…" was all Yuudai could force out of his numb lips. Assessing the situation the courier quickly wrapped an arm around the general's waist.

"Let's get you back to your tent," he said soothingly. "You can tell me what happened and I'll help you figure out what to do." He urged the older man along, soothingly running his hand up and down a tense arm, hoping to diffuse some of the anxiety the general was suffering.

Before long he was urging the shaken man into a chair and thrusting a strong drink into his hands. The courier waited until he had taken several swallows, shuddering as the alcohol coursed through his system.

"Better?" Akemi asked. When he received a small nod in response he continued. "So, what happened? You look like you saw a ghost."

Yuudai cradled his head in his hands, not able to look the other man in the eye. "I did the stupidest thing imaginable. I'll never be able to make this right."

"Start at the beginning and tell me all of it. Even if I can't help, it will let you see more clearly." The general sat very still for a moment, before slowly recounting everything, starting from when he woke up in his tent.

"This is my fault then," Akemi decided. "I should never have left you alone." He sobered, running his hands through his hair as he thought. "You fucked up, that's for sure. At least you're not dead yet. Your best bet is to just act normally, let some time pass before you see him again. I guess I'll just have to keep you here in this bed to make sure you don't screw up again."

The courier leaned forward and captured Yuudai's lips in a bruising kiss, reaching down to roughly stroke him to hardness before dropping to his knees and taking the now rigid length into his mouth, vigorously bobbing his head and swirling his tongue. The sensations caused the general to forget all about his near escape, concentrating, instead, on the pleasure building between his thighs.

Yuudai gasped when a talented tongue swirled around the head and the hot mouth surrounding him sucked hard, pulling a keening wail from his throat. He buried his hands in soft hair and rocked into the moist warmth, feeling his knees buckle when Akemi nipped lightly at his slit.

The courier deftly stripped the larger man before dispatching his own clothes and tugging the general onto the bed. He laughed when Yuudai took charge and pushed him onto his back, diving in for a fierce kiss. The general devoured Akemi's mouth as he tweaked his nipples harshly, causing the lean body to twist in his grasp, grinding their hard cocks against each other with abandon.

The courier was quick to grab the flask of oil still by the bed from earlier and pressed it into Yuudai's hand. He gasped when three fingers pushed roughly inside him, rubbing relentlessly against his prostate as he was quickly stretched. The fingers soon retreated, only to be replaced by the general's erection. Akemi whimpered as his prostate was brushed and a rough voice began whispering in his ear.

"So fucking tight. I'm gonna fuck you for a week, take a nap and do it again." Yuudai punctuated his words with hard thrusts that struck the courier's prostate dead on, making him squeal and clutch broad shoulders. Akemi dug blunt nails into scarred flesh as he shuddered under the onslaught, panting the general's name brokenly as he rocketed towards his release, ending in a broken cry as his cock was roughly fisted.

Akemi had heard the expression 'seeing stars' before, but he'd always laughed it off as romantic nonsense. Now, he needed to readjust that view because he was, quite literally, seeing stars with every powerful thrust. Finally he could take no more and he came with a strangled grunt, the world growing hazy and white as he shot his load across his chest. The convulsions of his release squeezed Yuudai's cock, the insistent clutch of molten heat sending him roaring into his own orgasm.

Finally they slumped to the bed, completely spent. Soon the general was snoring loudly as Akemi silently stroked his hair. "What am I going to do with you?" the courier wondered, kissing a broad shoulder and snuggling down for some much needed sleep.

Chapter Thirteen

Ryuu watched the unfolding confrontation in horror. He had never hated his status more than he did at this moment. What good was he if he couldn't even fight to defend the man he cared for? Despite the death that was sure to follow such a move, he couldn't restrain himself when Yuudai roughly thrust into Aoshi. A fierce wave of forbidden possessiveness rose up in him and he leapt to his feet to pull the general away, only to fall back and watch in shock as the warlord broke free and threatened to castrate his oldest friend. But what snapped him back into the real world was the kiss.

He thought hard about the relationship between the two men. Before Aoshi purchased the scribe he spent most of his time with Yuudai, training, discussing strategy, sharing meals. Now, aside from the occasional morning training session, they only met on official business. *He's jealous,* Ryuu realized, considering what this meant to him and the burgeoning feelings he had for his master.

He saw clearly what he knew his master did not, his status as a slave was a barrier preventing any kind of relationship. The general, though, was a perfect choice; strong, loyal and obviously attracted to Aoshi. *I need to encourage their relationship*, he reluctantly decided. *It's the best thing for everyone.* His heart, however, did not agree with his logical assessment.

He sat huddled against the wall, arms wrapped around his knees, tears running unchecked down his cheeks, trying to convince himself that he was making the correct decision. Ryuu reminded himself, yet again, not to give his heart so it could be broken on the auction block, but he feared it was too late. Even now, all he could think about was the way the warlord looked in the throes of passion. He took a deep calming breath and looked up, only to meet worried eyes.

Aoshi crouched in front of the huddled figure, sad chocolate eyes finally lifting to meet his gaze. "Are you hurt?" H gathered the scribe into his embrace, holding him close in the protective circle of his arms. Ryuu only cried harder, the concern making what he had to do much more difficult. "Please talk to me," the warlord crooned. "I can't help if I don't know what's wrong."

"We're what's wrong. What we were doing is what's wrong." The scribe hung his head in defeat. "I'm what's wrong, and I always will be."

"I don't understand." Aoshi was clearly puzzled. "How can we be wrong? How is caring for someone other than yourself wrong? As far as I can see, you're the only thing in my whole life that's right."

"I'm a slave, master. A possession, like a chair or a pair of pants, not something you get attached to. You can't treat me the way you have been, it's not right. You need to find someone worthy of you." The scribe paused, gathering his composure. "General Tanaka-san loves you, you know. He probably has for years and just didn't realize it. He's a good match, too, you already share so much. You should go to him and make this right, see if you can work things out." By the time he finished Ryuu was barely audible and his gaze was fixed on a point between his feet, but his eyes were dry and his voice was steady.

"No." The warlord took the scribe's face in his hands and turned it to meet his eyes. "This is not your choice, and it most certainly is not Yuudai's. It's mine and mine alone. If I wanted to I had years to get together with him, but I don't want that and he knows it. I chose you. I want you and only you. If you won't stay with me then I'll be alone, and so will you. Why do you want that?"

"Master."

"I won't say it again, Ryuu. Use my name."

"Aoshi, I want to stay with you, but I'm afraid. I'm afraid you'll get hurt because people won't accept this. I'm afraid you'll realize you've made a mistake," his voice dropped to a whisper. "I'm afraid you'll sell me and my heart will break."

Aoshi slumped at those words, knowing he could no longer delay the inevitable. "Ryuu, before you I was always alone, I never let anyone get close. I have come to depend on you, your intelligence and your tenderness. You've helped me become a true leader, not just a strong arm. Without you I would truly be lost. I've delayed doing this because I was afraid of being alone again." The warlord looked up and met the scribe's gaze. "I can't think of you as a slave and it's cruel of me to keep you one. You're free," he concluded bitterly. "Free to leave me behind like everyone else. I'll sign the papers in the morning. Will you stay with me till then?"

"I'm free? Really, truly free?"

"Yes," the warlord husked. "Free to do as you will."

The scribe didn't even stop to think before pressing himself against Aoshi and capturing his mouth in a passionate kiss. When they broke apart he smiled broadly. "Silly man, didn't I say my fear was you'd get rid of me? Do you really think I could leave you? If I'm truly free then I am free to stay, for as long as you'll have me, that is."

"I think that will be a very long time." Aoshi leaned in to nibble on a tempting throat. "I can't imagine my life without you now." He steered them back across the room to the bed, pushing the scribe to lie flat and climbing over him. "Now, if I'm not mistaken, we were in the middle of something when we were so rudely interrupted." He chuckled as he reached down to stroke the scribe back to hardness before positioning himself and slowly sliding down onto Ryuu's erection.

The scribe gasped as his erection was swallowed in the warlord's clenching heat. Aoshi bent down and captured plump lips in a tender kiss before lifting himself on powerful legs and dropping back down.

The warlord groaned as his prostate was struck dead-on. He quickly developed a rhythm, rising and falling on the thick length, faltering slightly when a soft hand wrapped around his cock and began to stroke.

He braced his hands on the scribe's smooth chest and used the leverage to speed up the pace, eyes dropping shut under the onslaught of pleasure.

Aoshi moaned and writhed in abandon, chasing his pleasure as he rode the scribe hard, muscles flexing and bunching under sweat slicked skin as his eyes fluttered shut. Finally he came with a strangled grunt.

Ryuu's eyes flew open when he felt something warm land on his cheek. More warm droplets pattered down and he realized that it was the warlord's come. The sight of the powerful leader riding out the last of his orgasm, coupled with the extremely erotic mental image of his face covered in the other man's come was enough to push the scribe over the edge.

"No more," the scribe choked out. The warlord bent and licked his come off of his partner's face. "Please, you'll kill me. Sleep now, I'm not going anywhere." With that he pulled Aoshi under the covers, cuddling close with a contented sigh before drifting off to sleep.

Aoshi contemplated the events of the day, gradually coming to grips with all the changes the last twenty-four hours had wrought. "It will all work out," he whispered. "I promise I'll make it work." Too exhausted to fight it any longer he slipped into sleep, comfortably curled around his chosen, the problems of tomorrow still far away.

Chapter Fourteen

Despite how well his day had ended, Aoshi woke the next morning with a feeling of dread. Simultaneously dealing with border incursions, takeover plots and now this mess with Yuudai was overwhelming. He cast a fond glance at the man still slumbering peacefully next to him. *Ryuu stayed, everything else I can work out.*

With a heavy sigh he untangled himself from the warmth of his lover and slipped out of bed, wincing slightly as the activities of the previous day caught up with him. *It was well worth it,* he decided with a smirk as he headed to bathe.

Washed, dressed and as ready as he would ever be, the warlord set off for Yuudai's tent. He hoped the normalcy of morning training would diffuse the tension he knew would accompany their talk.

He hesitated for a moment, then squared his shoulders and strode in confidently, stopping to survey the scene with pursed lips. Yuudai was sprawled out in bed, face down and snoring. Sitting next to him, partially covered with a sheet, was Akemi, silently drinking as he studied the sleeping form.

The courier raised a finger to his lips and pointed outside as he gathered the blanket around himself and climbed out of bed. Once outside he jumped right in. "Sir, about last night. He's really torn up over what he did…"

"He told you?" the warlord asked in a strangled whisper, horrified that someone else knew what had happened.

"Well, yes. I forced him to tell me. You should have seen him. I was really worried and so I asked what happened. To be honest, I wish I didn't know. For some reason I really like the jerk, and he only has eyes for you." He looked up at the warlord appraisingly. "No one can compete with you. I should know, I've been trying for years."

Aoshi looked at him through narrowed eyes, before replying in a carefully controlled tone. "So what would you have me do? I can't just ignore what he did."

"Of course not. But the way I heard it, if you were going to kill him you would have done it last night. Instead you sent him away. Are you sure it's retribution you're after?"

"You question my motives?" The warlord drew himself up to tower over Akemi. "His actions almost cost me everything. I've made my choice. If he interferes again I won't hesitate."

"Just let me deal with him for now, give me a few days before you talk to him," the courier implored. "Find someone else to train with, spend some time with your slave."

"He's not a slave," Aoshi remarked absently. "Not anymore. I freed him last night. And his name's Ryuu."

"Well then, go spend time with your Ryuu and let me deal with the idiot." The warlord nodded and the courier broke out in a wide smile. "Thank you." He leaned up to kiss Aoshi's cheek before slipping back inside.

Aoshi rubbed his cheek in bemusement as he headed back to his tent. He'd been kissed by more people in the last few hours than in the rest of his life combined. He chuckled softly as he lifted the flap to his tent and spotted the scribe, curled up around the warlord's pillow mumbling contentedly.

He slipped off his sandals and stretched out on the bed, relaxing now that he was back with Ryuu. He was grateful for the respite from dealing with Yuudai, trusting the courier to keep him informed. *I really should train,* he thought absently. *Ryuu doesn't look like he'll be waking any time soon.* He huffed to himself as he once again grabbed his gear and headed across camp.

This time he made sure to announce himself before entering, "Oi, Ken'ichi, up for some training?"

"This is a surprise," the general said as he stuck his head out through the flap. "You usually train with Yuudai."

"I thought you could use a break." The warlord grinned, motioning toward the tent. "How is Kotone doing, by the way?"

Ken'ichi scratched his head, "Her mood swings are driving me crazy. If she doesn't have this baby soon I'll be tempted to fall on my sword."

"Sshhh!" Aoshi waved his hands and tried to quiet his friend, "I do not want to be here when she kills you. Pregnant women are scary," he muttered under his breath.

"S'okay, she's in town. Probably listening to a bunch of old biddies tell delivery horror stories that'll have her yapping in my ear all night." Ken'ichi scratched himself absently. "Training sounds good. Come in while I grab my stuff."

The warlord lifted the flap and followed his general. Ken'ichi was a rarity, a married man whose wife traveled with them. Kotone's father had also been a soldier and she missed him greatly as a child; she had no intention of going through the same thing with her husband. He wondered if things would change for them after their baby was born. He hoped not. Kotone was a stabilizing influence on the hot-headed general.

The tent showed a woman's influence, colorful tapestries adorned the bed and fresh tatami warmed the floor.

"So." Ken'ichi turned, swords in hand. "Why are you really here Aoshi? You haven't come to train with me for years. Did I do something to upset you?"

"No, nothing like that. Yuudai and I had words. I am keeping my distance for the time being. Ryuu was still asleep and I usually train now, so I hoped, if you were free…"

"Oh, that's great." The general visibly relaxed. "Who's Ryuu?" he asked as they headed towards the training grounds.

"My companion. He was my slave, but I freed him. He's willing to stay with me though. He's a scribe. He's really smart, good with paperwork and stuff." The warlord trailed off nervously, studying Ken'ichi's face for signs of rejection.

The general thought hard about what Aoshi was saying: this relationship, with an ex-slave no less, was serious. "It's none of my business, of course, but you might want to keep it quiet. There are some who disapprove of two men together, not to mention the fact that every man with a daughter has had their eye on you for years. Besides, an ex-slave is hardly of your status. There will be a backlash."

The warlord's lips thinned. "So I'm to sneak around like some pathetic mongrel, is that it?"

"No," Ken'ichi hastened to reassure him. "Of course not, but you don't need to proclaim it either. Act as you wish, just say nothing. What's his background? How did he become a slave? He's young and educated, maybe he has a family you can dig up to elevate his status."

"I know his family, they sold him to steal his inheritance. I have every intention of making sure he gets it back, providing there's anything left. He's more than worthy of me, although I didn't know it when we got involved." The warlord stopped, lost in thought for a moment before catching up to the general. "He is precious to me. I want to make him happy."

"Oh boy, you have it bad." Ken'ichi laughed. "Come on, let's go sweat our troubles away." They continued on to the training grounds in companionable silence, each man pondering what had just been said and what it could mean for the future.

Chapter Fifteen

It was mid-morning when they returned from training, dirty, sweaty, bloody and laughing like loons. They pushed open the flap on Ken'ichi's tent to be met by an angry voice. "Leave your shoes outside unless you want to sleep on the floor tonight," Kotone yelled. "Oh, Aoshi, what a lovely surprise. It's good to see you, it's been far too long. You should have dinner tonight with us and catch up." She glided forward to give the warlord a hug.

"Yes, Aoshi," Ken'ichi snickered. "Bring the little woman."

Kotone's eyes lit up. "You met someone," she exclaimed with delight. "How wonderful, please bring her to dinner, I'd love to meet her." She cast a sidelong look at Ken'ichi. "It will be wonderful to have another woman to talk to. There's only so much manly grunting a lady can put up with."

The warlord scratched his head uncertainly. "I'm not sure that's such a good idea. Ryuu was still asleep when I left, I'll have to check."

"Aoshi, I hope you're not setting a bad example. Too many of the men want the pleasures of marriage without the responsibilities. I'm sure you're planning on making an honest woman out of your Ryuu."

"It's kinda complicated..." the warlord stammered, only to be cut off by his general's raucous laughter.

"Go home, get cleaned up, spend some time with the little woman and we'll see you back here at six," the general choked out.

Aoshi glared at him but didn't protest, heading toward his tent to explain their sudden dinner plans to Ryuu.

By the time he arrived the scribe had finally woken, although he had yet to get out of bed. *Just five more minutes,* he kept telling himself. *Then I'll straighten up before Aoshi gets back.* He was right in the middle of a giant yawn when he noticed the warlord watching him with amusement.

"Oh, Aoshi you're back." The scribe leapt out of bed and began to straighten the tent, not realizing the show he was giving as he scurried around naked, making the bed and then bending to scoop the discarded clothes from the floor.

He was so intent on what he was doing, in fact, that he didn't notice the warlord moving in behind him until he pressed up tight against him, grinding into his ass as strong hands pinched and rolled his nipples.

"Stop that." The scribe attempted to wiggle out of the warlord's encircling arms. "Don't you ever think about anything else?" He glared up at Aoshi, having no idea just how adorable he looked with the pout on his face and his hair all rumpled from sleep.

Aoshi leaned in to husk his response in a delicate ear. "How could I possibly think of anything but you, especially when you're running around like this?" He smirked as he ran a hand over a firm cheek before giving it a sharp smack. "Now, aren't you going to greet me properly?" The warlord bent to capture plump lips in a deep, devouring kiss, breaking away to nibble on a bronze shoulder. "Are you still sore?"

"Probably not as sore as you are. Why, are you going to ravish me?"

"Mmmhmmm," the warlord hummed. "At least until we have to get ready for dinner. We're eating with Ken'ichi and his wife."

"What?" the scribe exclaimed in shock. "I can't go to dinner with you."

"And why not?" Aoshi demanded. "You're free to do as you want. Don't you want to be seen with me?"

"Oh, Aoshi, no," Ryuu assured him. "It's nothing like that. My clothes aren't suitable."

"So wear some of mine," the warlord murmured as he nipped at a slender neck. "Or nothing at all, I don't care. Kotone wants to meet you and she won't take no for an answer. She hopes we'll get married."

Ryuu would have questioned this, if only he hadn't been so distracted by what Aoshi was doing with his tongue. "Aahhhhh, what time?"

"Later." Aoshi sealed his mouth in another deep kiss. He dropped to his knees and nuzzled and nipped the curve of a pelvis before burying his nose in chocolate curls and inhaling deeply. He greedily engulfed Ryuu's erection, lapping and sucking enthusiastically.

Aoshi forced the scribe's legs apart so he could slide lower, pulling the tight sac into his mouth and massaging it with his tongue. Bracing his hands on sturdy thighs he twisted his head and licked a wet trail up to the tight pucker, lapping and nibbling before darting inside.

Ryuu's knees gave out and he crashed to the floor. The warlord's wicked tongue never faltered and he found his face pressed into an impressive bulge. He scrabbled at Aoshi's clothes, freeing his rigid cock to bob enticingly in front of his face. The scribe took the head into his mouth, lapping frantically at the slit, before starting a long, slow slide down to the base. The taller man hummed in pleasure, sending ripples of vibration through his lover's softening pucker, making him moan around his mouthful.

Eventually they broke apart, deft hands quickly freeing the warlord from his clothes as their mouths met in another breathless kiss. Aoshi sat and pulled the scribe to sprawl across his lap. He stroked firm cheeks tenderly before pulling back his hand to deliver a sharp slap. He chuckled at the hurt look the scribe sent him. "It's only fair. As I recall you did this to me," he said, mirth apparent in his voice as he landed another stinging smack, enjoying the flush it brought to bronze flesh.

Ryuu relaxed when a slick finger caressed his opening, pressing in gently and pulling out before sliding in deeper, slowly easing the way. It pulled out and returned with a second, twisting and turning before scissoring, pushing deep to stroke over the scribe's prostate, making him arch and moan. A third finger joined in, and both men were soon panting as their hard cocks brushed against each other with every movement.

Aoshi could take no more, he lifted the scribe and positioned him over his dripping length, slowly lowering him until he sat securely in the warlord's lap. Soft hands clutched broad shoulders tightly as Ryuu was encircled by strong arms and plump lips were covered in tender kisses. "I want to stay like this for a minute, please," the warlord murmured. "I want to remember just how it feels."

Eventually Ryuu had to move so he started a slight rocking motion, pushing up slightly and falling back. The warlord joined in, rocking his hips up, striking the scribe's prostate, drawing a loud moan. Their rhythm gradually increased until, with one hard thrust, Aoshi came with a loud cry. It was too much and Ryuu came with a strangled sigh, the convulsions of his passage milking his lover of the last of his seed in a series of thunderous aftershocks that left him reeling.

Ryuu nuzzled the warlord's neck as he relaxed into the embrace. "We need to clean up. What time is dinner anyway?"

Aoshi peered at the light, trying to get his fuzzy mind to process what he was seeing. "Mmm, couple of hours I think."

At that the scribe reluctantly stood, hating the feeling of loss as their intimate connection was broken. "Come on you." He stuck out a hand to help his tall lover up. "Let's go take a bath."

The prospect of a bath with Ryuu was enough to get Aoshi up and moving, although a part of him was disappointed when it was limited to washing and a few stolen kisses. "We don't want to be late," the scribe reprimanded him when his hands wandered from scrubbing yet again.

"Don't want to go at all." The warlord suckled the shoulder that was taunting him. "Want to stay in with you."

"Tempting as that is, you said we'd be there." Aoshi found himself alone in the tub, the scribe already drying off and moving to dress.

Before long they were standing outside the general's tent. "Oi, Ken'ichi, Kotone, we're here," Aoshi called as they lifted the flap and stepped inside.

"Aoshi, you actually came." Kotone's voice preceded her as she stepped into the room. "I hope you brought your girlfriend."

"Well," he began hesitantly. "I brought Ryuu, but…"

"I'm not a girl," the scribe finished with a laugh as he stepped around the stammering warlord and extended his hand to the startled woman. "Hello, you must be Kotone. My name's Ryuu, I'm very pleased to meet you. Thank you so much for inviting us."

"Tiny, polite and pretty, I'd say he's close enough to a woman, Fujiwara!" a loud mirth-filled voice rang out as the general strode into the room.

"Ken'ichi," Kotone hissed. "I swear…" she faded off before turning to Ryuu. "I'm so sorry, my husband is an ill-mannered boor. It's lovely to have you. Please, make yourself comfortable." She threw a killing glare at her husband as she awkwardly moved to get drinks.

"Here, let me help you." The scribe moved to assist the very pregnant woman. Soon they were laughing and chatting as they moved from the makeshift kitchen to the table, leaving Aoshi and Ken'ichi to watch in wonder.

"You are in so much trouble," the general hissed as he watched his wife and Ryuu working in tandem. "She'll have you two hitched before the week is out."

"Huh?" the warlord grunted in shock, turning wide eyes on his friend just as Kotone called them to the table. He slowly rose and took his place, suddenly leery of what was to come.

Chapter Sixteen

Aoshi and Ken'ichi flopped onto their cushions, neither catching the pointed looks directed their way as Ryuu carefully helped Kotone get settled before gracefully kneeling on his own.

"Fujii Ken'ichi," his wife began in a venomous tone of voice as he lifted a piece of meat to his mouth. "What do you think you are doing?"

"Eating?" he queried around his mouthful.

"Guests first," she hissed as she slapped him hard, making him drop the food he was holding and look at her in astonishment.

"Yes dear," he said dejectedly, looking abjectly down at his plate.

"Whipped," Aoshi stated with a huge grin.

"Like you're any better," the scribe muttered under his breath, wiping the smile off the warlord's face and replacing it with an anxious look. "Kotone, everything looks wonderful." He gracefully served Aoshi and then himself. "So, what names were you thinking about for the baby?"

"Well, for a boy we've decided on Yuu. But if it's a girl…" Ken'ichi frantically began mouthing the word no and waving his hands back and forth, slowly trailing off as he observed the look on his wife's face. "…it will be either Aoi or Haruka. You do know we have a fifty percent chance of having a girl, don't you, Ken'ichi?"

The general mouthed 'save me' to his friend. "Yes dear, I know. You made that point very forcefully just last week." He rubbed his shoulder, remembering just how she had driven that particular message home.

"So, Aoshi," she began, rounding on her guest. "How did you and Ryuu meet?"

"Well," he began around a large mouthful of food. "Yuudai and

Ken'ichi and some of the guys took me to the market to buy a pleasure slave. They said I needed to loosen up."

"Don't talk with food in your mouth," the scribe hissed.

"Yes, Ryuu," the warlord said absently as he took a mouthful of tea to wash his food down and wiped his mouth before continuing. He paused, cocking his head to watch the scene playing out across the table with growing horror.

"You didn't," Kotone hissed, punching her husband. "Corrupting poor Aoshi like that." She turned to the man in question with a huge smile. "Please continue. I'm so sorry for Ken'ichi's interruption."

"Well, I didn't really want a pleasure slave, so I bought Ryuu instead. He's a scribe," Aoshi continued earnestly, "and really smart, he helps me with my paperwork." Ryuu broke out in a wide smile at the compliment, warming the warlord's heart.

"Anyway, the more time we spent together, the more I began to care for him, although I didn't realize it at the time…" he trailed off, not sure how much he should say about their relationship.

"Ryuu, you're a slave?" Kotone asked in surprise.

"Not anymore. Aoshi freed me, and I chose to stay with him."

"How romantic," Kotone gushed. "It's just like a story from one of my novels. The dashing warlord frees the wrongfully enslaved princess and they live happily ever after."

"Ryuu's not a princess," the warlord corrected her. "He was destined for a career in the government before his family sold him and stole his inheritance. We'll be fixing that."

"Aoshi," the scribe broke in. "You don't need to bother with any of that, you have much more important things to spend your time on."

"Nothing is more important than you. I will restore what they stole."

The sultry look the scribe aimed his way had the warlord twitching in his chair, ready to snatch his lover and head home. Kotone's voice finally broke through his lustful haze and he turned to look at her.

"Aoshi … Aoshi, hello, is anyone home?" their hostess asked as she waved her hand in front of the warlord's face.

"Yes, Kotone, I'm," his voice broke. He squealed, "sorry," as a strong foot began inching its way up his thigh.

"I asked if you and Ryuu were free next Saturday. We're

having one last get together before I have the baby."

"We'd be delighted," the scribe answered cheerily, taking pity on the now dumbstruck warlord as he slid his bare foot across a prominent bulge. Ryuu's agile toes wrapped around Aoshi's trapped erection and squeezed gently. His lover gasped, nearly choking. "What time?" he blithely continued, even as he ground hard into the now dripping length, before starting a teasing, light, up-and-down slide.

"Seven o'clock," she began before she was cut off by her husband, who was studying the warlord curiously.

"Say, Aoshi, everything alright?" The general inquired anxiously. "You look a little faint. Kotone, I told you all that talk about babies was enough to make anyone sick. Here, let me help you outside for some air."

The warlord almost passed out when Ken'ichi's hand wrapped around his forearm. The last thing he needed was to stand up and flaunt his little problem in Kotone's face. She was scary even before she got pregnant, and now her mood swings were a thing of legend.

"No, no I'm fine," he squawked, waving his arms frantically. "I was just," he searched his mind frantically for a worthy diversion, "thinking about how strong women must be to go through delivery. Yes, that's it."

"Ryuu." Kotone turned to face the scribe, a serious expression on her face. "You don't know how lucky you are to have someone who can empathize with what others are going through." She cast a dark glare at her husband. "Some people," poking Ken'ichi hard enough to crack a rib, "think everything's a joke."

"Now Kotone, I'm sure that's just his way of trying to put you at ease," the scribe soothed, making Ken'ichi look at him in a new light. "You're really being too hard on him. It's obvious he's crazy about you."

"Now," Ryuu continued as he rose. "you sit there and relax while I clear this table and bring in desert, it'll only take a moment." He gracefully gathered the dirty plates.

Kotone's voice rang out. "Leave the dishes, Ken'ichi will deal with them later. He needs to get into practice doing chores for after the baby comes."

Ryuu did as he was told and returned with a platter of sweet bean buns, noting the kicked puppy expression on the general's face and suppressing a laugh. He was glad Aoshi had gotten him to come, this was more fun than he could remember having in a long time.

Soon they were finished and Ryuu was thanking Kotone for a wonderful evening. Aoshi rose in a daze and clasped forearms with an equally shell-shocked Ken'ichi. "See you in the morning for training."

"Aaaaa, I'll need to work out the kinks; I see a night on the cold floor for me," the general replied. "See you then."

Aoshi merely hmm'd as he took Ryuu's arm and steered him outside, grateful to have survived the evening and eager to get home and pay his lover back for the little stunt he pulled during dinner. That thought in mind he pressed a kiss to the top of the scribe's head and quickened his pace, not wanting to waste any more time.

Chapter Seventeen

Yuudai woke in a panic. *Oh shit, oh shit, oh shit,* he thought as he tried not to hyperventilate. *I need to go try and explain.* He jumped out of bed and began to dress, completely confused when his clothes seemed to have shrunk.

"Those are mine," an amused voice piped up from the bed. "While it's kind of kinky you want to wear them, I really don't think they'll fit."

The general nearly broke his neck whipping around to look at the man in his bed and the clothes he was trying to squeeze into. "I-I-I," he stammered, completely unable to put together a sentence.

"You, you, you need to get back in this bed. I talked to Fujiwara this morning. Give him a few days to calm down before you see him," Akemi explained. "I'm supposed to keep you out of his sight and out of trouble, so get back here in bed so I can do that." He reached out, snagging the clothes that the general was struggling with, and yanked hard, toppling him back into bed.

"You talked to him?" Yuudai practically shrieked. "I have to go fix this now."

"You need to wake up and stop chasing someone who clearly isn't interested."

"You need to mind your own business," the general snapped back. "This is between Aoshi and I."

"You made it my business when you told me about it. Hell, you made it my business when you had sex with me even though you wanted him. You know what," the courier yelled as he began pulling on his clothes. "You do whatever you want. I'll make sure to come to your funeral. Other than that I wash my hands of you." He whirled and stormed out of the tent.

I certainly fucked that up. The general hastily pulled on his own clothes. *I'll go talk to him right after I fix things with Aoshi.* He rushed out of the tent and hurried toward the warlord's, eager to apologize and move past what he had done. As he drew closer, however, he slowed. *I can't fix this,* he thought in horror. *I raped my friend. We can't just pretend it didn't happen.*

His feet carried him relentlessly forward, even as his mind began to backpedal, and he looked up in surprise to find himself at his destination. He called out before entering this time. "Oi, Aoshi. You in?" He lifted the flap and peered into the gloom. He stepped inside, stopping when he realized the only occupant was Ryuu.

Yuudai studied the sleeping figure, recalling how he'd looked the last time the general had seen him, eyes closed in pleasure as he pounded into a clearly ecstatic Aoshi. *I was jealous*, he admitted. *I am jealous.* His heart clenched when he thought of everything he and the warlord had shared over the years, the easy camaraderie that would now be forever beyond his reach.

He rushed outside with a hand over his mouth, afraid that he'd let the scream that was building inside him loose and wake the man slumbering a few feet away. That's all he needed, to be found hovering over the warlord's sleeping slave. He headed toward the mess tent in a daze, hoping to find Akemi and apologize for being an ass.

Yuudai's luck was hovering between bad and worse. When he got to the mess he quickly spotted the courier, with someone else. A tall good-looking man he didn't know had his arm slung over Akemi's shoulder in a possessive manner as he whispered in his ear.

The general was surprised at the rage he felt watching another man touch his sometime lover. He walked toward them purposefully, hovering directly in front of them awaiting acknowledgment. "General, sir," the tall man stammered in shock. "Is there something I can help you with?"

"You can take your hands off Akemi, and get the hell out of my sight."

The soldier was quick to comply. "I'm so sorry. I didn't know." He darted out of the mess, leaving Akemi and the general staring after him.

"Just who the fuck do you think you are?" the courier growled. "I told you I washed my hands of you, and I meant it. Now, if you'll excuse me," he pushed past Yuudai, "I need to go catch my friend. I'd like to get laid tonight."

The general snagged his wrist as he passed. "I can help you with that. Come back to my tent, please?"

"No. I'd like to have sex with someone who sees me, and I know I'd like them to not run to someone else the moment we're done. You had your chance, too many of them, and now it's too late." He pulled his wrist from the general's grasp and headed after the tall soldier, leaving Yuudai wondering if there was anything else he could ruin that day.

* * *

The daimyo banged his hands on the table in frustration. "What do you mean he didn't buy a pleasure slave? What was Benjirou thinking?"

The soldier sitting across from him shrugged "We'll never know now, the dead keep their secrets close. In any event, it's too late. We'll have to find another way to get to Fujiwara-sama."

"But the plan was perfect. The pleasure slave we planted could still work. We just need to get them together. Maybe we should present him as a gift from the council."

"I doubt that would do any good. Apparently our warlord has a thing for his scribe. He even freed him. If he didn't have any interest in the pleasure slaves before, he certainly won't now."

"Well," the daimyo said, stroking his chin. "Then we need to lure the scribe away. He's free now, perhaps we can tempt him with a good position here in the palace. What is his name? I'll approach him."

"He goes by Ryuu. If he ever had a family name I haven't heard it. It should be on the manumission papers when they get filed."

"Ryuu ... no, it couldn't be," the noble murmured. "What does this Ryuu look like?"

"His coloring is very similar to your's, my lord, only he's smaller with a scar across his face."

"I will go and see him. This will work. We are tired of Fujiwara turning things upside down. By this time next month I hope to have power back in the hands of those who deserve to wield it, the nobles. After all, we have been trained for generations in the ways of leadership." His face twisted in an evil smirk. "With the army in the control of our friends we will have no problem cementing our position."

"I will convey your wishes to my superiors," the soldier replied with a curt bow. "If they have questions I will contact you again." He turned and swiftly left the building, heading back to camp to report on their meeting.

Oshiro Masashi sat silently for a moment after his departure before breaking out in a wide smile. *So cousin, you survived and landed on your feet. Too bad I'm going to wreck your world again.* He stood and headed for the market, he needed to pick up the pleasure slave and prepare him. Then he'd go find Ryuu.

Chapter Eighteen

Masashi finally found the man he'd been searching for. "I'm here to pick up the warlord's new slave."

"I thought he didn't want a pleasure slave." The slave dealer shook his head. "How did you change his mind?"

"I haven't yet, but I will. I have inside information that he's got a soft heart. He can take the slave he's presented with and make use of it, or I'll have it eliminated. Fujiwara won't condemn an 'innocent' boy to death, no matter what his wishes in the matter are." A slow smile spread across his face. "By this time next week he'll be out and we'll be in, and may the gods help anyone who tries to interfere."

Oki made no comment. He'd been paid well for the special training the boy had received. What happened to his charges once they were sold held no interest for him. "Let me go get him and you can be on your way."

He returned a few minutes later with a beautiful young boy in tow. "Kazuya." Oki squeezed the slave's shoulder tightly. "This gentleman will take you to your new master. Make sure you remember your lessons and work hard to please him."

"Yes, master. I live to serve."

Masashi took a moment to study the kneeling slave. He was beautiful certainly, long raven hair, smooth ivory skin and unusual violet eyes. He had a delicate, almost feminine quality which the noble found particularly attractive. "If all your stock is of this quality I may have to make a purchase for myself."

"I offer nothing but the finest quality, all physically perfect, each fully trained in the arts of pleasure, every one a virgin. I have yet to have a complaint." The slave trader bowed subserviently.

"Come, boy." Masashi snapped his fingers and motioned for the slave to precede him. On his way out he turned and said, "I will be in touch about the other matter." He swept out of the tent, slave in tow.

He headed for the military encampment. Once there he hurried the pleasure slave toward the warlord's tent, eager to set the next phase of his plan in motion.

* * *

Ryuu woke with a smile. He couldn't remember ever having as much fun as he had the night before at Ken'ichi and Kotone's. It had been years since he'd interacted with people in any sort of normal way. Although he had to keep reminding himself it was okay, he was slowly becoming used to the freedom he had now.

When he finished bathing he dressed, anxious to get to work on the pile of communications waiting for him. He hoped to have them ready when Aoshi returned from his morning training. He had just finished pulling on his clothes when the flap of the tent was thrown back and a daimyo entered, slave in tow.

"Good morning," Ryuu greeted him pleasantly. "Is there something I can do for you?"

"I seriously doubt that someone like you could manage anything useful," Masashi replied with a sneer. "I'm looking for Fujiwara-sama. I have a gift for him from the council."

"Aoshi is training. I'm not exactly sure when he'll return. Would you like to come back later? Or you could just leave the gift and I'll make sure he gets it," Ryuu replied politely, refusing to rise to the man's bait.

"I'll wait."

"Suit yourself." The scribe decided to get back to work and ignore the daimyo staring so intently at him. He was quickly absorbed in the correspondence he was sorting through, not noticing that the stare had turned predatory.

"So," the noble's voice broke his concentration. "Who might you be? I haven't seen you here before."

"I am the warlord's scribe, my name is Ryuu. I've been with him for several months now."

"Oh, so you're the slave I've heard so much about."

"I'm afraid you are mistaken, I am a free man," Ryuu retorted. "Now, if you don't mind, I have work to attend to."

"If you don't mind my asking," the noble interrupted with a sly smile. "What is your family name? You remind me of someone."

"Oshiro," the scribe replied distractedly. "Oshiro Ryuu."

"Cousin!" Masashi exclaimed. "We have been looking for you for years. I am your Uncle's son, Masashi. You must come stay at the house, meet the rest of the family. How did you come to be here?"

Ryuu's mouth dropped open in shock; this was his cousin, son of the man who had sold him so many years ago. The last thing he wanted was to spend time with anyone from that household. "While I would love that, I'm afraid I must decline. The warlord has need of me at all hours, and it would greatly inconvenience him."

"Not so free as you like to proclaim, eh," Masashi countered. "A truly free man goes where he will, he doesn't cater to the whims of another."

"I am free to do as I choose, and I choose to stay where I am," Ryuu stated. "I have no intention of changing my life at this time. Now, I really do have to get back to work. Are you sure you don't want to just leave the gift with me?"

"Fine." The noble snapped his fingers to summon the slave he had brought. "This is the council of noble's gift to the commander. It is our wish that he enjoy only the rarest of pleasures. If, however, he does not wish to make use of it, tell him to send it back and I will dispose of it."

"What do you mean by dispose?"

"It will be eliminated. It has been specially prepared for the warlord and will serve no other." A wide, cruel smile spread over Masashi's face. "It's really all up to him." He turned just before exiting the tent. "Think about my offer, Ryuu. You really can do better than this."

Ryuu turned to examine the boy. "What is your name?" he inquired gently, feeling nothing but pity for him.

"Kazuya," the slave replied. "I was named that for I am to be the start of a life of pleasure and ease for our esteemed warlord. I have been trained for five years to be the epitome of erotic service, ready to cater to his every whim."

"I'm afraid that won't be possible. I cater to his needs, and he to mine. There is no place for you here."

"That is for the warlord to decide," the slave declared. "But why condemn me so quickly? Perhaps you might enjoy me together." He reached out and caressed the scribe's face. "I would certainly like that."

The scribe struggled to suppress his shudder. This was the life he had so narrowly escaped; the last thing he wanted was to be reminded of it on a daily basis. He could not share with this slave, no matter how guilty it made him feel. He struggled to find an answer to the dilemma that would allow the slave to live while still keeping him away from Aoshi.

Half an hour later Ryuu reluctantly admitted to himself that he could see no way out of the trap his cousin had ensnared them in. He finally gave up and slumped on a cushion to wait for Aoshi's return, Kazuya kneeling gracefully at his side.

Chapter Nineteen

Aoshi finally returned from training early in the afternoon, surprised to find Ryuu sitting quietly, lost in thought, rather than working as he'd expected. "What's the matter?" he asked as his eyes adjusted and he toed off his shoes. Then he gracefully stalked over to the scribe, kneeling behind him and leaning over his shoulder, capturing his lips in a hard kiss.

"Ahhh," Ryuu squealed, startled out of his thoughts moments before the warlord began kissing him senseless. "Aoshi, wait…"

"I have no interest in waiting," he mumbled as he nipped a path down the column of the scribe's neck. "Let's take a bath and then go back to bed. I haven't been able to get my mind off of you all morning."

"That sounds wonderful, but we have company right now."

"Oh, you certainly shouldn't stop on my account. I'll be more than happy to lend a hand, or a mouth, or whatever else you'd like," the pleasure slave interjected as he rubbed sensuously against the startled warlord.

"Ryuu, what's going on?" Aoshi stammered as he pulled back, peeling the slave off of himself with both hands. "Who is this person and why is he touching me?"

"This," the scribe began grumpily, "is your new pleasure slave, Kazuya. A gift from the council of nobles; they wish you to have nothing but the best." He turned worried brown eyes on Aoshi. "My cousin Masashi delivered him this morning."

"And you allowed this because?"

"Well, let's see … in the first place it's not up to me to accept or reject any gift made to you, that would be totally presumptuous. Not to mention the fact that I was a little taken aback by the unexpected appearance of my cousin. Oh, and then there's the added problem that he'll be executed if you don't keep him."

"Not my problem." Aoshi grabbed the slave by the arm and shoved him outside the tent.

"Aoshi, you can't just throw him out. They'll kill him."

"Like I said, not my problem. I can't afford to accept anything from those snakes on the council. For all I know he'll kill me as soon as I shut my eyes. Unless you have some other reason to keep him? You don't prefer him to me, do you?"

"Don't be silly. How could I ever compare a boy like that to you? Believe me, the last thing I want anywhere near me is a pleasure slave. The thought gives me the shivers. I can't just condemn him to death, though. It could have just as easily been me."

The warlord wrapped strong arms around the scribe. "I understand. What do you want me to do?"

"Well, for the time being I guess you'll have to keep him, at least until we figure a way out of this," Ryuu answered, unhappiness clearly evident in his voice. "I just hope we can do it quickly. I don't like the way he looks at you."

"Well, if it makes you feel better, I haven't looked at him at all. The only person I want is you," Aoshi assured him. "Now, let's go have that bath, I'm all dirty from training."

"Kazuya, please wait here for us while we bathe. Make yourself comfortable, we shouldn't be too long." Ryuu was cut off with a squeak as the warlord grabbed him around the waist and dragged him off to the bath.

The communal baths were, thankfully, deserted. Most of the men were off performing their daily duties while those on the night guard slumbered. The pair quickly stripped and scrubbed themselves before slipping into the heated water.

The scribe found himself seated between long legs, a broad chest against his back and sure hands stroking every inch of his skin. He was coaxed to lean forward as a hot mouth began to nip and suck its way down his spine, before stopping to nibble and knead firm cheeks.

"We can't do this here," Ryuu hissed. "We'll dirty the water."

"Then I'll have it replaced," Aoshi assured him. "Just relax and enjoy. It isn't often we'll get the chance to have the bath to ourselves. It would be a shame to waste the opportunity."

Ryuu let out a loud groan when a finger slowly slipped into his tight pucker, stroking and loosening. It was soon joined by a second and they began stretching and scissoring, opening him up for what was to come. He moaned wantonly when the fingers were removed and replaced by the head of his lover's cock.

Aoshi paused when he was fully seated, the scribe bent over the side of the tub, knuckles white and back bowed as he adjusted to being filled. The warlord whispered reassurances as he stroked tense muscles, almost dizzy from the heady sensation of being surrounded by Ryuu's tight heat.

Finally the muscles eased and Aoshi started to move, slowly pulling out until only the head remained. He slid back in, twin cries ringing out as Ryuu's prostate was struck and his passage convulsed around the warlord's hard cock. "Gods, Ryuu," a deep husky murmur tickled his ear. "How did I survive before I found you?"

A strong hand wrapped around the scribe's bobbing erection and began to lightly stroke it, the calloused palm barely caressing the satiny skin as the thumb idly rubbed across the tip.

The warlord pressed his chest to Ryuu's back and increased the pace, a strong arm wrapping around to pinch and rub at his nipples. The scribe moaned wantonly and tossed his head back onto a broad shoulder, writhing as his prostate was repeatedly struck. "I'm so close."

Immediately the pace slowed and the hands stilled. "Not yet, I haven't had enough of you." Aoshi captured plump lips in a deep, devouring kiss, breaking apart for air, only to dive right back in. Ever so slowly he began to move again, gradually increasing the speed and force of his thrusts until they were once more teetering on the brink.

When Aoshi stopped the second time, Ryuu thought he might lose his mind. "Please, please," he mumbled into the pale column of the warlord's neck as he frantically nipped and sucked at the tender flesh. "I'm going crazy, please move."

"This time, I promise," his lover whispered as he once again began to move. There was no gradual progression, no slow build-up, instead the warlord immediately started a series of deep hard thrusts that soon had both men moaning continuously as they drew close.

Finally a strong hand grasped the scribe's tortured member and began to stroke in rhythm, making Ryuu squirm and shudder, endless cries of his lover's name falling from his lips, ending in a keening wail as he shot burst after burst of creamy seed onto their chests.

The look of abandon on Ryuu's face as it contorted in the throes of pleasure made a host of unnameable feelings course through the warlord, and he came deep inside his lover with a strangled shout. They lay sprawled in the tub, panting for breath as they recovered, only to be pulled back to reality by the sound of clapping.

"Well, that was certainly entertaining," Kazuya remarked from his position by the door. He strode forward, shedding his clothes as he moved, stopping next to the tub. "Now, master, if you're done with this camp whore, perhaps you'd like to experience real pleasure. Not only am I fully versed in the erotic arts, but I'm also a virgin—hot, tight and all yours." The slave practically purred the last as he came to kneel beside the tub, finishing with a sensuous lick to the warlord's ear.

Aoshi recoiled violently, pushing Ryuu away in the process. The scribe gasped, seeing it as a rejection, and quickly jumped out of the tub. He pulled on his clothes before rushing out of the baths, leaving the warlord and his new pleasure slave naked and alone.

Chapter Twenty

Ryuu raced mindlessly out of the tent, no destination in mind other than away. Halfway across camp he slowed as he realized he had nowhere to go. He finally came to a halt, staring mindlessly, tears streaming down his face. He nearly jumped out of his skin when a hand landed on his shoulder.

"Ryuu, are you alright? What are you doing over here?" Akemi asked softly as he peered into the scribe's face. "Did something happen to Fujiwara-sama?"

At the sound of Aoshi's name the scribe dissolved into a fresh round of tears. "It's ....it's ... it," he stammered, unable to compose himself long enough to get the words out.

"Come with me," Akemi crooned soothingly. "You need to sit down and have a drink, then you can tell me all about it." He wrapped an arm around Ryuu's shoulders and propelled him until they reached the courier's tent. "I'm afraid it's not as nice as what you're used to."

Soon he was pressing a cup into trembling hands. "Just drink and relax. I'm sure we'll find a solution to whatever it is."

"Why me?" Ryuu finally asked in a soft voice laden with self-loathing. "Why did he choose me in the first place. I was alright as a sensei, I didn't need this." He shook his head before straightening and looking the courier in the eye. "The council gifted Aoshi with a pleasure slave. They named him Kazuya because he was supposed to bring harmony to Aoshi's rule," he said bitterly. "They were going to execute the slave if Aoshi didn't keep him so I convinced him he had to. But, he's young, beautiful, and the way he looks at Aoshi..." The scribe trailed off into a fresh wave of sobs.

"He threw you over for a pleasure slave?" Akemi asked in a tight voice, but Ryuu only cried harder. "What the fuck is wrong with him? He lost his oldest friend over you. He whipped the men who raped you himself. Hell, I thought he was going to kill me when I told him. He worships you, and he threw you away over a pretty boy." By this point the courier was livid. All he could think about was how badly Yuudai had been hurt by the warlord's involvement with Ryuu, and now that didn't matter anymore. He was going to go have a talk with his commander.

"I'm going to go talk some sense into his dumb ass." The courier stalked out of the tent, fists clenched at his sides. Ryuu, however, had stopped hearing the courier at the mention of the rape he didn't remember. *That's it,* he decided. *I'm dirty, disgusting. That's why Aoshi doesn't want me.* He shuddered as a flash of memory assaulted him, jeering faces, blinding pain, rough heavy hands on him. A low keening wail escaped his throat as he realized those men were still here in camp, watching him, knowing what had happened. Who had they told? Did everyone know what happened? *I can't stay here, I can't. I have to get out.*

Yuudai paused outside the tent and looked at the bottle in his hand. *Just apologize for being a total ass,* he told himself. *Maybe he'll forgive you.* "Oi, Akemi," he called as he lifted the flap. "I brought you…" he trailed off in shock. Akemi was nowhere to be seen, the sole occupant of the tent was an obviously distraught Ryuu.

The scribe looked up at the call of Akemi's name. When he spotted the general he almost gasped in relief. *I'll be safe with him till I get away*, he decided. "General, I need your help. I need to get out of this camp and to my cousin's house in town. Can you take me, please?" he asked, tears still streaming down his stricken countenance.

Yuudai automatically asked, "Where's Aoshi?" But his only answer was a fresh bout of tears. "Fine, fine, I'll help you, please stop crying." He fumbled in his sleeve pocket, pulling out a rag for the scribe to wipe his face. "Who's your cousin?" he asked, hoping that this, at least, was a safe topic.

"Oshiro Masashi. I'm afraid I don't know his address."

"I know who he is. Are you sure that's where you want to go?"

"I have nowhere else," Ryuu replied. "Can we leave now? I really want to get away from here."

Yuudai nodded and headed out, holding the flap for the scribe before they set off for town.

* * *

Akemi stormed into the warlord's tent, fists clenched and eyes ablaze. "Fujiwara, I need to talk some sense into your sorry ass…" He trailed off at the sight that met his eyes. There stood the warlord, fully dressed and pulling on his shoes. Next to him on the floor was the pleasure slave, naked, bound and blindfolded.

"I can explain," the warlord began as he raised his hands in supplication. "I had to tie him up." He was cut off abruptly when Akemi's fist collided with his face.

"What is your fucking problem, Fujiwara?" he bellowed. "First you break Yuudai's heart, now Ryuu's. I'm gonna beat some sense into your sorry ass." His first blow may have landed, but the second never had a chance. The enraged courier found himself pinned to the floor by a muscular forearm.

"What the fuck are you talking about?" the warlord ground out, hard eyes freezing Akemi in place. "What happened to Ryuu? Do you know where he is?"

"He's in my tent. Crying his eyes out because you rejected him for that." He poked the clearly furious pleasure slave with his foot. "I get it, you're tall, handsome and powerful. You can do whatever you want, but you need to start thinking of other people and not just yourself before you lose everyone's respect."

"Reject Ryuu, for that?" the warlord sneered. "Have you lost your mind? I would never reject him, especially not for some toy the council stuck me with."

"Oh, really?" the courier snarked back. "Then why, pray tell, is he trussed up like that?"

Aoshi shot him a clearly puzzled look. "He kept touching me so I had to tie him up, and then I blindfolded him because I didn't like the way he looked at me." He shivered before continuing. "I tried to get rid of him but Ryuu insisted I keep him. Doesn't mean I have to like it."

"You mean you didn't fuck him?" the courier asked in surprise.

The warlord's face screwed up in distaste. "You have to be kidding me. I wouldn't touch that thing with a ten foot pole." The trussed slave wriggled and thrashed, trying to get free.

"I hate you," Kazuya yelled. "I'm not a thing, I'm perfect. You're supposed to want me."

"Well, I don't," Aoshi retorted. "And I never will. I will dispose of you in the morning. Akemi, take me to Ryuu now, please. I have to straighten this out."

The two left the furious slave writhing impotently on the floor and headed for Akemi's tent. When they arrived, however, it was empty. "Is this some kind of joke, Suzuki-san? Because I don't have time for your crap right now."

"No, he was right there." Akemi indicated the overturned teacup and discarded rag. Then he noticed the bottle sitting on the floor. "Someone else was here and left that bottle. They probably took Ryuu."

"Took him." The warlord swallowed around his suddenly dry throat. "Took him where?"

The courier just shook his head. "Away from here. We need to figure out who was here before we'll know any more."

Aoshi was already striding out of the tent. "Where are you going?" Akemi called after him.

"I'm going to get the dogs," he called back. "They can track them for us." With that he disappeared into the deepening gloom, leaving Akemi to fret and pace, unsettled by the events taking place and worrying about what it all meant.

Chapter Twenty-One

Yuudai kept shooting glances at the scribe walking by his side. Something had happened between him and Aoshi, of that much the general was sure. What he really wanted to know was what. He couldn't imagine the warlord giving Ryuu up voluntarily.

"Ryuu," he began tentatively. "What exactly happened between you and the commander? If you tell me maybe I can talk to him and straighten it out."

The scribe sighed deeply. "Not that it matters, but the council gave him a pleasure slave. He's beautiful and perfect, and I'm ugly and tainted. Not too hard to figure out now, is it?"

"A pleasure slave? He has no interest in pleasure slaves, that's how he ended up with you in the first place. I mean, someone suggested that he could use one, said he was too serious. When we took him to the market he didn't even glance at them, he bought you instead." Yuudai looked at the scribe appraisingly. "I don't know about tainted, but you're hardly ugly." He reached out and ran a finger along Ryuu's scar, starting on the right cheek and slowly tracing over his face to the other end. "Even this only makes you seem exotic, not like my scars."

"How did you get them?" the scribe asked. "You must be very strong to have survived, and very brave."

"There was a fire," the general said in a faraway voice. "I was trying to get the injured out when I was trapped in the burning building. I don't really know what happened after that. I woke up a few days later. I didn't know anything could hurt so deeply. Aoshi visited every day while I recovered." He thought for a moment. "It's always been like that. He can be very thoughtful, but he doesn't open up and he never lets go. You're the first person he's ever wanted more with, and I've been so jealous. I never once thought about his happiness the way he's always thought about mine."

"He doesn't hate you, you know. What you did confused the hell out of him, but he could never hate you." Ryuu shuffled his feet nervously. "I wanted to kill you for what you did, but at the same time I understand it. It's just, Aoshi, and he's totally oblivious to the chaos he leaves in his wake. I knew this was going to happen. I knew I'd get my heart broken and I tried to keep my distance. I just couldn't."

Yuudai stopped and turned to the scribe, grabbing his arm to hold his attention. "Are you sure you want to leave. We can go back right now. I'm sure that this is all some ridiculous mistake. I know he cares about you."

"That's very sweet of you to say," Ryuu replied in a soft voice. "But things have changed and it's better for him this way. No one would have accepted our relationship. It could only hurt him." He turned to the general and forced a smile. "Akemi really likes you, you know. He doesn't mind your scars. Maybe you should give him a chance; he's a really nice guy."

The pair walked on in silence, each thinking about what the other had said, until they reached the Oshiro estate. "Are you sure?" Yuudai asked one last time.

"This is best for everyone. At least until I get a job and find a place of my own. Don't tell him where I am, please. This is painful enough without dragging it out." With that he rang the bell, speaking quietly with the man who answered before disappearing inside.

* * *

Akemi paced while he waited for Aoshi to return. After what seemed like an eternity, but in reality was probably only about ten minutes, a pack of dogs flooded past him into the tent, snuffling around the bottle and spilled tea before racing toward the gates, the warlord hot on their heels. "Wait for me," he called as he hurried to catch up.

The dogs raced across camp and out the gate, pausing occasionally to snuffle the ground before taking off again, the two men impatiently following. When they stopped outside the gates to the Oshiro estate, Aoshi cringed when he realized how upset the scribe must be to come here rather than stay in camp.

He motioned for Akemi to stay with the dogs while he headed for the door. When someone finally answered he asked for the scribe, then waited. To say the warlord was less than pleased when Masashi appeared instead of Ryuu would be an understatement. "I need to speak with Ryuu immediately," he snarled.

"I'm so sorry," Masashi replied in an oily, patently fake, voice. "My cousin does not wish to see you. He says you should go back to your pleasure slave and leave him be."

"I can't do that, his services are vital," the warlord replied. "He needs to come with me now."

"I'm afraid not, Fujiwara-sama. He's neither a slave nor a soldier; you can't make him do anything. Now, if you'll excuse me, my cousin needs comforting," he finished with a smirk before shutting the door in the warlord's face.

Aoshi stood outside the door with clenched fists. *I'm going to kill that son of a bitch*, he decided. *Right after I get Ryuu back.* He pounded on the door, but no one responded. *Fine*, he thought, *I'll come back in the morning with troops. I will get back what's mine.*

He slumped at the realization that there would be no warm welcoming body to cuddle with in bed that night before returning to an impatiently waiting Akemi.

"He won't see me," the warlord whispered. "What the fuck did I do?"

"Come on, let's get you back to camp." Akemi slung a comforting arm around the warlord's shoulders and began guiding him in the correct direction. "We'll come back in the morning and straighten everything out after you've both had a good night's sleep."

Ryuu, unfortunately, was oblivious to the turmoil he was causing. The cup of tea his cousin offered him had been laced with powerful herbs. The scribe was locked in a nightmare, reliving his rape over and over again, made even worse by the hallucinations the plants induced.

Masashi watched with a slowly spreading smile as the scribe writhed and shrieked in agony, reveling in the tears tracking down now ashen cheeks. "Sorry, cousin," he hissed sarcastically. "But you got in my way yet again. Don't worry though, you and your beloved will be reunited on the other side soon." He chuckled to himself and took another sip of wine, relaxing back in his chair to enjoy the show.

* * *

Yuudai contemplated Ryuu's words as he headed back to camp. *I need to support my friend,* he decided. *I have to talk to Aoshi and straighten this out, they should be together.* He headed towards the warlord's tent, a tentative plan starting to form in his mind.

"Oi Aoshi," he called as he strode into the tent, "I need to talk…" he stopped short at the sight of the bound and blindfolded slave. *Shit, maybe Ryuu was right.* Angered at the very idea he roughly shook the bound figure. "You, slave, where's the commander?"

"Untie me and I'll tell you," was the gentle response. Yuudai quickly cut the bonds and removed the blindfold, blinking as the beautiful young man gracefully unfurled himself to stand naked before him. "My hero," the slave whispered breathily, before embracing the general and capturing his lips in a long passionate kiss.

Kazuya watched in amusement as the general slumped to the floor unconscious before quickly donning his clothes and slipping out of the tent.

Chapter Twenty-Two

Aoshi shuffled dejectedly into his tent, loathe to even set eyes on the pleasure slave that had started this whole mess. He was shocked to find, instead, a pile of rope where the slave's bindings had been cut, and an unconscious Yuudai.

"Yuudai, Yuudai," he called as he shook the limp form. *Oh shit no*, he thought, quickly dropping his head to the general's chest to check for a heartbeat. *Thank the gods*. He sighed in relief when he sensed a very weak flutter. He scooped his friend into his arms and headed for the healer's tent, calling for help as he raced in and deposited his burden on an empty table.

"He's ingested some sort of poison," the healer decided after examining the general, noticing some burn marks on his lips. "We'll have to try and identify it so we can prepare an antidote." He swabbed the area and disappeared, leaving the warlord to pace.

The sun was starting to peek over the horizon and the healer still had not returned. Aoshi watched his oldest friend slipping away and felt a profound sense of despair. *I need to do something. I'm going to explode if this keeps up.* He decided that he might as well round up some help to get Ryuu back, since he couldn't do anything for the general. "You hold on, I'll be back," he whispered in the unconscious man's ear before giving his shoulder a squeeze and leaving the tent.

"Ken'ichi. Oi, Ken'ichi," he called softly from outside his tent. "I need you." He was startled when Kotone's tousled head poked out instead of the general's.

"He's getting dressed, Aoshi," she said with a smile. "Would you like some tea while you wait?" She studied the man before her critically. He was obviously exhausted, dark circles clearly evident under bloodshot eyes. "Have you been up all night? Come in and sit down at least." She pulled him into the tent. "I'll hurry Ken'ichi along."

She disappeared behind the screen that hid the bed from view. "Ken'ichi, something's wrong with Aoshi, he looks terrible. He's waiting for you. Hurry up and get out there, I want to know what's going on."

"Yes dear." He finished pulling on his clothes and headed in to greet his friend. "Good morning, commander. What can I do for you?"

"It's Ryuu. He's at his cousin's and I need to get him back." Ken'ichi blinked and looked at Aoshi appraisingly.

"I think I deserve more explanation than that." The general leaned back patiently as the warlord proceeded to fill in the details of the previous day's events.

He stuttered to a stop when Kotone smacked him on the back of the head hard enough to rattle his teeth.

"Fujiwara Aoshi, I can't believe you did that," she hissed, face contorted in anger. "You are such an idiot." She smacked him again, unmoved by the hurt look he graced her with. "And don't try those puppy dog eyes on me, they won't work. You men are so hopeless, I'm surprised you get anything accomplished." She began pulling on her cloak. "I'll go get this straightened out. You just sit here and figure you how you'll apologize."

She turned and waddled out of the tent, dark hair streaming behind her. Aoshi turned to his general, astonishment clear on his face. "My gods, how do you deal with that on a daily basis?"

"Practice," Ken'ichi muttered. "I usually just say 'yes dear' and agree with her completely, makes it less painful at least. Seriously though, the woman's a force of nature. I pity anyone who gets in her way."

Kotone rapped on the door to the Oshiro estate, tapping her foot in impatience until it finally opened and a servant peered out. "I'm here to see Ryuu," she declared, sweeping past the man and into the entry hall. "Please tell him to hurry, I don't have all day."

A few minutes later Masashi appeared. "May I help you?" he asked in an overly polite voice.

"I'm here to see Ryuu," Kotone stated. "I've been kept waiting long enough, so go fetch him please. Tell him Kotone's here."

"I'm terribly sorry," the daimyo said with a sneer. "But my cousin is not feeling well. I'm afraid you'll have to come back another time. I will, however, tell him you called."

"He's sick? Well, I'd like to see him then. Make sure he doesn't need anything."

"I assure you my staff is doing an excellent job caring for him," Masashi informed her. "Besides, he could be contagious. You wouldn't want to take any chances in your condition." He grasped her elbow and began moving her towards the door.

"I'm not worried," Kotone said breezily. "I won't get too close, but I'm not leaving until I see him."

The daimyo ground his teeth in frustration. He needed to get this woman out of there before she ruined everything. "I really don't think..." he began before he was cut off by the very irate, very pregnant Kotone.

"That," she said between clenched teeth, "is painfully obvious. You really shouldn't agitate a woman in my condition. I could go into labor right here."

Masashi recoiled in horror at the thought. "Fine, follow me," he said coldly. "But just a peek and then you'll really have to leave. Ryuu needs his rest." He led her up the stairs and into a small, rather empty, room where the scribe lay, sweating and thrashing on the futon, apparently asleep.

"As you can see, he's quite ill," the noble pointed out. "Now, I really must insist that you go home. I'll be sure to tell him you stopped by when he recovers." With that he ushered her to the front door, handing over her cloak before rudely shutting the door in her face.

Kotone stormed back to camp, completely incensed. *I'll teach him to try and get rid of me*, she thought angrily. *Just you wait and see.* She threw open the tent flap and fixed the two men inside with a poisonous glare. "Why are you just sitting here?" she yelled at the hapless pair. "Go get Ryuu back ... now."

The men scrambled out of the tent, unwilling to even ask questions in the face of the woman's wrath. "You better hope to hell you fix this, Fujiwara," the general said. "Otherwise you get to explain it to Kotone. I spend enough time banned from my bed as it is."

"Oh, I'll get him back," the warlord ground out as they stopped to pick up some guards before heading into town. "Even if I have to raze the place to the ground." Ken'ichi shuddered at the look on the warlord's face. *I haven't seen him this angry since Benjirou. Gods help anyone who tries to balk him now.*

The party soon arrived at the estate and the commander banged on the door. When it opened he pushed past the servant and hurried inside, calling the scribe's name as he took the stairs two at a time.

He found Ryuu in the third room he tried, unconscious, wringing wet, and apparently in agony. "Hold on, Ryuu. I've got you," the warlord whispered as he stroked sweat matted locks. Scooping up limp figure he hurried back downstairs, only to be met by an angry Masashi.

"You can't just break in here and take him," the noble snarled. "I'll ruin you for this, Fujiwara."

The warlord shot a hand out and wrapped it around the man's neck. "You won't be ruining anything. One of my generals is near death, apparently poisoned by the slave you sought fit to gift me with. And now Ryuu is in much the same state."

He turned to the waiting guards. "Arrest this man and make sure you bind him well. I will deal with him later," he commanded before rushing back to camp with Ryuu.

Chapter Twenty-Three

Aoshi made his way to the healer's tent for the second time that day. "Help me," he called. "He's burning up and in so much pain." The healer rushed to Ryuu's side, quickly checking him over.

"It appears he's under the influence of some unknown substance," the healer stated slowly. "Although it's not the same one that was used on the general." He took some samples and hurried off to try and determine what had been done to the scribe, cursing under his breath at having two patients under the warlord's watchful eye and no answers as to what was affecting either of them.

Aoshi sat by Ryuu's bed, holding a trembling hand in his large ones, eyes riveted on the thrashing form. "Please, Ryuu," he whispered. "Please wake up. I need you and only you. Kazuya is gone, everything will be just like it was if you'll only wake up and look at me." He hung his head and sent a blind prayer to gods he wasn't sure he believed in. *Please, let him be alright. I don't want to survive without him.*

* * *

Akemi stumbled into the mess, looking worse for wear after the turmoil of the previous evening. He was immediately assaulted by a chorus of voices. "Hey, Akemi, did you hear? Fujiwara-sama found General Tanaka-san poisoned in his tent last night. I heard he may not survive."

The courier had to grab hold of the table to steady himself before heading to the healer's to get more information. He stopped dead at the sight that met his eyes. Aoshi was holding onto a thrashing Ryuu, using his greater size to pin him to the bed so he wouldn't hurt himself. In the next bed lay Yuudai, pale as death and unmoving.

Akemi's heart almost stopped when he saw how still the general was compared to the scribe. "Oh, you silly man," he said as he carefully smoothed a hand across his cheek. "What have you gotten yourself into now?" He pulled up a chair and sat down beside the bed, carefully clasping the still figure's hand in his.

The healer returned, a cup in his hand. "I think I've got an antidote for the general."

"Wait just a minute," Akemi protested. "What do you mean think? Could it be dangerous?"

"Well, I didn't have much of a sample to work with, so it may not be effective. As far as danger goes, normally it wouldn't be an issue; but with his vital signs so weak, anything could be fatal. However, if we do nothing he will most certainly die."

"Hurry up then," the courier urged in a tight voice. "I have some questions for his dumb ass."

Aoshi looked up from his vigil when he heard Akemi questioning the healer, sending a prayer up for his friend's recovery. *Kami, let this turn out all right. Let them both recover.* He turned his gaze back to the scribe, his heart breaking at the pain clearly etched on his face.

"Healer, what about Ryuu? Any idea what's wrong with him?"

"Unfortunately, I do know, and I'm afraid it isn't good. He was given an herb that causes hallucinations. It causes a person to relive the worst moments of their life. If left under its influence for too long, madness is generally the result." He regarded the warlord warily. "I've sent for the antidote, it should be here shortly. Do you know how long he's been under its influence?"

"I'm not sure." Aoshi frowned as he thought. "Probably since sometime last night, although I'm not sure when. It was after... Hey, Akemi." He turned to the courier. "What time did you come to my tent yesterday?"

"I'm not sure, five maybe?" he replied distractedly, eyes never leaving Yuudai's pale face.

"So, after five certainly. Probably a bit later than that." The warlord narrowed his eyes and glared. "How long does he have?"

"A few more hours, sir," the healer replied. "It will be close though."

"I just wish I could do something to help him."

"I'm afraid there isn't much you can do now. After he comes out of it," the healer paused and shot a wary look at Aoshi, "he'll need a lot of help."

"Not a problem," the warlord replied decisively. "Just get him the antidote and I'll take care of him after. He'll have whatever he needs."

A noise from the next bed caught their attention. Yuudai groaned several times before rolling to his side and vomiting. Akemi wiped his face with a damp cloth before bending to whisper, "You scared the shit out of me. Don't do that again."

"'m sorry," the general mumbled. "Was an ass to you. F'rgive me?"

"Forgiven and forgotten," Akemi assured him. "What happened to you, anyway?"

"Was lookin' for Aoshi," Yuudai slurred. "Untied the slave to find out where you were. Kissed me and then ... nothin' till now." His eyes shut and he seemed to drift back into sleep, before continuing. "Find the damn slave. And get Ryuu, he's at Oshiro-san's." This time the general began to snore, making it clear he was done with conversation for the moment.

The healer moved in to check his vital signs. "He's looking much better, his heartbeat and respiration are much closer to normal. I think he'll recover with rest."

"Akemi," the warlord ordered. "Get Fujii-san for me. We need to find Kazuya before anyone else ends up in here."

The courier nodded and stood to leave, giving Yuudai's hand one last squeeze before heading out to collect Ken'ichi.

"General Fujii-san," he called from outside the tent. "The commander has need of you."

"Come in Akemi," the general answered. "I'll be right with you."

Kotone was pacing, trying not to fret about Ryuu. Ken'ichi had told her that Aoshi had rushed him to the healers, but he didn't know anything more. And he forbad her from going to check on him, stating the healer's tent with all its sickness was no place for a pregnant woman.

"Is there any news on Ryuu's condition?" she asked as soon as the courier entered.

"They were waiting for an antidote to be delivered. Apparently he was dosed with a powerful hallucinogenic potion. Fujiwara-sama's with him, that's why he needs the general. Someone has to find the pleasure slave, Kazuya. He's the one that poisoned Tanaka-san."

"Hurry your lazy butt up, Ken'ichi," Kotone bellowed. "Aoshi needs your help."

"Yes dear." He planted a quick peck on her cheek before following the courier back to the healer's to meet with Aoshi.

Chapter Twenty-Four

"Ken'ichi," the warlord began as soon as he arrived. "I need you to track down the pleasure slave, Kazuya. He's dangerous, his saliva contains poison. They must have been feeding it to him for years to build up his immunity. Anyone he kisses could die."
 He gritted his teeth before continuing. "Put him in with Oshiro-san when you find him. I'll deal with them both once I'm sure Ryuu will be alright."
 The general hurried across the compound to the small jail. He was sure that if anyone knew where the slave would flee it would be Masashi.
 When he opened the door and strode inside he found both of the guards on the floor and the prisoner missing. *Shit*, he thought, rubbing a hand across his face. *Aoshi's going to have my head.* He debated for a moment then headed for the gate, calling to some men to get the guards to a healer. *If they haven't left the compound we'll track them down eventually. Where they're hiding could point out other snakes we need to get rid of.*
 When he reached the gate he was relieved to find the guards unharmed. "Has anyone passed through tonight?"
 "A few men have come back from town but no one has gone out," the guards replied. Ken'ichi was quick to fill them in on the situation and leave some extra men on guard. Once he was sure no one would be leaving camp he had his men spread out and they began searching tent to tent.
 The problems began when they reached the tent of Endo Nozomi. "Oi, Endo-san," Ken'ichi called. "We need to search your tent."
 The grizzled soldier appeared at the opening, a serious look on his face. "What do you mean, Fujii-san? These are my personal

quarters."

"There are dangerous prisoners loose in camp. We're looking for a pleasure slave and a noble, Oshiro Masashi, perhaps you know him?" Ken'ichi studied the veteran's face. He was older and had come to power while Aoshi and his friends were still coming up through the ranks. To say he resisted change would be an understatement.

"I knew his father," the older man rumbled. "We were friends when we were children. I haven't seen Masashi though. If I do I'll be sure to let you know." He turned to head back into his tent when Ken'ichi stopped him.

"We still need to check."

"You doubt my word? I've been a loyal officer since before you were born, pup."

"I never said I doubted you," Ken'ichi replied. "It's for your protection. General Tanaka-san is in critical condition, as is the warlord's scribe. Obviously we wish to prevent any more tragedies. Now," his smile disappeared, "if you'll excuse me." He pushed past and into the tent as his men spread out to surround it.

Ken'ichi glanced around, noticing three cups on the table but no occupants. He continued to the back, where found the pleasure slave hiding in a chest. "General, we've got one," a voice yelled from outside.

He hurried out, pulling the slave behind him, to find his men standing over a prone Masashi. He had been crawling out from under the edge of the tent.

"Endo-san," Ken'ichi said coldly. "I'm afraid you're guilty of harboring fugitives. Men, take him into custody. Escort them to the jail and triple the guard. Make sure everyone stays well away from the slave, his kiss is deadly. The commander will deal with them personally."

A collective shiver ran through the men at the last words, remembering how the warlord had 'dealt with' Benjirou. They quickly moved to do as Ken'ichi bid, not wanting to get consigned to a similar fate.

Ken'ichi hurried back to the healer's tent, anxious to let Aoshi know that he had the prisoners in custody and to check on the guards. The scene when he entered was pure chaos. Akemi was trying to keep Yuudai in bed, healers were frantically working on the two guards. In the middle sat the warlord, an island of calm, oblivious to the storm raging around him as he focused only on the man whose hand he held.

Ryuu tossed and turned. Although the antidote had been administered he was still lost in his own mind, whimpering as a particularly unpleasant memory surfaced. "I hope you have good news for me," the warlord said. "I could certainly use some."

"Oshiro-san and the pleasure slave have been recaptured," he hesitated. "They were hiding in Endo-san's tent. He's been taken into custody as well."

Aoshi frowned. "Were there others? Nozomi isn't the only one of the old guard who resents the changes I've introduced."

"I thought we could make an announcement at muster and see who reacts." The general paused. "How's Ryuu doing? Kotone's going crazy. I don't dare go home without a progress report."

"They gave him the antidote but he still hasn't come around. All I can do now is wait," the warlord explained. "Tell Kotone I'll send word when he wakes up. I know Ryuu would love to see her."

"Maybe you should go get some rest. It won't do anyone any good if you collapse."

"Once Ryuu comes around. I can't leave until I know he's going to be okay."

Ken'ichi clapped a hand on the warlord's shoulder, squeezing it in a show of support. "If you need anything just send for me. I'm going to go update the wife before she comes hunting for me." Both men shuddered at the thought.

"Hurry up then," Aoshi said as he ran a nervous hand through his hair. "I'm pretty sure that's the last thing any of us wants." He smiled at his friend before turning back to the unconscious scribe and recapturing his hand, once again falling into stony silence.

He was so lost in thought he didn't notice wary chocolate eyes watching him. When he realized that the scribe was conscious he smiled broadly and moved to embrace him. "I was afraid you wouldn't wake up. How are you feeling?"

The warlord was shocked when the panicked scribe shoved him away hard. "Don't touch me, don't touch me," he screamed over and over as tears streamed down his cheeks. The healer forced him to drink a sedative potion, watching as his eyes slipped shut once again.

"Well, it's good he came out of it." The healer checked Ryuu's heartbeat. "He didn't react as badly as I thought he might."

"What in kami's name do you mean?" the warlord yelled.
"He's scared of me. You saw him. How is this not so bad?"
"He's lucid, that's a good start," the healer replied. "I did say he'd need a lot of help."
"And I said I would give it to him. So, what do I do?"
"I'm going to keep him sedated so he can rest now that the hallucinations have faded. Go take care of whatever you need to. He'll need a lot of help when he wakes up again."

Aoshi nodded and rose. Before leaving he stopped by Yuudai's bed to check on him and ask Akemi to keep an eye on Ryuu. Then he strode purposefully out of the tent and headed for Ken'ichi's. He needed to make some plans for morning muster.

Chapter Twenty-Five

"Aoshi, sit down," Kotone fussed as soon as he arrived. "You look terrible. When's the last time you slept?"

"Night before last," he replied wearily. "And I won't be getting any for a few days. Price of the job, I suppose."

"Well, at least sit down and have something to eat while you and Ken'ichi talk. You can fill me in on Ryuu's condition." The petite woman skillfully maneuvered the warlord to the table and got busy fixing him some onigiri and miso soup while he slowly recounted everything that had happened since he left with Ken'ichi the night before.

"He pushed me away, Kotone." The warlord dropped his head and stared intently at his bowl. "He's scared of me. I don't know how to help him, especially if he won't let me get close."

"Why don't you let me go talk to him. You and Ken'ichi make your plans and I'll hopefully have good news when I get back." She grabbed her cloak and headed toward the door. "Ken'ichi, hurry up," she called. "Aoshi's waiting." She turned back to the warlord one last time. "Don't go easy on them Aoshi, what they did is unforgivable." Before he could reply she was gone.

When Kotone arrived at the healer's tent she was shocked at the turmoil she found. Akemi was trying to keep Yuudai in bed. The general was convinced he needed to go join Aoshi and Ken'ichi. One of the guards had died, while the other was in critical condition, the antidote not working as well as it had on Yuudai.

Ryuu lay very still in the bed next to the general. Kotone gracefully knelt in the spot Aoshi had so recently vacated and stroked his hair back from his face. "Excuse me," she called to the passing healer. "Could you update me on his condition?"

He stopped and glanced briefly at the scribe before pulling a packet of herbs from his pouch and adding it to a cup of water. "That will bring him around in a few minutes. You don't look very threatening. You may have better luck than the commander did." He turned to check another patient, leaving Kotone to watch and wait.

Several minutes later the scribe groaned and stretched. "Hello, Ryuu," Kotone said. "How are you feeling?"

The scribe motioned for something to drink, and after a few sips of water was able to reply. "Kotone, you shouldn't be here, it could be dangerous for the baby. I'll come and see you when I'm better."

"Don't be silly," she countered. "I've never seen Aoshi in such a state. I had to check on you myself." At the mention of the warlord's name Ryuu shivered. "What's the matter?"

"It's Aoshi … he's … I'm…" Ryuu started to cry. He didn't know how to explain what he was feeling; he cared for the warlord, but he didn't trust him. Right now he didn't trust anyone. Except maybe Kotone, she was obviously not a threat. He haltingly tried to justify his train of thought before he was interrupted.

"It doesn't matter why. What matters is that you're comfortable. You can come stay with me for a while. Ken'ichi can stay with Aoshi."

"Oh no," the scribe demurred. "The general shouldn't have to move out of his own home. I'll just get a room in town."

"Nonsense. I'd much rather spend time with you right now. Frankly, he's been getting on my nerves more and more as I get closer to delivery. This will do us all a lot of good." She looked him over critically. "You can help me get ready for the party on Saturday, and you can see Aoshi there, where people are around. How does that sound?"

"I really don't want to inconvenience you."

"It's no inconvenience, I want you to come," Kotone said with a wide smile. "So, it's settled. I'll pick you up here tomorrow morning."

"I can walk to your tent. I'll see you in the morning."

Kotone smiled widely and turned to leave, hurrying back home as fast as her condition would allow.

"Ken'ichi," she yelled before even stepping inside. "Grab your stuff. You're staying with Aoshi for a few days."

"What did I do now?" he asked in a hurt voice. "Whatever it is

I'm really sorry and I didn't mean it. I know it must be bad if I can't even sleep on the floor."

"No, honey, you're fine, but Ryuu's going to come stay for a few days. I don't think he'd be any more comfortable around you than he is around Aoshi." She began to pack him a bag as she continued to explain. "He's confused right now, and he's scared of anyone who looks threatening." She planted a kiss on her husband's cheek. "I may know you and Aoshi are just big pussy cats, but you'd never know it to look at you. All big and growly, it's no wonder he's intimidated."

"But I don't want to stay with Aoshi. He can't cook and he doesn't smell anywhere near as nice as you do," the general protested.

"I love you too," Kotone replied with a smile. "It's just for a few days, and I'll bring dinner by."

"Are you sure you'll be alright by yourself?"

"I'll be fine. I'm pregnant, not terminal. Besides, I won't be alone, Ryuu will be here. If there are any problems he can get help. It's very sweet, but you don't have to worry so much." Kotone leaned into the general's broad chest as he gently stroked her back.

"When's he coming?" the general whispered as he pulled her as close as he could.

"Not until morning," she replied lazily, enjoying the feeling of large hands massaging her aching back.

"Then why do I have to leave now?" Ken'ichi pulled back to look his wife in the eye.

"Because Aoshi is all alone and upset," Kotone replied in much the same tone she would use with a stubborn five year old. "He's one of your oldest friends. He needs your support now."

"You need my support too," the general insisted.

"And you'll be supporting me by doing as I wish." She ended the argument with a smile. "I'll see you every day. And this way you won't have to help with the party preparations, or gathering things for the baby."

All of a sudden this was sounding like a good idea. "If you're sure, honey."

"I think I can survive a few days without you." Kotone smiled and gave him a hug and a kiss. "This way you'll appreciate me more."

"I could never appreciate you more than I already do." Ken'ichi pulled his wife in for a thorough kiss.

When he finally released her, Kotone stumbled a bit, fanning herself and muttering, "It's just a couple of days."

Smiling widely at the effect he had on his wife, the general grabbed his gear and headed out, whistling as he headed for the warlord's tent.

"Yo, Aoshi," he called, throwing back the flap.

"Hey, Ken'ichi, what brings you by?"

"Kotone says I'm bunking with you til Saturday and Ryuu's staying with her. Says we're too scary for him." The general threw himself into a cushion and stretched. "I'm not thrilled with the idea … no offense," he hastened to add. "But I hate to argue with her now."

Both men fell silent as they pictured a hugely pregnant, incredibly angry, Kotone going into labor. "No, no, you wouldn't want to upset her," Aoshi agreed. "Stay as long as you like. It's too quiet without Ryuu, anyway."

Chapter Twenty-Six

Aoshi didn't even pretend to sleep, instead he spent the night sprawled in a chair, lost in contemplation. It was tricky suppressing a rebellion without inciting another. Too little force and he'd be prey to every man with aspirations for leadership, too much and there would be backlash.

Finally he came to the realization that there were variables he just couldn't account for, and that his plan was as good as it would get. He rose and stretched before ambling off towards the jail, intent on having a few questions answered before he levied punishment.

When he arrived he had the pleasure slave brought to him for questioning first. "Kazuya, I need you to explain some things to me. In particular, how long were you prepared for this assassination and who undertook your training?"

The slave seemed to shrink into himself at the mention of his training, appearing to be the young boy he actually was, rather than the seasoned whore he'd been taught to be. "My master was Narita Oki. I was with him for five years, and he always said I was to be yours."

So, the warlord thought, *they've been planning this for the last five years. How could I not have noticed so much dissatisfaction for so long?* "Other than Oshiro-san, who else had contact with your master about this?"

Kazuya smiled slyly. "What do I get if I tell you?"

"You won't suffer. Which is more than I can say for the two guards you killed."

"What about the general?" the slave asked. "Not so concerned about him, are you?"

The warlord surged forward and grabbed the slave by the throat. "General Tanaka-san is my right hand. I trust him implicitly, he is one of my oldest friends." He swallowed hard before continuing. "You are lucky he recovered, or we would not be having this conversation. Now, who else was involved?"

Kazuya squirmed and coughed, dropping his head to avoid Aoshi's hard stare. "There were several officers. Endo-san, they caught us with him last night, Ito-san and Saito-san. They each showed up right after Oki purchased me, after that they just sent aides. I could point them out, but I don't know their names. As for the nobles, as far as I know there are members of all the important families involved, but mainly younger men without power. I will write out a list of names if you give me a brush and paper."

Aoshi studied him critically before pushing a sheet of parchment and a brush his way, keeping a wary eye on the boy as he listed all those he could remember.

When he finished, Kazuya pushed back with a sigh. "That's everyone whose name I know. I can point out those soldiers to you now if you like, then we can finish this." He scuffed the ground with his toe. "I am sorry, you know. I didn't choose my life."

The warlord called for a guard to take him away and sat in contemplation for a long moment. He called to a guard and quickly ordered him to have Commander Saito-san arrested, and pondered for a moment before asking for Endo to be brought in to see him.

"Ah, Endo-san," he said as the disgraced officer entered the room.

"Fujiwara, what is the meaning of this? I can't believe you had me arrested. When I get out of here..." He was cut off by the warlord's angry reply.

"The meaning of this is questioning you about your role in the assassination plot against me. The plot you've been working on for five years, I might add. Did you honestly think you would get away with it?"

"I'll give you names," Endo begged. "I'll tell you everything if you spare my life."

"I already have all the names I need," the warlord replied. "There's nothing you have to trade, and I'm not in the mood to barter. I will announce your sentence at muster and it will be carried out before dark." He stood to summon the guard before turning and fixing the former officer with a hard stare. "What did I do that was so bad? The nobles I can understand, but my own men..."

"You changed things that have been in place for decades, like rising through the ranks based on time served. Older men resent serving under young officers."

"Even if those officers keep them alive?" Aoshi asked skeptically. "I highly doubt that. I think it's you, Saito-san, and Ito-san, who were dissatisfied because I expected you to earn your rank and not curry favors." He summoned the guard. Unfortunately he had left the worst for last. "Bring Oshiro-san here."

The warlord sat silently as the noble was brought in and secured in a chair. Several minutes passed in silence before Masashi finally broke and began to speak. "What do you want of me Fujiwara? You must have brought me here for a reason. Do you have questions about Ryuu, perhaps?"

"Do not say his name." The warlord snarled as his hands tensed on the edge of the table, the wood groaning under the strain. "It is obviously a distant kinship. He is far too good a man to be related to the likes of you."

"Ah, he is a sweet little whore, is he not. I'm only sorry I didn't sample him myself while I had the chance. Although the show he gave while reliving Benjirou's little party was almost as good."

Aoshi kept his composure, although the strain was obvious in the tightness of his smile. "So you knew about that."

"Of course, although I didn't know it was my dear cousin until later. How wonderful fate is to bring us back together like that, especially since I was the one who arranged he be sold in the first place. I convinced my doting idiot of a father I would be much better off with the lands and title than poor orphaned Ryuu." He smirked as he continued. "I had hoped he would end up as a pleasure slave so I sent word to Narita-san to be at the market on the day of his sale. It was just bad luck that got him off the hook. But, your pleasure slave is what he ended up as, so I guess I won in the end."

"He was never my pleasure slave," the warlord replied with barely leashed fury. "He is, and has been, my cherished companion. I have always treated him as my equal. He is gentle and wise and far more deserving of your title than you are. It will please me greatly to be able to restore it to him after your death."

"My death." Masashi gulped, he hadn't expected a sentence of death.

"What punishment did you expect for inciting a coup?" Aoshi asked. "I considered giving you to my men as a pleasure slave, since you see it as such a noble career, but I was afraid they'd get infected by your hatred. You will be put to death before sunset."

With that the warlord rose and left the tent, wanting to clear his head before morning muster, leaving the noble gaping behind him, dumbstruck at the realization of the consequences of his actions.

Chapter Twenty-Seven

The warlord and his generals stood and watched the troops assemble for muster. There was no way anyone could miss the very clear message this was going to send. Aoshi frowned as he examined his plan one more time; something was missing. "Ken'ichi, someone needs to pick up Narita Oki, the pleasure slave trader, and bring him to me."

"Certainly, Commander." The general whispered to one of his aides. The soldier ran off with several others in the direction of the marketplace as both men turned hard eyes on the soldiers assembling in front of them.

"They've been sitting for too long," the warlord decided. "As much as I'm enjoying the rest, it's time to start a new campaign. In the North I think, that's where the border's most troubled."

"I suppose you're right," Ken'ichi replied. "Although Kotone isn't going to be pleased. Still, it can't be helped."

"Well, someone will have to stay here and keep an eye on things. I think you'd be a good choice. Especially with the little woman to keep you in line."

"You'd go to battle without me?" The general's face fell in disappointment.

"No, my friend." Aoshi put a hand on the general's shoulder. "I'd let you enjoy your wife and child." Ken'ichi merely nodded in response, and the warlord turned to survey the gathering. "It's time," he said as he stepped forward to address the assembly.

"It has come to my attention, that some of you are dissatisfied with the changes I've made. So much so, that for the last five years some of you have been planning to have me murdered in my bed, so that power would change hands." Aoshi clasped his hands behind his back and began to pace. "If you are one of that group I am sorry to inform you that your plot has been uncovered. These men," he gestured toward the group of nobles, officers, aides and the lone pleasure slave with one hand, "are at the center of this web of intrigue. They are guilty of treason and shall be punished by death, immediately."

The generals fanned out across the stage as men were brought to kneel before them, Kazuya coming to kneel before the warlord. "You see, my lord," he said in a soft voice. "I said I was meant for you alone, even in this." He knelt gracefully and bowed his head.

As one the warlord and his generals raised their swords, as one the swords fell, and heads rolled. The bodies were thrown onto a pyre even as the next group was led into place. Aoshi gritted his teeth and said nothing as he dispatched both traitorous officers.

By now the ground was soaked in blood, the anxious prisoners churning the area to a red froth. The assembled troops watched with barely veiled terror as the heads were left to lay where they fell, gazing reproachfully into the ranks even as the bodies were burned.

Finally the last of the traitors was led out and the warlord couldn't stifle his growl as Masashi cowered before him, trying one last attempt to sweet talk his way out of punishment. "Please my lord, I beg you, as a favor to my cousin. Please spare my life."

He had picked the worst possible plea to use, since his actions had driven Ryuu out of the warlord's arms, perhaps permanently. "The biggest favor I could ever do him will be to get rid of you." With that Aoshi raised his sword one last time and neatly severed his neck, watching dispassionately as blank eyes seemed to catch his as they rolled lifelessly across the ground.

"Gather the heads and throw them in with the offal, let them feed the dogs we rely on." The warlord ignored the gasps from the crowd at such a dishonorable end. "Obviously we have been at rest too long," Aoshi continued. "So, Monday we march north to repel invaders on the borders and expand our boundaries. To ensure you will be in the proper state of mind I wish to give you a little treat before the campaign starts."

Aoshi turned and motioned to the men holding Oki. They dragged the slave trader over to the warlord, easily overpowering his efforts to break free. "Ah, Narita-san," the commander said. "I have a special treat for you. Rather than death I have decided to grant you a reprieve." He smiled widely. "I'm sure you'll enjoy your new role. It's one you've chosen for so many others, after all."

"Strip him," the warlord commanded, and the guards were quick to comply. Once Oki was naked, Aoshi studied him intently. "Something's wrong. I know, we need to prepare you." He motioned for the men to hold the slave trader still as he grabbed a sharp knife and thrust the blade into the flames. He grasped Oki's scrotum and pulled, slashing the connecting tissue, the hot knife cauterizing as it cut.

The warlord idly tossed the slave trader's testicles aside, nodding his approval at the sight of his panicked, tear-stained face. "That's better." He turned to address the troops again. "Men, here is your reward for loyal service. I gift you with this pleasure slave to use as you see fit. Just remember you need to be ready to march on Monday morning."

"Please, no," Oki begged, grasping Aoshi's clothing in an attempt to stop him from leaving.

"Mouthy, aren't you." The warlord forced the slaver's jaws open and yanked on his tongue, pulling it out as far as he could. "I hate to remove what could be the source of great pleasure for my men, but if you can't be quiet, I guess I'll just have to." He pulled his knife back out and thrust it into the flames yet again, watching the fear blossom on the cowering man's face.

"I-I-I'll be quiet," he stammered, and Aoshi let go of his tongue. Instead he pulled him up by his hair and shoved him into the waiting arms of the guards.

"Now, play nice boys. Make sure everyone gets his chance." The warlord turned and headed back to his tent, the generals following closely behind.

"They'll tear him apart, you know," Ken'ichi pointed out.

"Karma's a bitch," Aoshi replied without slowing. "Personally I wish I had taken his tongue." The general stopped dead; after a long moment he shook his head and hurried to catch up, although he wisely said nothing. This was, after all, the man he was stuck spending the next few days with. *Can't even sneak away to the bachelor quarters. Kotone's sure to find out. No, I have to stay with Aoshi 'Blood Will Spill' Fujiwara.*

Yuudai remained silent at the warlord's other side. For his part all he could do was thank the gods his friend had either forgiven or forgotten what had happened between them. In either case he was very glad to be where he was and not included in Aoshi's purge. He heard the yells coming from the other side of camp and shuddered. *I could have ended up like that poor sod*, he thought. *No one deserves to be thrown to the wolves like that.* He didn't even want to imagine what the slaver would look like by Monday morning.

The three continued across camp, each lost in his own thoughts, and no one dared intrude.

Chapter Twenty-Eight

Ryuu stood back to survey the work they had done. The room had been cleaned and scrubbed and fresh tatami had been laid on the floor. A fluffy rug was rolled out in front of a low chair. A baby basket sat ready in the corner. "This looks wonderful, Kotone. I'm sure your baby will be very happy here."

"If we stay. I'm a little nervous about making all these decisions without Ken'ichi's permission'"

"No one expected you to raise a baby in a tent," the scribe assured her. "It's a two minute walk into camp. I'm sure the General will be pleased with your decision to move to more permanent quarters."

"I'm not so sure. I think they'll be leaving on campaign soon and I have to make some hard decisions."

"What do you mean?" Ryuu helped her to sit and brought her a cup of cold water.

"The assassination attempt on Aoshi. They'll go on campaign to keep the men occupied after they eradicate the traitors. I've always traveled with Ken'ichi, but with the baby on the way I won't be able to. I don't look forward to waiting and worrying here on my own."

Ryuu had stopped listening at the words 'assassination attempt'. "What assassination attempt? Is Aoshi alright?"

"Yes, he's fine. General Tanaka-san was gravely ill and two guards died. It was that pleasure slave, Kazuya. Anyone he kissed was poisoned, it was in his saliva." She pursed her lips in annoyance. "It's just a good thing Aoshi has more restraint than his men. Otherwise he'd be dead right now."

Ryuu smiled as he realized this meant Aoshi had not been with the slave. The thought made him happy, even if he found the warlord himself terrifying. He knew it was ridiculous, he remembered how content he had felt in the commander's arms. But he couldn't stop the shiver of fear that traced down his spine as he thought about doing the same thing now.

He shook off his troubling thoughts and returned his attention to Kotone. "I'm sorry, I got caught up in memories," he said with a wry smile. "Now, what were you saying about a campaign?"

"I was just complaining. I know I shouldn't, but it's going to be hard raising the baby alone." She stroked the blanket in her lap. "I don't want my child to feel abandoned the way I did when my father was off on a campaign."

"Well," Ryuu began, "you shouldn't travel now, that's true. But soon you'll have the baby. You'll be able to travel again a couple months after that. I know it seems like forever, but the time will pass quickly. I'll need to find a place myself. You could stay with me until you feel up to rejoining Ken'ichi. I need to find a job, too. I'd better get started or I'll end up on the streets." He laughed, but it was hollow.

"You're not going back to Aoshi?" Kotone asked, concern obvious in her voice. "He'll be devastated. He's never cared about anyone like this before. He needs you to stay with him, even if you won't touch him."

"I couldn't do that. I won't do that, and you're wrong." The scribe looked up and locked serious orbs with Kotone's. "He doesn't need me, in fact, he's much better off without me. I'm nothing but a liability, a former slave, a joke. All the men know what happened to me, how can I stay without tainting him by my presence? Not to mention the fact that I'm a man. A pleasure slave is one thing, but for a companion, it just isn't done. He may not understand but I most certainly do."

"Ryuu, none of that matters. Aoshi loves you. He's been alone for a very long time and you're the one he finally chose. That's not going to change, whether you stay or not. The question you need to ask yourself is if you want to make him suffer." She shook her head and sighed. "Please don't rush into any decisions. At least wait until after the party tomorrow night."

"All right," the scribe agreed. "I promise I won't make any firm decisions until after your party. But early the next morning I'm looking for a job and a place to live. Let me know if I should make it big enough for three."

He stood and faced the obviously exhausted woman, hands on his hips. "Right now what you need is sleep, no arguments." He held up a hand as he continued. "You are going to lie down and take a nap while I make dinner. I'll wake you when it's ready." With that he helped her into the bedroom and covered her with a blanket. "Just rest."

As soon as she was sleeping he headed across camp to the warlord's tent. "Aoshi, General Fujii-san, are you in?" he called from outside. The warlord's head popped out, a huge smile etched across his face

"Ryuu, how are you feeling? Gods, it's good to see you here." He gingerly reached out and embraced the scribe, the smile dropping from his face as he felt his lover cringe at the contact.

"I'm looking for General Fujii-san. Kotone needs him."

Aoshi dropped his happy mask and wearily ran a hand over his face. "Hey, Ken'ichi," he yelled. "The little woman is calling, better run home and see what she needs."

The general appeared, yanking on his clothes with one hand as he rushed towards the door. "Is it time, is the baby coming?" he asked in a panic.

"No, no they're fine," the scribe explained. "She's afraid you'll be angry, we moved your things to one of the staff houses by the south checkpoint today. Add to that her fears about the campaign and you being so far away when the baby is born, and she's worked herself into a panic. She needs you to comfort her. I'll be back in a couple of hours when dinner's ready."

The general quickly finished dressing and rushed out of the tent. "So," the warlord began awkwardly. "What are you going to do for the next couple of hours?"

"I don't know," Ryuu replied. "Go look for a job, I guess. I can't impose on Kotone forever."

"You have a job. You work for me. I don't recall firing you."

"I can't work with you anymore. It just wouldn't be right. You'll have to go to the market and buy another slave."

"But I don't want a slave. I only want you. Please, Ryuu, what did I do? What can I do to change your mind?"

"I'm afraid you can't. This is for the best, although I'm flattered that you want to try. Right now I need time and space. I don't know when or if I'll be ready to be close to anyone again. You need to move on and find someone else, someone suitable. There's still

General Tanaka-san."

"I've already told you, I only want you." The warlord's expressive face twisted into a frown. "What do I have to do to convince you?"

"I believe you, Aoshi. But it doesn't change anything. Believe me when I say it's better this way." He shuffled his feet a bit. "I should get going. I'll see you at the party tomorrow night."

With that he turned and hurried out of the tent, leaving the warlord behind, shoulders slumped in defeat.

Chapter Twenty-Nine

Kotone smiled when she felt her husband slide into the bed beside her. *Ryuu is so smart when it comes to other people. Why can't he do as much for himself?* "What brings you home?"

"Missed you." The general wrapped his arms around his wife and pulled her as close as her condition would allow. "A little birdie told me you were worried about the campaign. Is that true, sweetheart?"

"Well, I've never stayed behind when you've been in the field. I know you could still be hurt if I'm with you, but I'll worry so much more if I'm not there. I won't know when it's safe to relax."

"Aoshi did ask me if I wanted to stay here and keep an eye on things while he's in the field. I have to admit I was disappointed at the thought of not going into battle, but you and the baby need me, too. I guess you don't have to worry, I'm not going anywhere."

"Then who's going to keep an eye on Aoshi?" Kotone worried, biting her lower lip. "Ryuu's not going back to him. He's determined to get a job and stay here."

"Why would he get a job?" the general asked. "Now that Masashi's dead won't he get his lands and title back? The house should be his too."

"His cousin is dead? What happened?"

"He was at the center of the conspiracy. He was executed this morning along with the other traitors, Endo-san, Saito-san, some of the nobles, and that damned pleasure slave," Ken'ichi explained. "It was unpleasant business, but necessary. The men are on liberty until Monday when we move out ... I mean they move out."

"Sweetheart, you want to go with them, don't you?" Kotone asked.

"I can't imagine not being there, but I want to be here with you, too. It's tearing me apart."

"Then we'll have to come up with a plan. Maybe we can even help Aoshi and Ryuu at the same time." She thought for a few minutes, tapping her finger against her chin, brow furrowed. "Well, it's obvious that I can't go anywhere right now. How long do you expect to be in the field?"

"I would guess six months, but it could be as little as three, or as long as a year," Ken'ichi replied, calculating the engagements in his head. "It really depends on Aoshi, how aggressive he's feeling. If Ryuu really leaves him, we could be out for years."

"Assume three months before I can travel. Plan A assumes Ryuu stays here and Aoshi leaves. In that case I can stay with him and you go with the troops. When I'm recovered the baby and I will join you. Ryuu can run things here, that gives the two of them a reason to get together and stay in touch." She climbed out of bed and began to pace. "With any luck Ryuu will come with me when I join you and they'll get back together."

"Now Plan B," Kotone continued, "is my convincing Ryuu to go with Aoshi while you stay here with me. It's my favorite, but I don't think I'll have much luck changing Ryuu's mind. He still needs time to sort out everything that's happened to him."

"So, what am I supposed to do to further your brilliant plan, dear?" the general asked.

"Make sure Aoshi comes to the party tomorrow night. I'll take care of the rest. By the end of the evening we should know which plan to put into effect."

Just then the scribe reappeared. "Kotone, General?" he called before entering. "I'm going to get dinner, come out whenever you're ready." He headed to the kitchen and began preparing plates and ferrying them to the table.

The couple entered the dining room a few minutes later, the general tenderly supporting his wife with a large arm looped around her waist. Once they were seated Ryuu excused himself, saying he needed to pack up the leftovers for Ken'ichi to take to the warlord. He hurried back into the kitchen, leaving the couple their privacy.

"To the plan," Kotone toasted as she raised her glass.

"The plan," Ken'ichi replied as he raised his own glass with a nod. He turned his attention to the meal in front of him, moaning in delight as he sampled the various dishes. "Wow, Fujiwara's a lucky guy. This is delicious. I'd marry Ryuu if I were single."

Kotone smiled widely. *Men are so predictable*, she thought

before turning her attention to her own meal. Plans or no plans, the baby wanted to eat.

A short while later Ryuu handed a bundle to the general as he prepared to leave. "Here are the leftovers. There should be enough for Aoshi's dinner and a snack for both of you later. I hope he likes it."

"I'm sure he'd like anything you made," Ken'ichi said. "It really was delicious."

"Thank you, you're very kind," the scribe replied with a small bow. "I picked it up over the years. It's always good to learn new skills."

"Any message for the commander?"

"Tell him ... tell him I hope he sleeps well," Ryuu said. "Now, if you don't mind, I'm rather tired. I'll see you at the party tomorrow." He excused himself and disappeared.

Kotone stood on her toes and kissed her husband on the cheek. "He's wavering," she whispered happily. "I'm going to go work on him. I'll see you tomorrow. Love you."

"Love you too." Ken'ichi gave her a kiss and a squeeze before heading out, whistling a merry tune.

Kotone headed into the kitchen after the scribe. "Ryuu, what's wrong?

"It's Aoshi. He begged me to stay with him. I wanted to, but at the same time I didn't. I'm scared," he admitted, tears coming to his eyes. "I don't think I can take much more. The last couple months have turned my life upside down. I don't even know who I am anymore,"

"I'm sure he'll give you as much time as you need," Kotone assured him. "But you need to let him know how you're feeling. If you keep pushing him away eventually he'll actually go, and I don't think that's what you really want."

"It's what's best. What I want shouldn't matter."

"That's the only thing that should matter. You deserve to be happy. Go after what you want. It will work out."

"I'll think about it," the scribe replied with a frown. "Now, let's get you settled. Tomorrow's a big day and the baby needs its rest." He ushered her into the bedroom and settled her in bed yet again, making sure she had a glass of water and some onigiri in case she woke hungry. "Pleasant dreams, I'll see you in the morning." He extinguished the lamp and left the room, already turning what she had said over in his mind, looking for a flaw in her logic.

Chapter Thirty

"You need to head them off," Kotone insisted. "This is such a bad idea, I can't go out there looking like this." She waved in frustration at her reflection before bursting into tears. "Please, Ryuu. If you're my friend you'll tell everyone the party is canceled."

"Calm down," the scribe said in a soft voice as he helped her to a chair and got her a glass of water. "You look beautiful. Ken'ichi is a very lucky man. He wants to show his gorgeous wife off one more time before they go out in the field."

"I look like a cow," the petite woman complained bitterly. "No, a big fat sow."

Ryuu laughed merrily, tugging her up and spinning her in front of the mirror. "Well, you have awfully nice legs for a cow and better cleavage than any pig I've ever seen. Not to mention a beautiful face, especially when you smile."

She smiled and covered her face with her hands. "I know I'm being ridiculous, pregnant women get big, the baby has to go somewhere. But then I see the girls the men are dating and I feel so old and ugly."

"You're more beautiful than any of them. Just you wait and see, everyone will be fawning all over you. Now, hurry up and get out there so you can check my work."

Kotone gasped when she finally tore herself away from the mirror and headed into the main room. The scribe had done a wonderful job decorating with bowls of fresh flowers. The food was picture perfect and the dishes and cups sparkled in the twinkling light. All that was missing were the guests, and they should start arriving any moment.

"It's lovely, Ryuu," she said as she gave him a hug. "Thank you so much for all your help. Now, you need to go change."

"I was thinking I would just go out for a few hours," he suggested, pointedly not meeting Kotone's eyes.

"Oh no, you will not. You will be at this party and you will talk to Aoshi. You cannot just avoid him. And no pushing him away either. I saw the way you look at him. If you need time I know he'll give it to you, but give both of you some hope." She shook her head at the stubborn look on the scribe's face. "All men are hopeless," she muttered, shaking her head. "Do you want to hurt him?"

"Of course not. I'm trying not to hurt him."

"Well, you're not succeeding. He looks like shit and he's scaring the men. I, personally, would like my husband to survive this campaign in one piece. So whether you stay or go, you need to make things right and be honest with him. He's been honest with you."

"Alright," he muttered sulkily. "I'll go to the party and I'll talk to Aoshi." His voice dropped to a whisper. "Not that I have any clue what to say."

"How about I love you, and I'll be here when you get back."

Ryuu just nodded, his face solemn. The sounds of the first guests arriving caused them both to turn with smiles on their faces. "Honey, I'm home," Ken'ichi called as he moved to kiss his smiling wife.

The warlord hovered in the doorway, not wanting to intrude on the happy scene. "It's good to see you, Aoshi," Ryuu said. "I hope you slept well."

"I can't sleep well without you in my bed. You've spoiled me." He smiled hesitantly. "But it's better now that I'm here with you."

The scribe blushed beet red at the compliment, and at the memories of the things they had done in that big bed. "I miss you too. I'm sorry for the way things turned out."

"You don't have anything to be sorry for," Aoshi retorted. "The people who hurt you have paid for their mistake. You did nothing wrong and you no longer have to worry about them."

"What do you mean?" Ryuu stammered.

"You got caught up in an assassination plot against me. It's really my fault you were hurt so badly. I'm so sorry, Ryuu." He grasped the scribe's hand earnestly. "Please forgive me. I never wanted you to be hurt because of me."

"It's not your fault. You didn't rape me or drug me. You've never hurt me, and I don't think you ever would. I'm not mad at you, but our relationship is going to hurt you. And now, every time you touch me I can't help but remember…" he trailed off with a shudder.

"I put them all to death, including your cousin and Kazuya." He gave the scribe a hard look. "Oh, and your old master Narita Oki is the troops' new pleasure slave, assuming he survives the weekend."

Ryuu just stared at him wide-eyed. His cousin was dead. Kazuya, the spark that started his current problems, was dead. He felt bad because a little voice inside himself was cheering at the news. "You know what that means, don't you?" the warlord continued conversationally.

"What, what does it mean?" the scribe asked.

"Your cousin is dead. Your title and lands revert to you. The clan compound is yours as well, and the seat on the council." Aoshi smiled. "It's good to know there will be at least one vote on my side in the future."

More guests began arriving and the two drifted apart, the scribe greeting the new arrivals while Aoshi sulked in the shadows. As Kotone had predicted, many of the officers escorted young attractive women, yet they all were careful to let the pregnant woman know how lovely she looked and how jealous they were of Ken'ichi.

Both Ryuu and Aoshi were surprised to see Yuudai and Akemi arrive together. The scribe was happy for both men, while the warlord was jealous that they had found happiness just when he had lost his. *But, I'm going to get him back*, the warlord swore to himself. *And once I do I'll never let go again.*

Ryuu fixed a plate and carried it over to where the commander was slumped. *He does look terrible. He hasn't been eating or sleeping, that's obvious.* "I brought you a plate," he said shyly. "You look like you could use a good meal, and a good night's sleep as well."

"It's … been hard." A haunted look blossomed on the warlord's face. "I never knew how out of touch I was. I really am a lousy leader."

"No, you're not. Your men worship you. They'd follow you into hell," the scribe retorted hotly. He lost his train of thought when Kotone suddenly wrapped her arms around her belly and doubled over.

"Ken'ichi, it's time," she hissed.

"Time for what dear?" he asked, not turning his attention from the conversation he was having.

"Time for the baby, you ass." She grabbed him by the ear, yanking hard before she was hit with another contraction.

One of the men ran for a healer while the girls fluttered around helplessly and the soldiers cringed. Ryuu took charge and helped Kotone into the bedroom, getting her settled in bed to await the healer's arrival.

Chapter Thirty-One

Ken'ichi stood off to the side of the room wringing his hands while Kotone lay in bed, cursing the day he was born and threatening him with castration as she was hit with another contraction. "They're coming pretty fast," the scribe told the general with a smile. "It shouldn't be long before the baby is born."

The healer finally arrived and pushed through the cluster of party-goers until he reached the woman laboring in the bed. "She's having a baby."

"Brilliant," Ken'ichi snapped. "Now do something to help her."

"I'm a field healer and she's not injured. I don't know anything about babies. What's she doing in camp anyway? She needs a midwife."

The general quickly sent a man into town to fetch the midwife. He hoped Kotone could hold on until she arrived. "General," the scribe's soft voice cut into his thoughts. "I'm afraid we don't have that long. The baby is coming now."

"It can't. The midwife isn't here yet."

"Well, the baby won't wait. We'll just have to take care of it. You get between Kotone's legs and tell me if you see the head."

"What!" His eyes bugged out at the thought.

"Just tell me when the baby starts to appear." The general turned grey and gulped, moving into position and cracking open an eye.

"Oh my gods," was all Ken'ichi managed to say before he passed out.

"Aoshi," Ryuu yelled. "Come help me please."

The warlord winced when he heard his name. He had no desire to see this baby being born, but he couldn't let the scribe down. He hung his head and shuffled into the room while the men sent sympathetic looks his way, although no one offered to take his place.

"Could you help me move the general out of the way?" Ryuu asked. "He's a bit large for me."

"That's right, move his fat, lazy, good for nothing ass," Kotone ground out through clenched teeth. "I swear Ken'ichi, I'm going to get out of this bed and kick your ass myself."

The warlord recoiled slightly at the outburst, narrowing his eyes and peering at the petite woman intently. *That confirms it*, he thought. *I don't want anything to do with this.*

"...shi ... Aoshi." He turned almost dreamily at the call of his name, the whole scene starting to take on a surreal quality most often found in his nightmares. He stopped where he was, bent at the waist to lever Ken'ichi up enough to drag him away.

"Hmmm," he replied absently as he pulled the general into the corner and propped him into a sitting position.

"Hurry up, I need you."

"What do you need, Ryuu?" The warlord stood and moved back to the bed.

"Hold Kotone's hand and help support her back when I tell her to push," the scribe explained as he positioned himself. "The head is just starting to show, Kotone. I need you to push on the next contraction."

She thrashed her head back and forth and gritted her teeth. "No, I'm not ready."

"Sshh, Kotone. Just relax." The warlord stroked a clumsy hand over her tangled hair. "In a few minutes you'll finally be able to hold your baby." He helped her into position, wincing at the death grip she had on his hand.

"Aaahhhhhoooooooooooo," she wailed as the next contraction gripped her.

"Push," the scribe urged, and Aoshi felt the bones compress in his hand as she tightened her grip and pushed. "The head is almost out," Ryuu said. "Just a few more pushes and you'll be done. You're doing wonderfully."

She keened again and pushed while Aoshi squeezed his eyes shut and murmured comforting phrases about how well she was doing.

"The head is out. You're almost there."

Aoshi cracked open one eye and risked a peek. *That's got to hurt*, was his only thought as his eye widened impossibly at the sight of the baby's head. When it swiveled in his direction he began to feel slightly light headed. "Uh, Ryuu…" he began, but he got no further before his hand was once again crushed as another contraction swept over the laboring woman.

Suddenly he heard a slap followed by a piercing wail. "It's a girl," the scribe announced. Aoshi opened his eyes to see Ryuu calmly holding up what appeared to be a blood and slime covered monster. "She's perfect," were the last words he heard as his eyes rolled up into his head and he fell bonelessly to the floor.

Ryuu quickly cut the umbilical cord and toweled the baby off before placing her in the proud mother's arms. "Say hello to your daughter, Kotone."

She smiled beatifically at the tiny baby and held her close while the scribe disposed of the mess. He then bent to shake Ken'ichi to consciousness. "General, general. You have a little girl," he said with a smile when his eyes finally opened.

Ken'ichi jumped to his feet and rushed to his wife's side while Ryuu helped the warlord to his feet.

"You were amazing," Aoshi bent to whisper in his ear, sending a shiver racing through the scribe as the hot breath brushed his skin. He automatically turned towards the voice, and his lips were captured in a soft kiss.

The warlord cheered internally when Ryuu melted into him. Their mouths opened and they leisurely explored each other, tongues dancing as breaths quickened. Aoshi tightened his arms possessively around the scribe as he reveled in the taste and feel of the man in his arms. When they finally broke apart for air they stayed in their embrace, foreheads resting against each other.

"Ryuu, I miss you," the warlord finally whispered. "Please come back to me."

"I miss you, too. And I want to come back, but I'm just not ready yet. Will you wait for me?"

"Forever," Aoshi husked with a smile before recapturing plump lips, tongues tangling sweetly, pulling back to nip teasingly at the scribe's nose. "So, will you be staying at the clan compound, my lord?"

Ryuu laughed, and the warlord's heart swelled at the sound. "Yes, I suppose I will be. Kotone and the baby can stay with me until they can travel. Then maybe we'll all come join you."

Chapter Thirty-Two

Ken'ichi interrupted them to show off his new daughter. "Isn't she beautiful?" He nervously held out the small bundle for them to peruse.

"She's perfect," Ryuu proclaimed. "You should be very proud, general."

"I am, and Kotone was amazing."

"I've never seen anything like it," the warlord admitted. "I wish my men were that strong." He chuckled at the sight of the tiny bundle in Ken'ichi's arms. "Hi, little one." He gently stroked her tiny cheek with his thumb, gasping in surprise at the strength of her grip when she latched onto his index finger. "You know you get to spend the rest of your life chasing the boys away." He smirked at the shocked look on the general's face.

"Just for that you two get to be her honorary uncles. You can help me beat the boys off," Ken'ichi replied.

Ryuu smiled at the picture the two made, the mighty warlord and his powerful general turned into piles of goo by a newborn baby. "You should go out and show your other guests the baby. I think a number of them stuck around to make sure everything was alright."

The scribe moved over to the bed, smiling widely at the woman lying there. "She's beautiful, Kotone."

"Thank you for everything. I'm so glad you were here. I don't know how to repay you."

"Right now, you need to rest. Come Monday you and that little darling can come stay with me while our men head north. It will be wonderful to have your company."

"Come on, Ryuu." The warlord wrapped an arm around the scribe from behind and rested his chin on his shoulder. "Let me walk you home. 'Night Kotone, you were amazing. Sleep well. I'll come visit before we leave."

With that the warlord skillfully maneuvered the man in his arms through the main room, waving to the general as they exited, stopping to breathe deeply of the cool night air. "So Ryuu, where to?" He slung an arm around the smaller man's waist, drawing him close.

"Uhhhh," the scribe stammered. "I don't know, the estate I guess, although I hate to show up in the middle of the night looking like this." He gestured to his stained and rumpled clothing.

"Well," Aoshi practically purred. "You could stay with me tonight. You could take a bath and then we could sleep together like we used to. I promise not to touch you, but I miss you in my bed."

Ryuu looked into haggard eyes, really seeing how worn the warlord appeared. "Alright," he said softly. "I've missed you too."

Aoshi's lips turned up in a small smile. "Thank you." He placed a gentle kiss on the top of Ryuu's head before turning toward his tent, his heart racing giddily at the thought of spending the night with his love in his arms.

In just a few minutes they were at their destination, Ryuu's mind whirling at the prospect of sharing a bed with the warlord. "You go get cleaned up," Aoshi said when he felt the scribe tense. "I'll find some things for you to put on."

Ryuu relaxed into the deep tub, slowly letting the tension seep out of his tired frame. It was mind boggling to think of everything that had happened since he'd woken that morning. He smiled when he thought of Kotone's beautiful little girl. The smile softened further when he thought of the kiss he had shared with the warlord after the birth.

He was startled out of his dreamy contemplation when the man in question appeared in the bathhouse, clothes in hand. "They'll probably be a little big," Aoshi stated. "But they're clean and dry."

"I'm sure they'll be fine," the scribe answered absently, not seeing the way the warlord's face lit up at the sight of him sprawled naked in the bath. "I'll be finished in a few minutes. Why don't you make us some tea?"

"Alright." Aoshi bent down to brush his lips against Ryuu's cheek. "I'll see you when you're done." He stood and headed to make tea, mind lost in memories of the scribe's face contorted in pleasure in that same tub.

When Ryuu returned a short while later he found the warlord stretched out in bed with a cup in his hand. "Join me," he entreated, patting the bed next to him. "Your tea's on the table."

"This reminds me of the first night I spent with you," the scribe said with a smile. "You patted the bed just like that to get me to lie down."

"It worked," Aoshi said with a shrug and a rakish lopsided grin. "Why mess with success. Besides, I love that look you get, caught between scandalized and longing. You look beautiful like that."

"Aoshi," the scribe said in a shocked tone of voice, waving his hand in dismissal. "I am not beautiful."

"I disagree," a low voice husked in his ear. "Right now, like this, you are the most beautiful thing I've ever seen. Now come get in bed, I want to feel you in my arms as I fall asleep." He tugged the blushing man into the bed, reaching over and pulling the covers up before handing him his mug of tea.

Aoshi nuzzled inky locks, breathing deeply. "I love the way you smell," he murmured before leaning in and capturing the scribe's lips in a gentle kiss. He tentatively slid his tongue along the seam of Ryuu's mouth, tempting him to open so a questing tongue could dip inside, smoothing carefully over plump lips before delving deeper, unable to get enough of the addicting flavor of his lover.

"Mmmmmm, you taste divine," the warlord mumbled when they broke apart for air, nibbling along the line of Ryuu's scar before stealing another passionate kiss. "I could do this all day."

"What happened to sleep?" the scribe asked with a smile.

"Changed my mind, I need kisses more." Aoshi chuckled. "After all, I can sleep out in the field, but I won't be able to get any of your kisses."

When they broke apart again the warlord noticed how Ryuu's eyes fluttered in exhaustion. He twisted them until they were spooned together, Aoshi's long body curled protectively around the scribe, muscular arms tenderly cradling him as he once again buried his nose in soft strands, nuzzling a bronze neck.

"Sleep my love," the warlord whispered as he watched Ryuu's eyes flutter shut. "I'll keep you safe." He tucked his head into his lover's neck and shut his eyes, drifting into the first restful sleep he'd had in days.

Chapter Thirty-Three

Ryuu woke flailing, trying to escape the circle of the warlord's arms. He broke free and whirled around to face the tall man with a snarl. "Don't touch me. Don't touch me," he screamed as he fought his way free of the covers to stumble out of the bed, grabbing a bottle from the table and brandishing it as he crouched defensively in the far corner of the room.

"Ryuu, it's me, Aoshi," the warlord crooned as he slowly approached the trembling figure. "I'd never hurt you. Please, I swear I'll protect you." He very slowly extended a hand toward the scribe, making sure it was palm up so Ryuu knew it was empty. "Come on, give me your hand. I'll keep you safe. I promise no one will hurt you. Please come back to bed and rest."

The scribe took the outstretched hand, although the look he cast the warlord was distrustful and his hand never loosened its hold on the bottle. "Sorry," he muttered. "I panicked without knowing who you were. I'm not afraid of you."

"Are you sure about that?" Aoshi eyed the bottle clutched in the scribe's hand so hard his knuckles were white. "You can be honest with me. I need to know."

"I don't want to be afraid of you." Ryuu's eyes remained trained on the patch of ground between his feet. "But that doesn't seem to matter much when I start to feel trapped. I'm sorry. Did I hurt you?"

No you didn't hurt me, Aoshi thought sadly. *You only broke my heart.* "No, I'm okay. I'm sorry I pushed you when you weren't ready. I just missed you so much."

"And I've missed you too." The scribe reached out to tuck some escaped hair behind his lover's ear. "You didn't push me, I wanted it too. Come on, it's late. Let's go back to bed and try to rest."

"Are you sure?" the warlord asked. "I can sack out on the floor, you take the bed."

"I will not turn you out of your bed. Just get in and stop complaining before I change my mind." The scribe climbed back in and held the covers up for the warlord to join him, the gesture eerily similar to the one Aoshi had used earlier.

The warlord slipped into bed, being careful to stay close to the edge and well away from the scribe so he wouldn't get spooked again. Ryuu, however, only saw rejection where he had been hoping for comfort. "I think I'll sit up for a while," the scribe said as he climbed out. "You go back to sleep."

"No. You can stay awake here in bed. Now get in." Ryuu huffed but did as he was told, sliding carefully into the bed, staying close to the edge. The two lay there, each isolated, the thin strip of bed between them indicative of a much wider rift. Finally they both drifted back to sleep, and drifted back together, gravitating toward the other's warmth until they lay legs entwined, the scribe's head pillowed on Aoshi's chest.

* * *

"Ken'ichi," Kotone whispered so as not to wake the baby.

"Yes, dear." The general jolted out of his light doze. "What do you need?" he slurred sleepily as he tried to untangle his legs from the bedding and get up.

"Stay where you are." She laid a gentle hand on his arm. "I just wanted to talk to you."

"Yes, dear," he said again, a little more coherently. "What did you want to talk about? Is something wrong?"

"No, no, everything's fine. I just wanted to ask what you thought about Ryuu and Aoshi. They left together you know."

"Well, I'm not surprised. You should have seen the way they kissed after the baby was born. Man was it hot." He trailed off when his wife smacked his shoulder hard.

"Ken'ichi, don't talk about them like that. I think they're sweet together. Do you know where they were going?"

"No dear, I didn't know I was supposed to follow them and eavesdrop. Next time." He chuckled, nudging her with his elbow. "You're one to chastise me for watching them."

"Ken'ichi," Kotone hissed, scandalized. "I can't believe you'd say something like that to me. I only want them to be happy. I have no interest in peeping on their private activities."

"Private activities," the general said with a smirk. "That's one way to put it." He wrapped an arm around his wife and pulled her close. "Want to try some private activities sweetheart?"

"I'd love to, but unfortunately I was nearly torn in two giving birth thanks to you and your private activities. I'm afraid we're going to have to wait a few weeks."

The general winced at the mention of the birth. He wasn't proud of the fact that he'd passed out and missed his daughter's arrival. He'd never anticipated seeing Kotone going through something so alien. He shook his head, glad that women had the babies and he would never have to endure anything like that. He pulled his wife into a tender hug, kissing her sweetly. "Love you," he muttered fiercely in her ear. "You did so well. I'm so proud of you."

"I love you, too," she whispered back, reveling in the tender affection the usually gruff man was showing. "Papa Ken'ichi, it's so sweet the way you melt when you hold Aoi."

"She's so tiny. I just can't believe she's real. She looks just like you, you know," he said sincerely as he turned to his wife with a smile. "Absolutely beautiful."

Kotone smiled and kissed her husband sweetly before snuggling down and resting her head on his broad chest. "Get some sleep, dear," she said with a yawn. "Aoi will be up and hungry before you know it."

Chapter Thirty-Four

Akemi and Yuudai drifted back to the general's tent after the party finally broke up. The courier noted Aoshi and Ryuu leaving together with satisfaction. *Good, they belong together.* He glanced at the man walking beside him as his mind continued down the same path. *Like we do,* he decided with a decisive nod of his head.

Once inside Yuudai pulled the courier in for a deep passionate kiss. "Thank you," he muttered when they pulled apart for air.

"For what?"

"For giving me another chance. I promise I won't let you down." The general proceeded to strip the courier, laving each bit of revealed skin, drawing mewls and whimpers.

Yuudai scooped the smaller man up and moved them to the bed, stretching out over the courier and languidly rubbing against him, reveling in the satiny skin sliding against his. Both men let out throaty moans as their cocks slid against one another, wantonly thrusting their hips together as they continued to kiss languidly. "Do you want to…" Yuudai trailed off uncertainly. "Would you like to be on top?"

"You want to see me ride you, baby?"

"No," Yuudai stuttered. "I want you inside me."

The courier went very still. "Are you sure? We don't have to."

"No, I want it. I want you," the general said as Akemi leaned in to seal their lips in another kiss.

"Well then lay back and relax," the courier said with a smile. "I promise I'll take good care of you."

Akemi bent his head and began to lick and nip along the edges of the scars on the general's neck and chest, making him squirm at the contact with such a previously ignored and surprisingly sensitive area.

"Stop, you don't have to do that," Yuudai tried to protest, suddenly embarrassed by the sight of his naked body.

"I know." Akemi twirled his tongue around a perked nipple, drawing a startled whimper. "I want to. I like your scars. I think they're sexy, shows how strong and brave you are. I think it's very hot," the courier purred before switching his attentions to the other nipple.

"You know," he continued conversationally as he ran his hands slowly over the general's chest before coming to rest on his hips. "I find everything about you sexy, especially this." He ducked his head and took Yuudai's erection deep in his throat, making him keen as he tried to thrust further into the moist heat.

Akemi skillfully licked and sucked the straining length, making sure to tickle the ridge with his tongue and thrust into the slit, causing Yuudai to whine his name and scrabble for something to hold on to.

The courier shifted his lover's legs onto his shoulders and dropped his head further down to lap and suckle his sensitive balls, nipping and rolling them before swiping a slick trail to his tight pucker, lapping and thrusting until the large man was tossing his head from side to side. He added a slick finger, pressing deep to stroke across the general's prostate, making him shudder with the unexpected jolt of pleasure.

"Oh gods, do that again."

"You mean this?" the courier asked with a smirk as he stroked the sensitive gland again, fascinated with the reaction he got.

"Yes, that. Keep doing that." Akemi pulled his finger out, only to slip two inside, twisting and scissoring, gradually spreading the tight channel. When the time came to add a third finger the courier took Yuudai in his mouth again, skillfully teasing the slick member with his tongue to distract him from any discomfort.

"Don't stop," Yuudai stuttered as the fingers were pulled out.

"I'm not stopping. Don't worry. I won't stop unless you want me to. Do you want me to?" the courier asked. "We don't have to do this."

"Please, please," the general begged. "I want you, Akemi."

"You know, it would probably be easier if I took you from behind," the courier whispered heatedly. "But I want to see your face while I bring you pleasure."

Yuudai let out a deep ragged moan as his lover slowly pushed into his virgin entrance. This was much bigger than the fingers had been. He struggled to relax around the rigid length penetrating him, dizzy from the combination of pain and pleasure teasing his already taut nerves.

"Do something," the general whispered. "I feel like I'm going to explode."

Akemi slowly pulled out of the constricting passage until just the head remained, and just as slowly pushed back in, watching the general's face in fascination as pleasure brought a flush to his features, giving him a rugged wanton beauty the courier found endlessly arousing.

He dropped one burly leg to wrap around his waist, twisting them slightly so he could drive even deeper into Yuudai. The change in angle resulted in his prostate being continuously stimulated, making the general writhe and pant, digging his nails into Akemi's shoulders as he pulled him down for a wet passionate kiss.

"Harder."

The courier raised a brow in surprise before picking up the pace, slamming into the general as he pistoned his hips to meet every thrust.

Akemi felt his release rushing towards him, fueled by the utterly arousing sight of the powerful commander begging for his touch. He wrapped a slim hand around the general's cock, spreading the dripping precum and stroked, rubbing his thumb across the head, adding a twist to his strokes when Yuudai started keening.

The general suddenly arched and shrieked Akemi's name, his eyes fluttering shut and his hands clenching as he shot his cum between them. The courier bent and swallowed his cry, thrusting his tongue into the kiss swollen mouth as he continued to pound into the clenching passage, determined to draw out his pleasure for as long as possible.

Finally the sensations overwhelmed him and he came, shooting his load inside the thrashing body before slumping forward in exhaustion. He gingerly pulled out of Yuudai's tender pucker, watching the thin trickle of his seed leaking out with a sort of bemused pride.

"I need to rest," the courier panted. "Then it's your turn."

* * *

Aoshi woke to find Ryuu's head on his chest, their legs tangled together. *Oh shit, I need to untangle us before Ryuu wakes up.* He tried to carefully untwist their limbs, but every time he worked one of his long legs loose the scribe would snag it with one of his own and pull it back into the fray.

Finally the warlord succumbed to the inevitable and lay back to enjoy the sensation of holding his lover, even if it was while he was sleeping. He stroked thick raven locks tenderly as he contemplated the situation he found himself in. Soon Ryuu would wake and leave to go start his new life in the clan compound.

The warlord's shoulders slumped in defeat when he realized that this might well be the last time he got to lay so intimately entwined with his love. He kicked himself for rushing things last night, knowing it was his own impatience that led them into the situation in the first place. *I'm so sorry, Ryuu. Please give me another chance.*

Ryuu snuggled more firmly against Aoshi's warm body. *I missed this*, he thought sleepily, *I wish I could do it every day.* He lay still for a while, drifting in his thoughts, lost in the rise and fall of the strong chest beneath his head and the comforting thrum of the warlord's heartbeat.

He'll be fine. Aoshi's strong and skilled, he'll come back from the campaign and we'll work everything out. A small part of Ryuu, however, worried that the warlord might not return from battle and he would never get another chance to lay together. He slowly took a deep breath and released it, willing himself to relax. *I have to stay positive*, he reminded himself. *No reason to assume the worst.*

Ryuu quietly tried to free himself from the tangle of limbs and bedclothes without waking the warlord, never realizing he was being studied intently by bottomless onyx eyes. "Morning, Ryuu." Aoshi winced at the startled jump the scribe made when he spoke..

"Good morning, Aoshi. I was just going to go make breakfast." Burly arms blocked his path, keeping him where he was.

"Five more minutes, please. I want to remember this feeling."

"That would be nice," Ryuu agreed. "I'm going to miss you, too." So they snuggled back down in the warm cocoon of blankets, as close as they could be without merging, and yet so far apart, pondering ways to bridge the distance between them as they drifted back to sleep.

Chapter Thirty-Five

Monday morning came all too soon for everyone. Camp was a flurry of activity as tents were struck and belongings packed for travel. Ken'ichi carefully escorted Kotone and the baby across the muddy remains of the campground on the way to Ryuu's. "Now are you sure you have everything you need?" he asked for the hundredth time.

"We'll be fine, sweetheart," Kotone replied. "Ryuu will be there to help us. And in only a few months we'll be coming to join you."

"She'll be so big by then," Ken'ichi said with a sigh. "She won't even remember me."

"Of course she will, silly. Her goal in life is to wrap you around her little finger. She'll never forget her Daddy."

The general broke out in a broad grin. "Daddy loves you, Aoi," he crooned as he rubbed her soft cheek with calloused fingers. "I'll always protect you." He bent to rub noses with her, only to gasp in pain when tiny hands fisted in his beard and pulled. "Ouch. That's attached little one, please let go." He tried in vain to pry her fingers out of his hair without hurting her.

"Let me help you," Kotone said with a laugh, knowing that her husband would never free himself that way. She plucked the dangling kanzashi from her hair, skillfully distracting the baby and chuckling at the look on Ken'ichi's face when she finally let go. "Come to Momma, baby girl." She plucked Aoi out of the general's grasp and skillfully positioned her on a shoulder, bright eyes still trained on her father's face.

"Gods, I'm gonna miss you two," the general admitted. "We've never been apart for so long."

"I'll miss you too. But it's just for a little while, and Aoi isn't up to traveling yet. Before you know it we'll be joining you. Besides, Ryuu needs us. I want to make sure he and Aoshi get back together."

Ken'ichi merely grunted in reply. He owed the scribe a lot. There was no way he could ever repay him for helping Kotone during the birth. "How'd Ryuu learn about delivering babies, anyway?"

"Well, he'd never actually done it before, so he was glad there were no complications. Apparently you learn about a lot of things very young as a slave." She wrinkled her nose as she continued. "You have no privacy. Ryuu said he'd seen a woman give birth before; there was no way to avoid it. You should have seen his face when he told me. I've never seen anyone that red. When I reminded him that he'd seen me that way too, I thought he might burst into flame."

Ken'ichi smiled at the thought, then frowned deeply. "I'm not sure I like the fact that he saw you that way."

Kotone smacked her husband hard. "Don't be an idiot. In the first place, there was no one else to help me; you weren't exactly useful. As I recall, he wanted you to be the one to see me 'that way', as you so quaintly put it, but you passed out. And in the second place," she continued, incensed, "it's not like he cared. He's sleeping with Aoshi, remember? He's not interested in girls."

"Are you sure? Maybe he just never had the opportunity. He was a slave after all. He wasn't exactly encouraged to date. Maybe that's the real issue between him and the commander."

"I don't think so. I've seen the way they look at each other. But I'll see what I can find out. And you," she said, rounding on her husband and poking him fiercely in the chest, "don't go putting any foolish worries about things like that in Aoshi's head. I don't want him distracted. Be positive about the two of them getting back together. And don't let him do anything stupid."

"I'll try dearest, I'll really try." They reached the door and rang the bell, the general wrapping an arm around his wife and daughter and pulling them close, bending to kiss his wife. The door was immediately thrown open, Ken'ichi pouting over his lost kiss as the scribe cheerfully ushered them in, clearly delighted to have Kotone and the baby staying with him.

"You're here." Ryuu swooped in to kiss baby Aoi, who immediately buried tiny fists in his long hair. "Guess I should start pulling this back," he said with a wince as he carefully disentangled her hands, twisting his hair and tucking it into his collar for the time being.

"Thank you for doing this, Ryuu." the general said. "I'd be worried sick about my girls if they were on their own."

"It's my pleasure, general," the scribe replied, making faces at Aoi as he spoke. "It would be horribly lonely here by myself. This place is a bit cavernous for my tastes."

"Well," Ken'ichi said. "I'd best be going, there's a lot to be done. Bye bye, sweetheart." He gave his wife a loving kiss. "You too, baby girl, I'll see you soon." He kissed his daughter and rose.

"Be safe, beloved," Kotone said with a sniff, burying her face in the baby's blanket and not looking up again.

"I'll take care of them," Ryuu assured him. "Take care of yourself and you'll see them very soon."

Kotone composed herself while Ryuu showed the general out. By the time the scribe returned she was fussing over her daughter, a smile firmly in place. "Why don't I show you to your rooms," he suggested. "You can settle in and rest until dinner. I can even watch the baby for you if you like."

"That sounds lovely, Ryuu. It's amazing how tired I got just walking over here. But I think I'll keep Aoi with me."

Shortly after Kotone settled down for her nap the bell rang again. *Kotone must have forgotten something*, the scribe decided as he went to answer it. He was shocked to open the door and see the warlord lounging there, stretched lazily against the door frame. His mouth went dry at the commanding sight of his lover dressed for battle.

"Hi," the scribe said shyly. "I wasn't expecting to see you."

"I couldn't leave without seeing you again. I don't know how I'll survive without you."

"Oh, Aoshi," Ryuu began, tears in his eyes. "I'll miss you too. We'll see each other soon, I promise."

"You'll come to me?" the warlord entreated. "You promise?"

Ryuu nodded, "How could I stay away? I just need some time. Stay safe for me."

Aoshi nodded as he wrapped his arms around the scribe and pulled him close. "You hold my heart," he murmured as he captured Ryuu's lips in a slow deep kiss. They melted together, the scribe clutching the warlord to himself almost frantically.

"I have to go," the commander mumbled when they finally broke apart. "I'll be looking for you." He dove back in for another long exploration of the scribe's mouth.

"I'll come with Kotone," Ryuu assured him, nibbling the pale column of the warlord's neck before recapturing his lips in yet another searing kiss.

"Enough you two, get a room," Kotone joked from behind them.

The pair broke apart, the warlord suddenly studying the floor with great interest while Ryuu blushed beet red. "I was just leaving, Kotone," Aoshi explained. "I wanted to say goodbye to Ryuu first."

"And now you have. But if you keep this up they'll all be waiting for you. Now get out of here, and keep an eye on that big lug of a husband for me, will you?"

"I'll do my best, Kotone," the warlord replied with a smile. "Take care of yourselves." With that he set off at a brisk pace, whistling as he strode across camp. *He promised to come, and those kisses.* Lost in thoughts of his lover, Aoshi allowed himself to just enjoy the moment before regretfully pushing it all aside and falling into combat readiness. No longer a lover, he was once again the seasoned warrior whose name inspired fear in his enemies and loyalty in his men.

A short while later he and his generals watched as the ranks moved past them in an orderly fashion, leaving only a skeletal encampment behind. They fell in behind the last of the troops, Ken'ichi and Yuudai flanking the warlord, all three men lost in their own thoughts.

Chapter Thirty-Six

Aoshi walked through the bustling encampment on his way to the command tent, greeting the men he passed even as his thoughts turned to the coming engagement. His intelligence hinted at dissension in the enemy's ranks. If that were really the case he had a clear advantage.

"Report," he said briskly, slouching lazily in a low chair as his generals updated him on the latest information coming in from their scouts.

"There has been a steady trail of defectors heading north, commander. Apparently their men have been out in the field too long and are fed up with the losses and poor conditions. The ones leaving are heading home as far as we can tell." Yuudai finished his report.

"Any hint they may be massing to flank us, swing around and attack from the rear?" the warlord probed.

"No, they're slinking off in ones and twos and heading north as fast as they can," Ken'ichi replied. "We've followed a few of them to be sure. They want nothing to do with this battle. The camp is too quiet, their men are afraid. We need to strike now."

"No," Aoshi decided. "Let's give them a few days to stew. Fear will make them weak, they'll make mistakes." He turned a knife in his hand contemplatively. "How's our morale these days? Do the men resent my actions?"

"Quite the contrary," Yuudai assured him. "They love their new toy. The healer is patching him up as we speak. I told them he's off limits until after the engagement, then they can celebrate."

"Aaaa, it's good to know he's being useful for once," the warlord remarked laconically. "Tell them to keep him out of my sight, will you? It'll be better that way."

Both generals shuddered at the implications behind the mild request. Ken'ichi pondered Kotone's mission to bring Ryuu here with her. *Good luck sweetheart*, he thought. *Can't be soon enough.*

Yuudai studied his friend with concern. Although they saw each other daily, they had not been alone together since that ill-fated night. *The night I raped my best friend*, the general thought with a groan. *He looks like shit and I'm probably only making things worse.*

"I'm going to go get some rest while I can," Yuudai announced, rising to take his leave.

"Hold up a minute, I'll walk with you." Aoshi stood, moving towards the door. "See you later, Ken'ichi. And stop worrying, Ryuu will take care of your girls," he finished with a smile before turning a serious face to Yuudai. "Let's get going, we have things to discuss."

Oh shit, today is not the day I wanted to die. The general followed his friend out, sweat running down his spine. "What did you want to talk about?" he asked nervously, glancing at the unreadable face for any clues as to how this might go.

"Let's go to my tent so we can talk privately," Aoshi said after a long pause. "I have no desire for this information to go any further than it already has."

Yuudai followed the warlord, looking exactly like a condemned man on the way to the gallows. When they finally found themselves in the relative privacy of Aoshi's tent, the general just stood there, his mouth opening and shutting like a goldfish out of water. Finally he blurted his thoughts out. "Shit, Aoshi, what am I supposed to say. I'm sorry? Oh hell yes, I'm sorry. Was it stupid? Stupid doesn't even begin to describe it. Am I ever going to do something like that again? Not if you let me live."

"And if I kill you?"

"Then I'll haunt you and make faces while you and Ryuu are having sex and you'll start laughing and he'll throw you out of bed," the general said with a snort of nervous laughter.

"You went too far. I thought I could trust you. Hell, I do trust you. But things can never go back to the way they were, and I kind of hate you for that." The general hung his head in shame. "I need you with me, but I need to know nothing like that will happen again."

"It won't, I swear. I'm … seeing someone. I really am sorry,

Aoshi. I miss the way things were too. If I could go back and undo it, I would. But that isn't going to happen. I'll do whatever you want, whatever you need, to make things better."

"Give me some time." The warlord raised his head and fixed the general with a sly grin. "How is Akemi anyway? I haven't seen him since Ken'ichi's party."

"He's good, really good," Yuudai replied.

"Gods, you should see yourself. Talk about a love struck fool," the warlord chortled. "Next thing I know you'll be batting your eyelashes."

"You should talk. You were making googly eyes at Ryuu all night at the party. Oh, Ryuu," he mimed in a simpering voice, "you're soooo beautiful, I just want to hug and kiss you all night." He jumped to the left to avoid the warlord's fist.

"I do not. At least I know when I have it good."

"Yeah, I really am an idiot," Yuudai admitted. "I just never realized I was attracted to men until I saw you with Ryuu that first morning. You're really good-looking, you know. It just seemed to build and build and then I just snapped." He looked down at the ground in embarrassment. "Just so you know, I do love you. You're my best friend and I can't imagine my life without you. But I'm happy with Akemi. I care for him and I won't jeopardize that again."

"As long as we understand each other," Aoshi said with a small smile. "Now, let's go get something to eat. I'm starving."

"Sounds good," the general replied, internally sighing in relief at the outcome of their confrontation. It was good that things could return to near normal for them. He swore that one day his friend would trust him completely again. Yuudai smiled as they strode out of the tent, chatting easily with the warlord about supply lines and pack animals.

"General Tanaka-san," a healer called as they passed. "May I speak to you a moment?"

"Certainly. What can I do for you?"

"It's about that whore the men brought in. Should I waste supplies on him?" the healer asked. "I mean, shouldn't I be saving it for the men?"

"Oh, I don't know," the warlord cut in coldly. "I'd say Oki deserves a long life to pursue his craft. After all, he's getting such a late start." He sneered openly, causing the healer to pull back in alarm. "Do everything possible to keep him alive and pleasing the men. No arguments," he snapped to Yuudai when it looked like he was going to say something.

"You heard the commander," Yuudai said. "Patch him up and get him back in the barracks." He shuddered at the thought of what the former slave-trader had been through over the weekend. "You have until after the battle. They'll need stress relief then."

With a curt nod the healer scurried off, leaving the pair to continue silently on towards the mess.

Chapter Thirty-Seven

"Ryuu, can you bring me some clean diapers?" Kotone called, exhaustion apparent in her voice.

"Here you go." The scribe entered the room with some clean laundry, plucking a cloth off the top and handing it to her with a smile. "It's amazing how much mess such a little thing can make." He briskly started folding the armload of tiny clothes, diapers, washcloths and blankets.

"I'm so lucky to have you to help me," the tired new mother replied. "I thought this was supposed to get easier."

Ryuu chuckled. "It is easier. Aoi is sleeping through the night a few times a week now. But it's only been a couple of months. It takes a while to recover completely, especially when you keep yourself up worrying."

"Well, what do you expect? I haven't heard from that idiot in almost a month. The first few weeks he wrote all the time. I can't help but worry. Aren't you worried?"

"No, I refuse to worry," Ryuu said. "Aoshi said there could be breaks in communication and not to fret, so I'm not. We'll be joining them in another month. I'm just looking forward to that."

Kotone finished changing the baby and handed her to the scribe. "Could you watch her for a few minutes while I clean up? I'll feed her when I'm done."

"I'll give her some sweet water now. You relax in the tub and then you can both take a nice nap."

"All I seem to do is sleep," she complained. "I don't know what's wrong with me these days."

"Well, you need more sleep because you're still recovering from the birth. You need more sleep because you get up with Aoi so often." He paused for a moment. "And you may be sleeping because it fills up the time until you see the general. It's even harder than it normally would be, because the baby reminds you of his absence. It's okay, Kotone. You're doing fine. I'm sure we'll have news soon."

She smiled sadly and shuffled off towards the bath. Ryuu looked at the baby in his arms, smiling sweetly at her as he crooned. "Let's get you fed, sweetie-pie. Then you and Momma can take a nice nap together."

She wrinkled her brow and studied him with all the concentration her two month old brain could muster before stretching both arms up and grabbing for the hair that had escaped his low tail. "No, no. Play with this instead." The scribe quickly replaced his hair with a small carved dog.

He soon had the syrupy treat ready and settled in to feed her, singing softly to her as she greedily sucked it dry. Then he swung her up on a shoulder and efficiently coaxed out a gigantic burp before carrying her into Kotone's room and settling her into her basket. "Sleep well," he said with a smile before bidding her mother the same and heading back downstairs.

Ryuu was idly reading a scroll of poetry to keep himself from worrying. However, the paper lay abandoned in his lap while he daydreamed about the warlord. *I wonder what Aoshi's doing?* he thought, the concern he'd masked in front of Kotone coming to the forefront. He startled from his thoughts by the distinctive click of the door sliding.

Sweat drew streaks of tan in the pallid dust coating Akemi. "I have news." The courier moved inside and collapsed onto a cushion.

"Do you need something to drink?" Ryuu asked.

"Water, please," the courier replied before slumping back into silence. When the scribe returned he accepted the cup and drained it in a single draught, placing it carefully on the table when it was empty.

"There was a rock slide. General Fujii-san's been injured. His leg is badly broken and may never be quite right, although they don't think he'll lose it."

"I'll go wake Kotone. I'll be back in just a minute." Ryuu stood and began to leave the room, pointedly not wanting to hear anymore. The sick feeling multiplied in his stomach as he feared more bad news was forthcoming, news he didn't want to hear.

"Ryuu, wait." The courier stood and caught his arm. "Sit back down, there's more."

The scribe reluctantly retook his seat, glaring at Akemi with hard eyes as if daring him to deliver bad news. "It's Aoshi. He was riding with Ken'ichi. It looks like he threw himself over the general. He was still unconscious when I left but it didn't look good."

Akemi watched the scribe's face carefully, hating to deliver such hard news. He flinched inwardly when normally bronze skin turned the color of cottage cheese. "Ryuu, put your head between your legs and breathe." He reached out and pushed him into the suggested position, repeating his advice, "Breathe. That's it, nice and slow."

When a few minutes passed some color had returned to Ryuu's face. The courier let him sit upright, keeping a steadying arm around him. "Are you ready for me to go on?" Akemi asked, continuing when the scribe gave an almost imperceptible nod.

"As I said he's unconscious and injured. And, in my opinion, what he needs is you. Will you come back with me?" the courier hesitated. "I should warn you it won't be pretty. He might even be gone by the time we get there."

"Then we have to hurry." Ryuu rose and wiped his eyes. Aoshi needed him. He was not going to let the warlord down. "Kotone." He headed towards her room. "Kotone, you need to wake up."

By the time the scribe reached her room she was up and at the door. "What's the matter, Ryuu?"

"Akemi's here with news. There's been a rock slide. Ken'ichi's broken his leg and Aoshi is in very bad shape. I need to leave now so I can see him." Ryuu visibly pulled himself together. "Will you be alright on your own?"

She was already moving into his room, packing a bag with some essentials. Kotone pulled the shell-shocked scribe into a tight hug before sweeping downstairs with him in tow. "Akemi. I hear you have news of my husband."

"Yes, ma'am," the courier replied. "I'm afraid the general was injured in a rock slide. His leg was broken. The plan was to move him back here once it was set. He's probably already on his way."

"Hire some help," Ryuu said in an overly calm voice. "You all can stay here, there's lots of room. I'll bring Aoshi back as soon as he can travel." He refused to even consider the alternative. "Hurry up, Akemi. Let's get moving."

Kotone watched the courier's face and her heart ached. If Akemi's expression was any indication, Aoshi was in very grave shape indeed. She sent up a silent prayer for the warlord and Ryuu both. The scribe hurried to ready fresh horses for himself and the courier. They headed off at a gallop, Kotone turning back inside with a heavy heart when she heard Aoi begin to stir.

Chapter Thirty-Eight

Ryuu stepped into the warlord's tent and stopped, stricken at the sight before him. Aoshi looked almost frail, swathed in bandages and lying so still in the large bed.

"He's hanging on," the healer said. "It's more than I expected. The next few hours will tell, that will mark five days. If he hasn't developed a fever by then he should survive. I have no idea if he'll ever regain consciousness."

The scribe slowly sank to his knees next to the bed, stroking lank strands off a pale forehead. "I'm here, Aoshi. I won't leave you, I promise. Now you need to promise to stay with me." Tears streamed down his face unnoticed. "Please come back to me," he whispered before falling silent, idly stroking his thumb over the back of the large hand he clutched too tightly.

The healer shook his head disapprovingly. This sort of emotional display was unseemly. "Sir," he began, placing a hand on Ryuu's shoulder. "This really isn't appropriate. I'm sure the commander would not approve..." He was cut off with a strangled squawk when Yuudai's heavy hand landed on his shoulder.

"I think these two could use some privacy." He steered the healer outside before giving him a piece of his mind. "What the fuck do you think you're doing?" he demanded as soon as the flap fell behind them.

"I was just trying to salvage the commander's dignity," the healer replied with a huff. "He doesn't need his memory tainted by some sordid affair."

The general took a deep calming breath. "Good gods, man, he may be dying. Like it or not those two are in love, and only a cruel bastard would deny them this time together." He fixed the healer with a piercing stare. "Are you a cruel bastard?"

"No, sir," the healer replied with a gulp. "I didn't fully understand the situation. I should go and check on my other patients."

"You do that," Yuudai replied with satisfaction as the healer disappeared into the night. He lingered outside the tent, not wanting to disturb the couple, but unwilling to be too far away in case his friend's condition worsened.

Ryuu sighed. He was glad the warlord was still holding on, but he was so badly injured. Even more frightening was how still the pale man lay. He squeezed the hand he was holding tightly, willing his strength into the man who had come to mean so much to him.

He stood and began pacing to try and work off his agitation, pausing by the worktable when a scroll tagged with his name caught his eye.

Closer inspection revealed a stack of scrolls, all addressed to him. He picked one up and unrolled it.

'My Dearest Ryuu,' it began in the warlord's familiar shaky script. 'There's so much I want to say to you, but I don't know how. You encouraged me to keep a journal to improve my writing, so I'm writing down all those thoughts. One day, perhaps, I will be brave enough to let you read them.'

Tears ran freely down the scribe's face as he read words of confusion, anger and despair. Through it all ran a thread of such loving devotion that Ryuu feared he could never live up to it. He finally dropped the pages and covered his face with his hands, shaking silently as he realized just how much his fear and indecision had hurt the warlord.

"You've given me so much, Aoshi," he whispered fervently. "And all I've given you is heartache. I swear I'll never leave your side again." He ran his hand through his hair and decided to try and make the warlord more comfortable. He fetched a basin of cool water and a cloth and began to gently clean Aoshi's exposed skin, tenderly scrubbing off the blood and dirt which remained from the accident. As he washed he sang the lullabies he'd been using to soothe baby Aoi, the now familiar melodies lending a sense of normality to the nightmarish situation.

Akemi ghosted up behind Yuudai and put his hands over the general's eyes. "Guess who?" he asked with a chuckle.

"My interfering lover?"

"No," the courier replied with a large smirk. "Your brilliant lover who brought the one person Fujiwara will wake up for." He studied the large man carefully. "Are you jealous?"

"No I'm not," Yuudai assured him. "But it's killing me to stand here and not be able to do anything. I'm glad we cleared the air before this happened, though. What I'm really worried about is screwing up. With Ken'ichi and Aoshi both out of commission I'm making all the decisions on my own. To be honest, I really don't want the responsibility. The men don't trust me the way they do the commander. Hell, I don't trust me the way I do Aoshi."

"Stop it," Akemi insisted. "Stop putting yourself down. You are doing an excellent job. Casualties are still very low and we should be able to overpower the rest of the opposition very soon. And you are helping the commander by handling all of this for him." He grasped Yuudai's shoulders and began to rub. "What you need is a massage, and I'm just the man who can give it to you."

"I don't want to leave. What if something happens?"

"If something happens Ryuu will be there. I don't think he's ready for company, although he may welcome it in a day or so." Akemi hesitated for a moment. "You won't be helping anyone if you drop from exhaustion, so come on. You need a bath, a massage and some sleep. I won't take no for an answer."

Yuudai reluctantly allowed Akemi to steer him to the bathing tent. He stripped quickly and climbed into the tub, immediately relaxing into the warm water, head nodding and eyes growing heavy. The courier immediately began to scrub the larger man, slapping his hand away when he tried to help. "Let me do this for you." Akemi said seriously. "Please. I want to, so just relax."

"You're dirtying the water," the general groused. "I hope you plan on cleaning this tub."

"Don't worry about the tub. Besides, you're the one who climbed in without washing first."

Once the general was clean, the smaller man helped him out of the tub and back to his tent. He coaxed him to stretch out on the bed, kneeling beside him and rubbing tense muscles. Yuudai groaned as strong fingers found each knot and worked until it eased. Before the massage was half done he was snoring blissfully.

Akemi finished and surveyed the sleeping man with satisfaction. *At least he's finally relaxing. Wish he could have stayed awake for some stress relief. Next time*, he decided with a leer before stretching out beside his lover and joining him in sleep.

Chapter Thirty-Nine

Yuudai studied the man in front of him critically. "Ryuu, you need to eat. You've lost weight."

"I can't leave him. What if something happens?" the scribe said. "Besides, I'm really not hungry.

"You're never hungry. You haven't been sleeping either. You won't be any help to Aoshi if you get sick," the general insisted. "It's been two weeks, and you need a break. Come on, Akemi is cooking. We'll have you back in an hour." Yuudai turned a deaf ear on the scribe's protests and towed him across camp to his tent, calling out to his lover as they entered.

"I'm back and I brought Ryuu."

"Wonderful," the courier called. "Sit down. I'll be right in with food." A few moments later he appeared, plates in hand, and moved to deposit them on the table. "Ryuu, I'm so glad you could join us. I hope you like eel."

"That sounds wonderful, Akemi." The scribe smiled for the first time in weeks. "Thank you so much for having me."

"You're always welcome," Yuudai replied. "I just wish I had dragged you away before this."

"I know I need to take better care of myself," the scribe admitted. "But I'm so afraid something will happen the moment I leave. I've never been very good at waiting."

"Well, sit down and try to enjoy at least one meal," Akemi said. "The healer will come get you if anything changes."

Aoshi sat down to eat, the scribe appreciating the effort they were exerting to lift his spirits. He studied Yuudai intently. *It can't be easy for the general. Aoshi is important to him, too.* "General, you know you're welcome to come visit whenever you like. I'll take a break and give you some privacy if that's the problem."

"That's very kind of you. And I'd love to come visit, but I won't need any privacy." He reached out and squeezed Akemi's hand reassuringly.

They soon finished eating and the scribe excused himself, hurrying back to the warlord's side. He dismissed the obviously bored healer and settled in for his nighttime vigil, softly recounting the evening's events. "Night, Aoshi. Come back to me soon." He bent to kiss a pale cheek before settling into his usual spot beside the futon, Aoshi's hand firmly clasped in his.

At some point the scribe's eyes slipped shut and his breathing slowed. He lost his battle to stay awake, head falling onto the bed next to their clasped hands. He jumped when a husky whisper of his name broke the silence. He instantly passed from sleep to waking, head snapping upright to see long lashes flutter as the warlord struggled to open his eyes.

"Ryuu," he rasped. "What happened?"

"You were caught in a rock slide with General Fujii-san. He's been sent home to recover with Kotone and the baby. You've been unconscious for over two weeks. I was afraid you'd never wake up. I'm so sorry. I hurt you so much. Believe me, I didn't mean to. I swear I'll never leave you again."

"Love you," the warlord mumbled. "Get up?"

"No, don't try to get up." The scribe laughed through his tears. Getting out of bed the instant he woke was exactly what he expected the stubborn warlord to try. "Let me go fetch a healer." He started to pull away but Aoshi grabbed his hand and held it tightly.

"Tomorrow?" he whispered hopefully. "Please?"

"I don't know," the scribe said. "I think you need to be checked now that you're conscious. But I guess it can wait until morning."

The warlord broke out in a broad smile, patting the bed beside him. "Come on. Get in."

"I haven't been sleeping with you because of your injuries. I wouldn't want to cause you more pain."

"Need you. Please." Aoshi pleaded.

"Alright, but you have to let me know if anything hurts."

"You won't hurt me," the warlord replied confidently, closing his eyes in bliss as Ryuu slid under the covers. He winced slightly when the bed dipped, but quickly hid it, relaxing when the scribe was finally settled, gently nestled up against his side with an arm draped across his chest.

Ryuu lifted his head and placed a soft kiss on pale lips, startled when Aoshi's hand snaked into his messy hair, pinning him in place and deepening the kiss. The warlord groaned when their tongues clashed, desperate to never let this moment end even as he felt sleep pulling at him. "Mmm," he hummed when the kiss gentled. "Don't leave me. Please."

"I'm not going anywhere," the scribe replied with a smile. "At least, not until I go fetch the healer in the morning. Now, you need to rest. You're still healing."

"Yes, Ryuu," the warlord slurred sleepily. "Love you." He finished with a mighty yawn before dropping into a deep restful sleep.

Ryuu sent up a silent prayer of thanks as he gingerly snuggled into the sleeping form, almost immediately falling into the first real sleep he'd had in weeks.

* * *

"Ken'ichi," Kotone called from down the hall.

"Yes, dear. What is it?"

"Why haven't we heard anything about how Aoshi's doing? I understand Ryuu's too busy to write, but you're a general. You'd think they'd keep you informed."

"They're on the border, sweetheart. They have more to worry about than keeping an injured man who's miles away up to speed."

"Well, I'm worried," Kotone admitted. "How can we find out?"

"If it will make you feel better why don't I go get some news?" Ken'ichi suggested.

"Why, is there someone in town you can ask?" Kotone wrinkled her nose in puzzlement.

"No, I thought I could ride back to camp and check in…" he trailed off at the deadly look she sent him. "I mean, I can't walk but I can ride. Yuudai would probably welcome someone to talk things over with."

"You're injured," Kotone reminded him. "They sent you away from the front, remember?"

"So I could recuperate, and I am. I have a broken leg. I promise, I'll be back in less than a week."

"You better be." Kotone shook her head, still not convinced this was a good idea.

Chapter Forty

Ken'ichi arrived in camp just before dusk, dusty, sore, and happy as hell to be back. He loved his wife and daughter dearly, but he was a career soldier. The thought of his men going into battle without him was more than he could take. Still, the long ride in a stuffy palanquin was not something he wanted to repeat. The sooner his leg healed, the better.

They pulled up outside Yuudai's tent and he called out, knowing there'd be hell to pay if he tried to get down on his own. "Yo, Yuudai. Give me a hand, will ya?" He was pleasantly surprised when both Akemi and the general appeared to help him into the tent.

"What the hell are you doing back?" Yuudai asked. "Baby too much for you?"

"Aoi's wonderful," Ken'ichi replied. "Although Kotone's bossier than ever. She wanted news about Fujiwara and I needed to find out what was happening. Suffice it to say she's really pissed at me right now. She expected me to send someone else." He rolled his eyes at the thought, sending Yuudai into fits of laughter.

Akemi clutched his sides as his eyes watered. He could picture Kotone lecturing the general, hands on her hips. "You're gonna be sleeping with the dogs for a month," he chortled.

"Yeah, yeah. Easy for you to laugh," Ken'ichi grumbled. "So, what's the news?"

"At least sit down and have a drink with us. We're celebrating," Yuudai said.

"Celebrating what?" Ken'ichi wasn't sure if he trusted the slightly intoxicated pair not to be setting up some elaborate joke.

"The commander regained consciousness," Akemi said. "He'll be out of commission for a while, but he's going to survive. He's been out for over two weeks so you can imagine how relieved we are. I guess we went a bit overboard with our celebration."

"That's fantastic news. I certainly don't blame you for celebrating. How are things at the front?"

"We've pushed them back to the far side of the river," Yuudai explained. "A little more pressure and they should be ready to negotiate."

"I guess you didn't need me after all," Ken'ichi huffed, frustrated by the progress made in his absence.

"Don't be ridiculous," the courier exclaimed. "Yuudai's been driving himself crazy worrying over every decision. With you here maybe he'll finally lighten up." He glanced at the taller man briefly. "After what happened between the commander and Yuudai, he lost his confidence. He's doing fine but he won't believe it. He looks almost as bad as Ryuu. It's a good thing Fujiwara finally woke up. Now maybe they'll both start taking care of themselves."

"What did they fight about anyway?" Ken'ichi asked. "Aoshi would only say they were taking a break."

"It's not important. What is important is the fact it was Yuudai's fault. They still weren't really talking when this happened. He feels responsible."

"That's ridiculous," Ken'ichi said. "It had been raining for a week, that rock could have gone at any time, or not at all. If anyone should feel guilty, it's me. Aoshi saved my ass and almost died."

"What are you two whispering about?" Yuudai asked.

"I was just telling the general how thin Ryuu's gotten," Akemi replied.

"Hmmmm." Yuudai peered into his lover's eyes. "Why don't I believe you?"

"Because you're naturally suspicious. That's what makes you such a wonderful leader." The courier turned to their guest. "So, Gimpy," he said, adroitly changing the topic. "Want us to help you over to Fujiwara's? We were planning on heading over soon anyway."

"I can walk," the general insisted, wobbling and almost falling when he went to stand. "A little." He took a few tentative steps, dragging the heavily bound limb before groaning in defeat. "Fine, I could use some help."

Yuudai and Akemi each wrapped an arm around Ken'ichi's waist, easily supporting him between them. "I hope Kotone won't be jealous," the courier quipped.

"If you ever tell her I'll skin you alive," the general replied through gritted teeth. "You have no idea what a truly terrifying thought that is." He shuddered and then shook his head. "Let's just go. This is embarrassing enough without dragging it out."

* * *

"Aoshi, we can't." Ryuu removed the warlord's wandering hand. "You just woke up and you're still injured. There will be plenty of time for that later."

"But Ryuu, I've missed you," Aoshi purred. "I need to touch you to convince myself you're real. Besides, I can tell you want it, too."

"I never said I didn't. But I don't want to put you back in a coma."

"Well, at least come cuddle with me," the warlord said with a pout.

He looks too cute like that, Ryuu thought fondly. "Alright, but just for a few minutes. Then I need to get up and fix you something to eat."

Aoshi lifted up the covers with a smile, pulling the scribe in for a deep kiss the instant he was in bed. "That's what I need to recover." He began to nip and lick at Ryuu's neck.

"Wait a minute, you said cuddling," the scribe squeaked when a strong hand palmed his hardening cock.

"But, I need you. It's been so long, and I've missed you so."

Ryuu rolled his eyes at the commander. "You are such a brat." He thought for a moment and seemed to come to a decision. "Fine, but you are going to lay there and not move. Understand?"

"Yesss." Aoshi hissed as the scribe's talented mouth began to trace a path down the parts of his chest not covered in bandages. "Oh, yess." Ryuu's hot mouth blew gently on his trembling erection before swallowing him to the root.

The warlord's eyes rolled up into his head as Ryuu's tongue twirled up the length of his straining cock before flicking over the tip. The scribe's cheeks hollowed as he sucked hard, sliding the length smoothly into his throat until his nose was nestled in soft smoky curls. He hummed as he retreated, making Aoshi arch and groan gutturally.

Determined hands held lean hips down as the scribe continued his slow slide, twisting and humming until the warlord thought he would go insane. Just when Aoshi thought he couldn't take anymore a slick finger slid into his entrance, sending shivers of pleasure zipping up his spine. "More. Please, need more."

The scribe brushed Aoshi's prostate firmly as he twirled his tongue around the head. The tip of that wicked tongue dipped into the slit, and the warlord screamed his pleasure. *One more hard suck and the crook of a finger should do it*, Ryuu thought.

Aoshi buried his hands in the scribe's hair and tried to still his movement "Wait. Stop or I'm going to come before you get inside."

"That is not happening," Ryuu replied tartly, dropping his mouthful to lecture his lover. "There's no way you're in any kind of shape for that. Take what you can get. Once you recover we'll do whatever you like."

"Anything I want?" the warlord asked with a leer.

Ryuu just gave him an indulgent look, giving his prostate a firm stroke before bending down to take Aoshi's cock back in his mouth.

* * *

The combination of Ken'ichi's broken leg and the drinks Akemi and Yuudai had indulged in meant it took longer than usual to reach the warlord's tent. "Hey guys, we've come to visit," the courier sang out as they stumbled inside.

Yuudai immediately clapped his hands over his eyes and moaned while Akemi and Ken'ichi stared, transfixed at the sight that met their eyes. Just then the warlord let out a warbling shriek of the scribe's name and came.

Ryuu sat up and licked his lips. "Feeling better dear?" he asked his lover with a smile.

"Great," Aoshi managed to stammer. "But I think our guests could use some help.

Ryuu turned around and blushed beet red at the sight of the three gaping visitors. "Uh,excuse me." He dashed out of the room, leaving Aoshi alone with his friends.

Chapter Forty-One

Aoshi stared hard at the three men standing in the doorway. Akemi was practically licking his lips as he leered at him, Yuudai looked like he might pass out at any moment and Ken'ichi tottered unstably between them waiting for the other shoe to drop.

"Can I help you with something?" the warlord snarled, upset at having his lover flee so abruptly.

"Dear god in heaven Kotone's gonna kill me." Ken'ichi effectively derailed everyone else's thoughts. "I might as well just move my things to the kennel permanently."

"What are you babbling about?" Aoshi asked.

"If Kotone finds out I interrupted you two she'll have my balls," the general moaned. "Getting you back together is all she can talk about." He slumped to the floor awkwardly, broken leg sticking straight out in front of him, and dropped his head in his hands. "You don't know what she's been like. One minute she's crying her eyes out, the next she's ready to take my head off. I didn't care if it killed me, I had to get out of there. And please don't tell her I said that."

The other three men just stared at him in shock. "You ran away from home?" Yuudai jibed. "I never thought I'd see the day..." he trailed off when Ryuu's voice suddenly cut through the tent.

"Fujii Ken'ichi, did you leave Kotone and the baby all alone? What in kami's name were you thinking? You've probably set your recovery back by weeks." The scribe headed toward the trio. Yuudai and Akemi clung together while Ken'ichi tried to scoot across the floor, unable to get his leg under him and stand.

The warlord collapsed in laughter, thoroughly enjoying the sight of his powerful generals cowering in the face of his scolding lover. "And you," Ryuu rounded on Aoshi, causing him to try and compose himself. "You just woke up last night. Do you want to end up in a coma again?"

"I think if that was going to happen it would have been while you were sucking his—" Akemi's voice cut off abruptly when Yuudai's hand slapped over his mouth.

"Shut up. I don't want to end up like Narita-san," the general hissed in his lover's ear.

"Narita Oki?" Ryuu said. "What about him?"

"Nothing at all, Ryuu," the warlord interjected. "Yuudai was just babbling again." He gave the general a pointed look, guaranteeing he wouldn't be contradicted.

"Hey, Fujiwara," Akemi spoke up. "Don't take it out on Yuudai just because you didn't tell Ryuu what you did. That's hardly fair."

"You," the warlord stated through gritted teeth, "have a big mouth, Suzuki. Perhaps I should find something better for you to do with it."

"Don't you threaten him." Yuudai jumped in front of his lover. "Just because I screwed up is no reason to punish Akemi."

"So, Ryuu," Ken'ichi cut in, trying to get the conversation back on safer ground, "when Aoshi's able to travel, I figured we'd all go back together. If I try to head back without you, my wife will certainly kill me."

"That will be a few days," Ryuu said, glancing fondly at the warlord as he considered their options. "Aoshi just woke up. We need to make sure he's stable before we attempt a trip. I need to be sure nothing will happen to him."

Aoshi's heart lifted when he heard the scribe's concern. *I did it, I got him back.* He smothered another snicker when he heard his lover sniff the air around their 'guests'. "Have you three been drinking?" Ryuu asked. "It's only ten o'clock. What kind of an example are you setting for the men, waltzing around camp drunk in the morning?"

"A confident one?" Yuudai slurred, leaning heavily on Akemi.

"Confident my ass," the scribe retorted. "Ridiculous is more like it. I'm going to make something warm to drink. You two," he pointed at Akemi and Yuudai, "sit down. And you," he pointed at the cowering Ken'ichi, "sit properly, you look like an idiot. Wait until I tell Kotone what you were doing."

"Oh gods, please don't tell her," the general implored, wrapping his arms around the scribe's leg and resting his forehead against Ryuu's thigh. "She's already mad at me."

"I don't blame her. A father needs to show more common sense than you're using right now. You will get checked out by the healer when he gets here. Then Akemi will take a message to Kotone letting her know you arrived safely and when we should be returning."

"Can't someone else take it?" the courier whined, not wanting to ride so far after drinking so much.

"No, the fresh air will do you good." Ryuu turned on his heel and disappeared to fetch tea.

"Ouch, Fujiwara. He's brutal. How do you put up with that?" Ken'ichi groaned, cradling his head in his hands. "He's worse than Kotone at that time of the month."

"Watch it," the warlord growled. "It's not like you don't deserve it. After all, you're the ones that burst in here and interrupted us. He's embarrassed."

Akemi decided that was his cue. "I'll go talk to him." He stood, swaying slightly, and headed towards the kitchens. The commander and his generals watched him go, silently commending his bravery as they turned their conversation to what had been happening on the front since the rock slide.

"Hey, Ryuu," the courier called as he slipped into the kitchen. "Are you okay?"

The scribe turned, keeping a tight grip on the counter. "I'm alright," he said, blushing a deep crimson. "I just wasn't expecting visitors so early."

"There's really nothing to be embarrassed about. Aoshi walked in on us a while back. I was so worried about what he'd think of me, but he didn't seem to even notice." He stared at the ground pensively before looking up and gracing the scribe with a wide smile. "I can tell you when a good time is to walk in on us. Then you can even the score."

Ryuu blushed even brighter at the thought, covering his eyes. "No thank you, Akemi. Although I appreciate the offer."

"Anything to help a friend." The courier poured hot water over the leaves and placed the teapot on a tray with some cups. He nodded at Ryuu and took his tray into the main room, placing a cup in front of each man before plopping into his chair. "Crisis averted," He announced. Aoshi and the generals all sighed in relief.

After the healer had come and gone, Akemi was dispatched with a letter for Kotone while Yuudai dragged Ken'ichi back to his tent. Once they were alone Ryuu turned to the warlord and fixed him with hard eyes. "What about Narita-san?"

"He trained Kazuya," Aoshi replied. "He spent five years feeding him poison with the intent of killing me, not to mention what he did to you …. to all those young boys." He was cut off by the low voice of his lover.

"Aoshi. What did you do?"

"I cut off his balls and gave him to the men as a plaything. I almost cut out his tongue as well." The warlord turned troubled eyes on his lover. "He hurt you, I could never forgive that. He more than deserves his fate."

"You mean he's still alive?"

"Last I heard. Apparently the men are pleased with his performance." Ryuu stared at him in shock, unsure what he felt about this new information.

Chapter Forty-Two

Kotone yanked the door open hard. *This had better be good.* She tried to comfort the frantically squalling infant in her arms. "Ssshh, baby girl," she crooned. "Mama will make the loud idiot go away."

"I have a message from Ryuu and a letter from General Fujii-san, ma'am. I'm sorry if I woke the baby." Akemi reached out and tapped the tip of Aoi's nose with his finger. She stopped crying and stared at him in startled fascination.

"Come in, come in." Kotone forgot her bad mood at the thought of news. "Would you like something to eat or drink?"

"I'd love a drink, ma'am. I can hold the baby." He took the tiny bundle in his arms. "Hi, sweetie," he whispered, dissolving into a pained groan when Aoi managed to fist both hands in his dangling hair and pulled.

"No, no, baby girl." Kotone tried to untangle the courier's long locks. "No pulling hair." Aoi just stared at her curiously and tightened her grip.

"Here's your letter from the general, ma'am," Akemi said once Aoi was finally detached and settled in her basket.

"Please call me Kotone. Ma'am makes me feel very old."

"Yes, ma'am, I mean, Kotone. Ryuu said to tell you the three of them would be coming back together once the commander can travel, which should be in a few days. And to let you know he would not be letting the general do anything else stupid, so you shouldn't worry."

Kotone smiled at the last part of the message, it sounded just like Ryuu. She missed the scribe. Although they hadn't known each other for long they had become good friends. It was nice to have someone to talk to about matters other than soldiering and war.

"If you'll excuse me a minute." Kotone rose, wanting to read her husband's message in private.

"Why don't I go into town, get a meal and get cleaned up. I'll come back later to see if you have anything for me to take back."

"No, no." Kotone stopped him. "Go upstairs and use one of the guest rooms. There's plenty of space here. Ryuu would be hurt if one of his friends was turned away." She saw he was still hesitating. "Please, I insist," she urged before shooing him up the stairs and settling in to read the letter from her husband.

* * *

Ryuu woke with a smile. In fact, it seemed like he hadn't stopped smiling since the warlord woke up a few days ago. He breathed deeply, enjoying the older man's unique scent. Smoky and spicy, like cinnamon and sex. *I can't wait until he's well enough to make love.* The scribe groaned when his cock twitched with interest at the thought. *Oh great.* He tried to will away his erection by thinking of unpleasant things, to no avail.

I need to go take care of this, Ryuu decided, slipping out of bed to head for the bathroom. "Don't go," a sleepy voice chimed in. "I can take care of that for you."

The scribe blushed bright red at being caught. "No you can't, you can barely sit up. You are not supposed to be exerting yourself."

"How would I be exerting myself? I promise to just lay here and enjoy it while you take me," the warlord coaxed with a rakish grin. "Please. I've missed feeling you inside me so much." He brought pleading eyes into play, rapidly eroding the scribe's tenuous self-control.

"I don't know," Ryuu said, wracking his brain for reasons why this was a bad idea.

"Pretty please?" That handsome face implored, long arms reaching out to pull the scribe back into bed, tightly wound in the warlord's arms.

"You swear you'll tell me if it's too much? I don't want to risk hurting you."

"I promise I won't overdo it. I'll leave that up to you." Aoshi lay back to sprawl temptingly across the bed. "I'm waiting," he sing-songed. "Come ravish me."

Ryuu couldn't help but smile in return, stretching out beside his lover and kissing him passionately, breaking away to lick and nibble at the warlord's neck. "Stop that." He pushed away Aoshi's wandering hands. "You promised you wouldn't exert yourself. If you don't cooperate I'll have to tie you up."

"Yes, sir," the warlord replied. "I promise not to cooperate so you can bind me." He smirked when the scribe roughly manhandled him to lie flat, pulling his hands up over his head and binding them together with the sash from his yukata. Ryuu deftly passed the strip of silk around and between the commander's arms, starting at the elbow and working his way down to the wrists. *Gods he's sexy when he's angry.* Aoshi whimpered when his knees were pushed to his chest and spread before being similarly tied.

"Now, are you going to do what I say?" the scribe asked, hands on his hips as he glowered down at his lover.

"Anything and everything." The warlord craned his neck to try and steal a kiss.

Ryuu took pity on him and closed the distance, sealing their lips together and easily dominating the kiss, sweeping inside to sample the delights of his lover's mouth. When the need for air forced them apart he moved to the warlord's chest, licking and nipping the defined ridges of muscle peaking between the tightly wrapped bandages, delighting in the tremors that raced through the lanky frame.

The scribe traced a wet path over a jutting hipbone, drawing a moan from his lover. Aoshi's leaking erection twitched with every swipe of that hot wet tongue, begging for attention. Ryuu finally ran his tongue up the underside, circling the head before sucking the length into his mouth to the root. The warlord strained to buck up into the moist heat.

Ryuu pulled back slightly and narrowed his eyes at his lover, waiting for him to settle back onto the bed before he continued. It didn't take long before the scribe's talented tongue had the warlord begging for release, so he slowed his pace before stopping.

Aoshi practically shrieked in frustration when the scribe pulled off his cock. "Please, I'm so close."

"But I'm not," Ryuu retorted. "Don't worry, I'll take good care of you." He blew lightly across the warlord's slick cock, fascinated by the way it jumped.

"Stop teasing. If you don't pick up the pace I'm going to die."

"Oh, I'd never let that happen." The scribe nipped at his lover's sac as he kneaded his ass, lifting and spreading the cheeks to lap at his puckered entrance. He reveled in the moaning growls the warlord let out when he thrust his tongue through the tight ring.

Ryuu squeezed his erection hard, desperately trying to stave off his climax at the sight of the warlord wantonly tossing his head from side to side, every growl and groan going straight to his erection, driving him to the brink before he could even slide inside.

The scribe took a deep calming breath before slicking his fingers and sliding two into Aoshi's tight heat, pushing them deep to stroke across his prostate, making the powerful man keen his pleasure. "Hurry, I'm going insane," the warlord panted. "I'm ready, please."

"Not yet." Ryuu added a third finger and continuing to twist and stretch. "I don't want to hurt you."

"You won't hurt me, but I'm going to come without you if you don't hurry up."

"Can't have that." The scribe finally removed his fingers and oiled his cock, tremors running through both men as the head nudged the softened pucker.

Ryuu took a deep breath and carefully began to push inside, ever so slowly sinking deeper until his balls brushed taut cheeks. He paused when he was fully seated, as much to allow him to strengthen his control as to let Aoshi adjust.

When he finally began to move he pulled out just as slowly, beginning a measured pace that soon had the warlord begging for more. "Harder, I need to feel all of you." Aoshi moaned, spurring the scribe to quicken the pace until he was slamming into his lover's hungry ass, hips snapping up to meet his every thrust.

Ryuu felt his orgasm approaching and finally reached out to stroke the dripping cock bobbing in front of him. The warlord let out a needy keening noise, building in intensity with each thrust until he finally exploded, screaming the scribe's name as he shot his seed between them.

The sight of that too serious face in the throes of pleasure, combined with the convulsions of the warlord's tight passage, was more than Ryuu could take. With one last powerful thrust to Aoshi's prostate he exploded, vision wavering as he came harder than he could remember.

When he finally gained control of himself he rolled off and quickly untied the warlord's hands, berating himself when he saw bruises on his wrists. "I'm so sorry. I hurt you. I knew this was a bad idea."

"It was my idea," Aoshi retorted. "I'm not complaining. In fact, I'm planning on misbehaving so we can repeat it."

"Mmmm, maybe later," the scribe decided. "For now, sleep." He received no protests when he maneuvered them until they were curled tightly together, both men drifting off into a sated slumber.

Chapter Forty-Three

When Ryuu woke again it was lunchtime. He slipped quietly out of bed and cleaned up, planning on getting them something to eat before waking the warlord.

He headed across camp on his way to the mess, whistling as he walked, at peace with himself and the world. He changed direction and veered off towards the healer's tent, deciding that Aoshi should be checked out after the morning's exertions.

His whistle died in his throat at the sight that greeted him inside the healer's tent. His old master Narita Oki lay on a pallet directly opposite the door. The former slave trader was covered in bruises and bandages, with a wild, wary look in his eyes.

The scribe's heart clenched, warring with itself, torn between hatred for Oki and sympathy for his plight. He moved forward, almost against his will, until he was directly in front of his former master. "Hello, Narita-san. Do you remember me?"

The broken man studied him cautiously, stopping at the scar on his face. "Ryuu?" he croaked. "So, you ended up as a pleasure slave despite your aspirations."

"No," he replied. "I'm a scribe. I heard about your sentence." He realized his next question would not be well received. "Are you badly injured?"

"I'll live. I don't plan on being stuck here forever."

"Really?" Ryuu inquired, curious as to what he meant.

"My friends are working to rescue me," Oki continued more confidently. "Then Fujiwara will find himself here instead of me."

"You have friends in camp?" The scribe worried about the implied threat to his lover.

"Of course, Fujiwara's a fool. He only scratched the surface. He's not as popular as he'd like to believe," Oki said with a grim smile. "I just wish I had more freedom. It's impossible to make plans when I have no control over who I see or when." He paused and studied the scribe, considering his next words. "Maybe you could help me, and take a message to my friends?"

"I suppose," Ryuu replied, not really wanting to deal with this man, but desperate to make sure the warlord was safe. "What is the message and who is it for?"

He listened carefully as Oki gave him the name of his contact and their meeting place. He headed back out of the tent, original plan forgotten. The scribe decided to head for Yuudai's tent, confident that the general was the one person who could help him with this.

"Hello, General Tanaka-san?" he called from outside. "It's Ryuu. Can I talk to you?" He hesitated, unwilling to enter without an answer, remembering all too well the interruptions he'd suffered through.

He was just turning to leave when Akemi's head popped through the flap. "Hey, Ryuu, what's up? Sorry to make you wait."

"That's quite alright. I need to talk to the general. It's about the plot against Aoshi."

Akemi quickly ushered him inside. "Yuudai, hurry up. Ryuu's here and he needs to talk to you."

The general appeared, towel wrapped around his waist. "Hey Ryuu, what can I do for you?"

"I just had a rather disturbing conversation with Narita. He asked me to get a message to his 'friends'. Apparently they're still plotting against Aoshi. Oki seemed fairly confident that he was going to be rescued. We need to figure out who else is involved. Maybe I should deliver the message and see what I can find out."

"I don't know if that's such a good idea. What if they recognize you? They'd never believe you changed sides. If anything happened to you, Fujiwara would have my head."

"I haven't been seen around camp much," Ryuu said. "But I guess they could have heard about me. I'm willing to try, though. If we can find the other conspirators you can eliminate the threat."

"I guess we have to risk it." Yuudai tried, and failed, to come up with an acceptable alternative. "But you can't go alone, take Akemi with you. He can stay out of sight nearby in case of trouble."

"Okay," the scribe agreed. "I'll come back later and pick you up on my way. Right now I better hurry before Aoshi wakes up and wonders where I've gone." He turned to leave, cursing internally when he realized he still had to fetch the healer and pick up lunch.

*　*　*

Aoshi rolled over and opened his eyes, incredibly disappointed to find himself alone. He smiled broadly when he realized his soreness was due to their very pleasurable activities earlier rather than his injuries. *I guess I'm getting better*, he thought gratefully. *I haven't felt this good in weeks.*

He worked himself into a sitting position before calling out. "Hey, Ryuu. What's going on?"

"Lunch," was the brief answer from the man just lifting the flap.

"You went out?" the warlord asked. "Have you been gone long?"

"I just went to get lunch." Ryuu made a decision not to fill Aoshi in on his conversation with Oki or his part in Yuudai's strategy to uncover the conspirators. "And to ask the healer to come and check you out. I was afraid maybe you'd overdone it."

"I'm fine, silly," the warlord replied with a heart stopping smile. "How could I not be after the wonderful way you took care of me. I'm just impatient to return the favor."

Ryuu sat on the bed and gathered Aoshi in his arms, tangling his fingers in a cloud of messy hair and kissing him sweetly. "I can't wait for that either," he whispered when the kiss finally broke. "Hopefully you'll be able to travel in a few days. I can't wait to get you home and have you all to myself."

"All to yourself. In a house with Ken'ichi, Kotone and a baby?"

"It's a big house. You'll never even know they're there. Besides, you know you'd go crazy without at least one of your buddies around."

"The only person I want to be around is you," Aoshi retorted. "I'm looking forward to spending lots of uninterrupted time with you."

"I just hope you don't get tired of me."

The warlord took Ryuu's face in his hands and turned it to look at him. "Ryuu, I love you. I'll never get tired of you."

"I believe you. I love you too." The scribe wondered if the warlord would still feel the same after he found out about what he was planning.

Chapter Forty-Four

Ryuu left when the healer arrived to check Aoshi. The warlord continued to moan and complain that he was just fine and didn't need a checkup. The scribe headed to Yuudai's to pick up Akemi. When he arrived the general studied him seriously. "I'm not sure about this Ryuu. If they recognize you it could be dangerous."

"Well, that's true. But Oki didn't know about my relationship with Aoshi. He recognized me from when he was my master." The scribe sucked in a harsh breath and clapped his hand over his mouth. *How stupid am I,* he berated himself. *Yuudai and Akemi didn't know about that part of my life.* "I'd rather not talk about that. Just believe me, he doesn't know I know Aoshi."

"If you say so," the general grudgingly agreed. "I don't want to even think about what the commander will do if I send you into a trap."

"Come on, Akemi. Let's go," Ryuu urged, impatient to get this over with.

"All right, I'm coming." He turned to the general. "Don't worry, I have his back." Akemi planted a kiss on his lover's cheek and following the scribe out of the tent, a cheeky grin stretched across his face.

"I'll be watching." The courier looked around for a good vantage point to watch the meeting. Once he had settled on a spot, the scribe headed across the open expanse until he reached the edge of the forest.

Ryuu almost jumped out of his skin when a man suddenly ghosted out of the trees and appeared at his side. "Dear gods, you startled me." His hand grasped his chest to calm his racing heart. "Are you Kudo Seiya?" he asked when his voice was under control.

"Yes," the man replied warily. "And who are you that you

know my name?"

"Oki sent me. My name is Ryuu, Oshiro Ryuu. Masashi was my cousin," he added, hoping that a connection to the traitor would convince this man to talk to him.

"Ah, a good man. It was a real shame he got caught. He got greedy and rushed into things, just like Oki wishes to. For myself, I prefer to let things settle out on their own. It's generally just as effective, but a lot safer."

"So you aren't planning on helping Oki to escape?"

"I didn't say that," was the glib reply. "I said I wasn't going to act against Fujiwara. It's a death sentence. Oki is a sweet little whore though. I won't mind having him all to myself."

"Did you tell him that's all it is?" the scribe asked. "Is that what he wants?"

"Who cares what he wants? Besides, it has to be better than his life is now. What's the problem, do you want a turn? I could be convinced to share."

"No, no that's quite alright. He's a little too used for my taste," Ryuu replied, stomach turning at the thought. "So what should I tell Oki?"

"Tell him I'll come pick him up tomorrow while he's still at the healer's. It should be easy to smuggle him out of camp." Seiya smiled. "I'm sick of war and campaigning, it's time for a change."

"Alright, I'll tell him," the scribe agreed, suddenly anxious to get away. He headed back into camp. Akemi waited until Seiya was out of sight before catching up with him.

"So, what is the plot?" the courier asked.

"He says there's no plot. He just wants Oki all to himself so he played along." Ryuu frowned. "I don't know whether to believe him. I certainly would love Oki as far from me as possible, but I don't know if Seiya's trustworthy."

"Who?" Akemi asked with a puzzled frown.

"Kudo Seiya. At least, that's the name I was given. Do you know him?"

"Never heard of him. I think we need to tell Yuudai and see what he says."

The two hurried across camp, intent on informing Yuudai about the meeting. When they reached the tent they hurried inside, happy to find that Ken'ichi had joined the general for a game of shogi. They quickly filled the pair in on all that had happened, hoping they could shed some light on the situation.

"That sounds like Kudo," Ken'ichi admitted. "He's one of the laziest men I've ever had under my command. A born slacker. He doesn't seem the type to get involved in rebellion. Of course, I would have thought he was a bit old to risk his neck for a whore, too."

"Lazy is just another reason for him to be dissatisfied," Yuudai countered. "He would have been better off under the old system, like Benjirou. He can't advance under Fujiwara without performing."

"The man I met with wasn't much older than I am," Ryuu insisted. "You must be thinking of someone else."

"Or he's hiding his identity," Akemi suggested. "We really don't have enough information to know who this mystery man is."

"So what should we do?" Ryuu finally demanded, hands on his hips. "I need to get back before Aoshi starts wondering where I am."

"You should go take care of the commander." Ken'ichi blushed brightly when he realized how his comment sounded. "Er, I mean, go help him out…" he stammered to a halt, overwhelmed by the unwanted images his mind was conjuring up of how the pair had looked when he, Yuudai and Akemi had walked in on them. "Just go. Yuudai and I will handle this. Aoshi doesn't need the hassle right now."

"But I need to pass the message on to Oki," Ryuu reminded them. "You can't just cut me out of this now."

"I can and I am," Yuudai insisted. "This is really too dangerous. You don't have any training in this kind of thing."

Ryuu rolled his eyes. "I was a slave for over fifteen years. Trust me when I tell you that I've handled much worse than this. I'm going to the healer's tent to give Seiya's message to Oki now, and then I'm going to check on Aoshi. I expect you to fill me in on what you decide." With that he tossed his head and stormed out of the tent, hellbent on following his own course of action.

"Follow him, Akemi," Yuudai asked as soon as the scribe left. "Make sure he gets back to Fujiwara, and keep an eye on him. No heroics." He ran a hand through his hair and sighed wearily. "I'd like to keep my balls another week."

"Yes, dear. Anything else I can do for you?"

"I'm sorry," the general said, pulling him in for a kiss. "I'm just distracted. Could you please keep an eye on Ryuu for me and make sure he's okay. I'll make it worth your while."

"Now that's more like it," the courier replied with a smile. "I'd love to. See you later." He headed out with a wave while the generals settled back down to finish their game and talk about a strategy for handling the threat.

Chapter Forty-Five

Ryuu slipped into the healer's tent and knelt next to Oki. "I talked to Kudo-san," he whispered. "He'll pick you up here tomorrow night." He was surprised by the lack of an answer, so he grasped one shoulder and gave him a firm shake. "Oki, wake up. It's Ryuu." But there was no response.

"Healer," he called. "This man's unconscious." The healer moved to Oki's side, checking his pulse before dropping his head to his chest.

"This man's dead," he finally announced. "His injuries must have been worse than they seemed."

"Are you sure? I spoke with him earlier today, he seemed to be on the mend."

"Whatever," the healer muttered. "He's just a whore, who cares?"

Ryuu turned on his heel and headed back to Yuudai's tent, anxious to let the generals know about this new development. "Yuudai? Ken'ichi? Akemi?" he called nervously, unwilling to just walk in.

"Come in, Ryuu." He pushed back the flap to find the two generals still lounging around the shogi board.

"Oki's dead. Now what do we do?"

The generals looked at one another, seeming to come to an unspoken agreement. "You go back to Fujiwara," Ken'ichi said. "We'll come talk to him about all this later."

"If you think so," the scribe replied doubtfully.

"I think Aoshi's going to wonder where you are," Yuudai replied. "We'll see you in a little while. Please, please make sure you both have your clothes on this time."

"Give us some warning," the scribe retorted. "You're the one that's always bursting in unannounced."

Akemi had been listening from the doorway. He lingered, eavesdropping on the conversation so Ryuu didn't realize he'd been followed. "Why don't you both calm down," he interjected. "Ryuu go home. Don't make the commander wait." The courier turned to address Yuudai. "You and I will have a little chat about manners, or, in your case, lack thereof."

Ryuu stormed back to the warlord's tent, angry at being left out of the generals' plans and even angrier at the memory of Yuudai seeing Aoshi naked yet again. "I'm home," he snarled, causing Aoshi to pull back and look at him askance, wondering what he had done to earn this reaction.

"What's wrong?" he asked, wanting to clear up whatever the problem was.

"Nothing's wrong. Why on earth would you think something was wrong?"

"Well, you snarled at me, and then nearly bit my head off. I've been good, I did exactly what the healer told me to. So why are you mad at me?"

"I'm not mad at you. I'm just frustrated with Yuudai's high and mighty attitude."

"Is he bothering you?" the warlord growled. "Because I warned him in no uncertain terms…" he trailed off at the look on the scribe's face. "Did he hurt you?"

"No, no, no." Ryuu shook his head and waved his hands in denial. "Nothing like that, really."

"Then what is it like? If you don't mind my asking, that is?"

"Well," the scribe began. "I don't think I should tell you."

"Oh, you don't? Hmm. I guess I need to see what Yuudai has to say about all this. Guard," Aoshi yelled, waiting for a head to pop through the tent flap, "Bring me General Tanaka-san."

Ryuu kept his eyes down and studied the warlord through his eyelashes. *He's really angry now. Let Yuudai explain this*. Minutes later the general called out a greeting, waiting for a reply before walking in.

"You wanted to see me?" he asked, eyeing the angry warlord and the smug scribe and trying to put the pieces together. "I swear it was Ryuu's idea. I tried to talk him out of it, I knew you'd be mad."

"Oh you did, did you?" the confused warlord grumbled. "And yet, you did it anyway." He fixed Yuudai with an icy glare. "This time you've gone too far. I'll not forgive you."

"I had Akemi keep an eye on him the whole time to make sure he was safe," the general babbled, not exactly sure if that made it better.

"You what! That is sick. I can't believe Akemi went along with you."

"Well, he was pretty mad at me at first, but I convinced him." The general gave a triumphant smile. A smile which slowly melted in the face of the warlord's all too visible rage.

"Aoshi, calm down," the scribe urged. "You're still recovering. Besides, all I did was take a message to Kudo-san from Oki. It wasn't nearly as dangerous as everyone makes it out to be."

"You what? I thought … oh," Aoshi trailed off in embarrassment.

"What did you think?" Ryuu asked. "You were really angry."

"I thought he forced you to have sex with him." The warlord wasn't surprised when the scribe smacked him.

"I can't believe you thought something like that."

"Well, you were so angry, and you wouldn't tell me why." Aoshi quickly changed the subject. "When did you see Oki?"

"He was in the healer's tent when I went there this morning. He recognized me from before. He wanted to get a message to his friend. I talked to the generals about it and then delivered the message so we could see who was involved."

The scribe took a deep breath before continuing. "When I went back with the reply Oki was dead."

"Actually," Ken'ichi's voice piped in from the doorway. "Oki is missing. As is the healer that was on duty. I went to see what he had died of and found them both gone. We need to talk." He hobbled into the tent and flopped awkwardly onto a cushion.

"Ken'ichi and I have come up with a plan," Yuudai began. "But I don't think you're going to like it."

"We think you should take a break. You need time to recover and we need time to root out the conspirators in our midst," Ken'ichi continued. "So, Yuudai's going to be in command of the troops. I'm going to run civilian affairs. And you're going to relax with Ryuu and advise us on what to do."

"I don't know," the warlord said. "I've never been anything but a soldier. I can't imagine not staying with my troops."

"Well, at least some of those troops don't appear to feel the same way." Ken'ichi was blunt. "We've been campaigning almost continuously for the last ten years. The men are ready to settle down, even if you aren't."

"I've almost wrapped up the negotiations here," Yuudai assured him. "We'll be pulling back to the capitol in another month. Just go home with Ryuu and Ken'ichi. We'll know more by then."

"Alright," Aoshi reluctantly agreed. "But I want to be kept informed of everything that's going on."

"Certainly, Commander," both generals replied, happy that their plan had been accepted, however unenthusiastically. Ryuu, on the other hand, was ecstatic. He was going to take the warlord home. He smiled at the thought, certain he could keep Aoshi busy enough not to fret about what was happening in his absence.

Chapter Forty-Six

Ryuu fidgeted impatiently, the enclosed palanquin was too small for one man, let alone two. *We could have walked home faster,* he thought with a sigh, pulling the warlord more tightly against his body and stroking a gentle hand through his unbound hair.

"We there?" Aoshi mumbled sleepily as he tried to burrow deeper into the warmth surrounding him.

"Soon," the scribe assured him. "Just relax, enjoy the ride."

"Enjoy everything with you," the warlord muttered, eyes squeezed tight against the shafts of sunlight filtering through the door hangings.

So handsome. Ryuu dipped his head to kiss his way up the warlord's throat until he reached his mouth. He nipped at the tempting curve before slanting his lips firmly against the slightly chapped pair and losing himself in the addictive taste of his lover's mouth.

"Mmm, want more," Aoshi demanded, eyes still shut, when the scribe broke the devouring kiss to nuzzle the nape of his neck. He stretched out to give Ryuu more room to work, his gasps and muffled groans fueling the scribe's ardor. The warlord's upper garments quickly disappeared, allowing a torturous tongue to dance across his chest, nibbling peaked nipples and tracing defined pectorals before gliding further down to test his patience, dipping below his waist and sending ripples of gooseflesh racing over his form.

"Why'd ya stop?" the warlord slurred huskily as he tried to urge the scribe to resume what he'd been doing.

"Someone might hear us. The bearers are just outside, after all. And the general's palanquin is right behind us."

"Which means no one can walk in on us. The curtains are

drawn so no one can see us. All you have to do is gag me and then no one can hear us." The scribe sat still for a moment, head cocked, as he considered the suggestion.

"Remember you asked for it." He grabbed a sash and bound the warlord's mouth before pulling off the rest of his garments and licking a wet path up the inside of a long leg to the joint of a hip. He smirked into a tender inner thigh before biting down hard, making Aoshi groan unintelligibly and thrash his head.

Ryuu pushed aside the warlord's wandering hands. "Uh uh. If you can't hold still I'll have to tie you up again." The scribe carefully searched his lover's face for any signs this wasn't alright with him before quickly binding his hands to a roof rib. "Now I have you at my mercy." He stayed at arm's length, eyes raking up and down the bound figure, appreciating the way the movement of the palanquin made his engorged cock bob and twitch.

He knelt and blew lightly across Aoshi's erection, leaning in close enough so the motion caused the tip to brush across his lips, loving the way the warlord's entire body strained to move closer. When Ryuu finally took pity on him and wrapped his lips around the head, sucking gently, the growling groan it elicited was audible even through the gag.

"Ssshhhhh," he cautioned, the vibrations sending the warlord spiraling even higher. Ryuu slowly slid down the thick length, flicking his tongue over the prominent vein before coming to rest with his nose buried in dark curls and sucking hard. He slid back up just as slowly, dipping his tongue in the slit at the same time he slid a saliva slicked finger through Aoshi's tight pucker, making him buck uncontrollably, torn between the pleasure in front and behind.

"Calm down, I want to make this last." The scribe slid a second finger into his lover's heat, taking the warlord's sac in the other hand and massaging it as he continued to stretch his passage.

Aoshi keened when a hot wet mouth engulfed his balls, sucking and nipping, so distracting him he never noticed when a third finger was added. Ryuu deliberately scraped his fingers across the warlord's prostate, making him shake and whine, hips snapping, his now neglected erection spattering drops of precum as it bobbed and jerked.

Ryuu pulled away completely, reveling in the shudders racing through the lean form as he oiled himself, stroking his erection absently as he carefully studied his lover. He knelt behind the warlord, and drew him down into his lap, spreading him wide as gravity ever so slowly settled him on the scribe's aching cock.

When he was fully seated Ryuu wrapped his arms around his lover, holding him in place while the scribe nuzzled his neck, infinitely patient as he waited for the tremors wracking the pale body to subside. Once Aoshi stilled he began a slow rhythm, pulling out until just the tip remained, then a maddeningly long pause before slowly sliding balls deep again, making sure he rubbed across the warlord's prostate with each stroke. He gradually increased the pace, grasping his lover's erection in an oily fist and beginning a slow stroke in counterpoint to his thrusts.

The scribe watched in fascination as his powerful lover's muscles bunched and jumped as he came, shooting his seed across the seat as he twitched and swayed on the thick length impaling him. Lifting a long leg he spun the warlord to face him, tearing off the gag and tangling his fingers in messy strands as he pulled Aoshi's mouth to his and proceeded to lose himself in a desperate kiss. His tongue swept into the tall man's mouth, tasting and teasing, tempting the warlord's tongue to join in the game. When the kiss finally eased he once again began a slow regular pattern of thrusts, gradually coaxing Aoshi back to the edge.

"Please," the warlord rasped as the scribe slowed yet again, squeezing his lover's erection to prevent him from coming.

"I'm not done with you yet." The scribe tightened his grip on lean hips as Aoshi tried to lift himself off the length still piercing him.

"Then move," the warlord barked, frustration flashing in his eyes. "Or I swear by all the gods I'll make you move."

"Awfully pushy for someone in your position, aren't you?" The scribe chuckled, although it turned into more of a squeal as Aoshi toppled him with a fierce twist and began to ride him.

The warlord watched as Ryuu bit his lip, shutting his eyes at the onslaught of pleasure. "Now touch me," Aoshi demanded. "You're taking too long." He slowed to a halt, resuming his motions when a slick hand wrapped around his cock and began a twisting stroke that had him slamming himself onto the scribe as he tried to get more, deeper, anything that would topple him over the edge he was perched on.

Ryuu finally reached up and unbound the warlord's hands, using the distraction to flip their positions yet again. Lifting one long leg onto his shoulder he spread his lover wide, the angle allowing him to sink deeper than before. He shut his eyes and breathed deeply of Aoshi's scent as he drove into him, lost in the wet slap of flesh against flesh and the low trembling moans building in the warlord's throat.

With one unbelievably deep thrust to his prostate and the pressure of a slick thumb dipping into the slit of his cock Aoshi came with a long loud moan. Ryuu continued to thrust into the warlord's passage as it tightened almost to the point of pain, finally exploding deep inside his lover with a garbled cry.

"You okay?" Ryuu managed to pant as he scanned the limp form worriedly.

"Mmmhmm," the warlord hummed. "Do that again?"

"We'll be home soon. Then we'll do whatever you want." He missed the smirk on Aoshi's face as they both slid seamlessly into sleep.

Chapter Forty-Seven

"We're here," Ryuu called when he, Aoshi and Ken'ichi finally struggled into the house.

"Oh thank kami. I've missed you all." Kotone swept into the room with Aoi in her arms and was immediately pulled into her husband's embrace.

"How are my girls?" Ken'ichi kissed his wife and daughter, marveling over how big the baby had gotten. "She's grown so much in just a few weeks."

"That's how babies are," Kotone replied with a smile. "It's why you need to hang around and not go gallivanting off again."

"Ken'ichi and I will be staying here for the foreseeable future," Aoshi assured her. "He won't be going anywhere." *At least, not without me.*

"Let's get you settled in, Aoshi," Ryuu insisted. "This trip probably took a lot out of you."

"I'm fine, really," the warlord replied, although exhaustion was obvious in his voice.

"Well, fine or not, you're going to go upstairs and rest. To humor me, if for no other reason."

"Yes, dear." Aoshi rolled his eyes, making Ken'ichi break out in gales of laughter.

Kotone slapped her husband hard on the back of the head. "Ryuu is right, don't make fun of Aoshi because he's listening to good advice. Maybe you should try it more often."

"Yes, dear." The general sighed, knowing any other answer would just lead to more argument. He looked up to see Ryuu helping the warlord up the stairs, growling when Aoshi turned to mouth 'whipped'.

Once they reached the bedroom Ryuu began bustling around,

helping his lover undress and slide into bed.

"Aren't you going to join me?"

"You need to rest. I'm going to take a bath and wash off the dirt from the trip, then I'll see if Kotone needs any help before I make us some lunch. I'll be back when it's time to eat."

"But I don't want to sleep alone. I've missed you so much and I hate waking up without you."

"Let's compromise," the scribe said. "I'll sit with you until you fall asleep, then go shower and get lunch before I come back and wake you up."

"If that's the best I can do," the warlord replied sullenly.

"It is." The scribe slipped between the covers, pulling Aoshi to him and running soothing fingers through his hair. "I promise I'll be here when you wake up."

Ryuu slid silently out of bed, undressed and headed into the bath. He efficiently went about scrubbing his hair and body, feeling much more like himself with the dirt of travel removed. When he slid into the heated water of the furo his muscles began unknotting, letting him release the tension that had been building since the warlord's accident.

When he finished the scribe headed downstairs, stopping halfway to listen when he heard Ken'ichi and Kotone talking.

"I feel bad about it, sweetheart, but it had to be done. Aoshi's been too erratic lately. The men don't trust him since the Benjirou incident," Ken'ichi said.

"But to relieve him of his command. Poor Aoshi," Kotone fretted. "He must be horribly depressed."

"I'm not sure he realizes what actually happened. He thinks it's because of the conspiracy. And it is, just not in the way he thinks."

"If he finds out he'll never trust you again," Kotone insisted. "You have to tell him the truth."

"And have him execute me for treason? I think not. Look, what he doesn't know, he can't be upset by. I'll tell him in my own time."

"I think you're making a big mistake. I only hope I don't end up a widow because of this stupidity."

"Look, you need to just stay out of this. I love you like crazy, but you can't always expect me to just buckle under to what you want. In this case I believe I know best. End of discussion."

"Oh really? Well, I just hope you enjoy sleeping with the dogs Mister I-Know-Best, because I don't really want your company right now," Kotone hissed.

"I don't want your company either," Ken'ichi grumbled. "Maybe I should see if Yuudai is willing to trade places with me."

"You do that. But don't bother to come back. Good riddance to bad rubbish."

Ryuu decided he'd heard enough. He needed to step in before they did something they'd regret. "What about Aoshi?" he asked as he stepped into the room. "What didn't you tell us, Ken'ichi?"

"There have been threats," the general admitted. "We didn't know about Narita and his friends, but some of the men have been agitating for a change since Ito was put to death. It only got worse after your cousin and the others were executed for treason. We've been in the field for too long. The men are tired and Aoshi's spread too thin." Ken'ichi looked Ryuu in the eyes, hoping to convey his sincerity. "Believe me, it's not what Yuudai or I want. It was the only way we could see to salvage things."

"I understand." Ryuu realized his greatest fear had just come true. His relationship with the warlord was going to cost his lover everything. "This is all my fault, isn't it? If he hadn't been protecting me, Aoshi never would have gone after Benjirou and his friends."

"That's not exactly true. The plot against Aoshi was put into motion long before you came along, though it was revealed because of what happened to you. In reality, you probably saved his life. That pleasure slave might well have killed him. You were the reason he rejected Kazuya."

"If you say so," Ryuu reluctantly agreed. "Now I just need to figure out how to explain all this to Aoshi. Kotone's right, he needs to know now."

Chapter Forty-Eight

"Hello, handsome. How are you feeling?" Ryuu asked as the warlord's eyelids fluttered before slowly opening.

"Better," he croaked. "I think I need a bath though. I feel filthy."

"That's because you are. Good thing I don't mind. Why don't we get you into the tub and then after you're clean we'll have lunch." He slowly eased the warlord out of bed and into the bathing area, settling him on a small stool to be scrubbed and rinsed. When he was clean, the scribe helped his lover into the tub, smiling at the blissful expression on his face. "I love you, Aoshi," he blurted, flushing beet red as he fretted that perhaps the commander didn't feel the same way.

"I love you, too," Aoshi replied without opening his eyes. "I'd do anything for you."

"So would I," the scribe replied.

Should he leave for the warlord's own good? Ken'ichi had as much as said Aoshi's problems were Ryuu's fault. *No*, he decided. *That would hurt him even more, and it might not solve the problem.* "There are some things we need to talk about while we eat. I just found out some information that's been kept from you. I think you have the right to it."

He helped the warlord out of the tub and toweled him off, tying a simple wrap around lean hips before helping him back to the bedroom. "Sit down and eat. You must be starving."

"I am, but you're crazy if you think I can eat after you dangle information under my nose. Tell me now, then we'll eat."

"All right." The scribe hesitated. "I heard Ken'ichi and Kotone arguing when I went downstairs. Apparently your injuries were just an excuse to relieve you of command. The men don't trust you since Benjirou…" he trailed off, before turning a teary visage to the warlord. "I'm so sorry. I feel like this is all my fault."

"Well, it's not," Aoshi insisted. "They'd been preparing Kazuya for five years, long before I met you. The fact is they're probably right." He sighed as he ran a strong hand through his messy locks. "I haven't given much thought to anything but conquest. It's just a good thing you're rich. I may have tamed an empire and united a country, but I don't have two coins to rub together. I'm afraid I'll have to mooch off of you until I figure out what else a broken down ex-soldier can do."

"Aoshi, please don't talk about yourself that way. You're hardly broken down, and this is only temporary. General Fujii-san and General Tanaka-san want you back in charge."

"You're very naïve, Ryuu. It's more civil than most, true. But a coup is a coup. I've been replaced by my so-called friends." He almost spat the last word. "Are you going to support them? I wouldn't blame you. It makes sense to stick with the side in power."

"Of course not. I said I'd never leave you again and I meant it. This will all work out. Now hurry up and finish eating so I can take you back to bed and remind you of my promise. You're mine and I'm not letting go without one hell of a fight."

"Mmm, that sounds nice," Aoshi hummed. "You're on my side, aren't you?"

"I only want what's best for you. So, yes, I'm on your side, even if I may not always agree with you. We can discuss all of this later. You're still healing, remember?"

"Yes, dear," the warlord replied with a grin, digging into his food. A few minutes later he pushed his empty plate away, leering at the man across the table. "I'm finished and I'm ready for my desert."

"Oh you are, are you? Far be it from me to keep you waiting." He helped the warlord up, pulling the wrap off his hips before pushing him back to tumble onto the bed. "You look good like that. All wild and wanton."

Ryuu quickly stripped and joined his lover, rubbing sensuously against the paler figure, entranced by the contrast between their skin tones. "You're mine, Aoshi," he said as he leaned in to capture the warlord's lips. "And I won't let you go without a fight."

The kiss was deep and needy, and Aoshi returned it with the same force, whining deep in his throat when the scribe's hand wrapped around him roughly and began to slowly stroke his rapidly hardening cock. "I want to be buried inside you," the warlord groaned. "It's been so long."

"We can make that happen. But you have to promise not to overdo. Let me be on top so I can do most of the work."

"Only a fool would complain about that," Aoshi replied. "I can't think of anything sexier than watching you ride me." He looked up and was met with the heart stopping sight of Ryuu preparing himself. The warlord licked suddenly dry lips. "Okay, that's really close."

Aoshi let his head drop back onto the bed, he didn't want to risk coming before they started. The vision the scribe made with his head thrown back in pleasure as he fingered himself was more than he could take.

"Oh gods." His erection was suddenly engulfed in Ryuu's tight heat.

"Look at me," the scribe commanded, locking gazes with Aoshi's lust hazed pair. "I love you and I will never leave you," he said as he began to slowly raise and lower himself.

Aoshi growled ferally as he bucked up into the velvety sheath. "I want to pound into you so hard you can't walk. I want to come so deep inside you can taste me."

"Oh gods, yes." The scribe panted, hanging his head back so his long hair tickled the warlord's thighs. "Take me hard, make me yours." They rocked frantically together, racing at breakneck speed toward release, unwilling, or unable, to slow down and savor the moment.

Ryuu was practically throwing himself down on the rigid length impaling him, while cords stood out in the warlord's neck as he thrust up, snarling and tossing his head. Both men were soon soaked in sweat, yet the pace kept increasing until the warlord wrapped a large hand around the scribe's erection and began to stroke. The added stimulation was more than he could take and Ryuu came with a strangled shout of the warlord's name.

Aoshi thrust up hard one more time into that impossibly tight heat and exploded, capturing his lover's lips in an oxygen depleting kiss as he filled him to overflowing with his seed. "Mine," he gasped weakly before his eyes fluttered shut and he joined Ryuu in unconsciousness.

Chapter Forty-Nine

"Aoshi, Aoshi, wake up. It's time for dinner," Ryuu crooned as he stroked the warlord's hair. "Come on. Ken'ichi and Kotone are waiting for us."

"Let them wait," was the cold response. "Come to think of it, I'd rather eat here. I'm not in the mood to play nice."

"What's all this about?" the scribe asked. "You aren't mad at Ken'ichi because of what I said, are you?"

"No. I'm mad because of what he and Yuudai did. I don't think I'm up to being civil to a man who took advantage of my injury to take my place. If we're all going to stay here it's best we steer clear of each other."

"Then I guess they'll need to find somewhere else to stay," Ryuu decided. "I'll miss Kotone and little Aoi, but this is your house, too. I won't have you feeling uncomfortable. You rest, I'll bring a tray. And I'll let them know they need to start looking for another place to live."

"Are you sure? It's really okay with me if you want them to stay."

"No, this is best. You are the most important person in my life. This is the least I can do to prove it to you."

"I never doubted you."

"I know," the scribe said with a smile. "You've always been there for me. Now I'm just doing the same thing for you. I'll be back in a few minutes. Can you get up, or do you need help?"

"I could use a hand," the warlord admitted. "I think I might have overdone it a bit." He looked properly chastised when his lover rolled his eyes at him. "And don't tell me it wasn't worth it. Because I don't believe you."

"Oh, it was worth it." The scribe leered. "In fact, I can't wait to do it again. But first I believe we need to eat and replenish our energy." He headed downstairs, trying to figure out the best way to tell Ken'ichi and Kotone what was happening.

"Hi guys," the scribe began as he entered the dining room. "How does it feel to be back, general?"

"I missed my girls. I won't be leaving them again."

Kotone smiled at her husband's answer. For all the grief she gave him, she was devoted to the gruff soldier. While he always treated her tenderly when they were alone, she was overjoyed when he gave any obvious indication he felt the same, especially in front of someone else.

"I'm going to fix a tray," Ryuu explained. "Aoshi's a little tired from the trip."

"I'm sure he is," Ken'ichi teased. "The way he was moaning and groaning. Although I'm sure you did everything you could to relieve his discomfort." He waited a moment until a light blush rose in the scribe's cheeks. "He certainly was praising you to high heaven a couple hours ago."

Ryuu felt like he was going to combust. Kotone glanced from the scribe to her husband. The only thing she'd heard coming from upstairs was what sounded like... *Oh my*, she thought when she realized what must have happened, *and in the palanquin, too. Ryuu, you sneaky little devil.* She smiled serenely and smacked her husband on the back of the head, causing him to break off his chuckles with a choked gasp. "So Ryuu, is there anything special Aoshi needs to eat while he recovers?" She effectively changed the subject, much to the scribe's relief.

"Clear liquids, easy to digest foods, no red meat or alcohol," Ryuu replied. "Could you come in the kitchen and give me a hand?"

"Of course." She sensed he really wanted the opportunity to speak to her privately. "I'll be back in a minute, dear. Keep an eye on the baby for me." She thrust the swaddled infant into her husband's arms and followed the scribe into the kitchen.

"I'll never understand women," Ken'ichi murmured to Aoi as he nuzzled her cheek. "But I love you both anyway."

"So, what did you want to talk to me about?" Kotone asked while the scribe put some onigiri and miso broth on a tray.

The scribe marveled at her ability to know what he was thinking. "Aoshi isn't really tired. I mean, he is, but that's not why he didn't come down. He feels betrayed by Ken'ichi and General

Tanaka-san, and he's very angry right now." He paused uncertainly, sighing before he continued. "I hate to do this, but I need you to find somewhere else to stay. I don't want Aoshi to think I'm betraying him, too. I'm really sorry." He looked up, tears in his eyes, and was surprised to see understanding on Kotone's face.

"Of course, Ryuu. It must be very hard for him knowing we're here. Don't feel bad," she hastened to add when his face fell. "I told my idiot of a husband he should have been honest with Aoshi from the beginning. We'll be fine. Besides, judging from the noises you two were making earlier I'm not sure I want to be around when the commander recovers his full strength."

The scribe blushed crimson, a strangled "Kotone," all that could make it out of his traitorous throat.

"Don't be embarrassed. What I mean is you'll want your privacy, and we'll want ours." Kotone decided never to have sex in her friend's house now that she knew how easily they would be overheard. *Ken'ichi is going to be pissed, but that will get him inspired to move quickly.* "Here you go." She placed the last few items on a tray. "Get back upstairs and calm Aoshi down. I'll go explain things to Ken'ichi."

"Thank you, Kotone. I'm going to miss you."

"And I'll miss you too," she replied, tears coming to her eyes as she realized the finality of what was happening. "I'll see you in the morning. I'll let the cook know to prepare a tray." She turned and headed back into the dining room, running through scenarios trying to find the best way to break the news to her husband.

"What was that all about?" the general asked as he passed the baby back to his wife.

"It's what I was afraid of. Aoshi feels like you betrayed him, and he's angry. Ryuu and I decided it would be best if you and I move out as soon as possible. I don't think the commander's going to come downstairs again until we're gone."

"Shit, I need to explain things to him." Ken'ichi ran a hand through his hair. *I need to let Yuudai know what's happening. His relationship with Aoshi was already rocky.*

"No." Kotone caught her husband's arm and held him in place. "He's not going to listen to you. You know him, honey. Loyalty is very important to Aoshi, always has been. In his mind you've been disloyal. He won't trust anything you do or say now."

This has gone from bad to worse. The general shuddered when he realized just how tenuous everything was. *I just hope this is the right course of action*, he thought grimly. *Otherwise I'm going to have a lot of explaining to do.* He turned silently back to his meal, lost in his thoughts. Kotone concentrated on feeding Aoi, at the same time keeping an eye on her husband.

Chapter Fifty

Yuudai wearily watched the last of the men assemble for muster. *I'll be so glad when this campaign is over*, he thought wearily, anxious to have command back in someone else's hands. "Hey, Akemi. Have we heard from Ken'ichi or Aoshi?"

"Nothing yet. Did you want me to go check?" the courier replied, willing to do whatever he could to bolster his lover's confidence.

"Well, I don't want you to go. But I'm going crazy waiting for news."

"Fine. I'll leave now, be back tomorrow. Just relax and concentrate on what you've got going on here." The courier turned and headed out with a wave, leaving Yuudai to brief the men on the day's strategy.

* * *

Ryuu sleepily raised his head. *Someone's knocking.* "Leave it outside the door," he slurred, sure it was someone with their breakfast tray.

"I can't," Ken'ichi's voice came back. "I need to see him."

"General Fujii-san?" Ryuu struggled into a yukata and slid the door open a crack. "Aoshi's asleep."

"He's making a huge mistake. I would never betray him. He has to know that."

"I'm afraid he knows nothing of the sort," the scribe retorted. "You did relieve him of command, and you weren't honest with him about it. Why should he trust you?"

"Because I'm trying to protect him. Look, Ryuu, I like you, but you have no real understanding of the forces at work here." He ran his hand through his hair. "Yuudai and I are trying to balance what's best for everyone. Taking the risk of possibly having the commander assassinated is not on our agenda."

"Even if I believe you, that doesn't mean Aoshi will, or that I should for that matter. I'm sorry, but I won't second guess him on this. He doesn't want to see you. At least give him a couple days to wrap his mind around things before you confront him. Then, maybe, he'll be willing to listen. If you try now I guarantee it'll fall on deaf ears."

"I just hate the idea that he feels we betrayed him."

"Aoshi's right, even if it wasn't in the way he thinks. You did betray him. You went behind his back and plotted all this out with Yuudai. Go back to Kotone and the baby. I'll tell him you stopped by when he wakes up. Right now though, I'm going back to bed." The scribe shut the door on Ken'ichi, slipping quietly back into bed.

"Thank you for standing up for me," Aoshi said.

"You're awake? Why didn't you say anything?"

"You were doing such a wonderful job defending me. It made me happy to hear how you stood up to him."

"He's very upset. But that doesn't excuse what he did. Thinking about it for a few days will do him good."

"My hero," the warlord quipped, leaning in to capture the scribe's lips in a tender, loving kiss. "How can I possibly fret over anything else happening to me when I'm lucky enough to have you?"

"You can't. So just kiss me and don't think about anything else."

"My favorite idea yet." Aoshi recaptured his lover's lips. The kiss grew more passionate as he pushed Ryuu onto his back, rolling on top of him and grinding their erections together. "Let's see how distracted I can get."

"Aoshi," the scribe interjected. "You need to sleep, you're still recovering."

"Then help me relax so I can," he whispered, rocking his hips insistently and smiling in satisfaction when Ryuu responded.

"You'll never heal if you keep this up," Ryuu warned.

"Good, then I can stay in bed and have you dote on me forever."

"No. Then you'll never be strong enough to do what I've been thinking about," Ryuu teased. "Wouldn't you like to know what that is?"

"Are you going to tell me? Or should I guess?"

"Why don't you demonstrate your guesses. It will make the game more fun."

Aoshi husked a single word, "Alright," before capturing his lover's mouth again. The scribe writhed and squirmed as the warlord continued his ministrations, rolling him onto his stomach and moving down the smooth expanse of his back to nip and suck pert buttocks. Ryuu moaned loudly as agile fingers eased him open. When the broad head of Aoshi's cock finally pushed inside, the scribe wailed his pleasure and pushed back.

Aoshi kept up a constant stream of endearments, bending his head to husk them into a delicate ear. That tender growl, coupled with over stimulation inside and out rocketed the scribe to new levels of arousal. Ryuu screamed his pleasure as he shook, clamping down hard on the cock inside him, velvety walls milking the warlord dry.

Aoshi gently pulled out and rolled to the side, pulling the scribe with him, holding him in the protective circle of his arms as their heartbeats slowed. "That wasn't what I was thinking of, try again." Ryuu quipped.

"Sleep now. Then I'll be happy to," the warlord mumbled, eyes already slipping shut.

* * *

Akemi paced back and forth in the entryway. "So what, exactly, am I supposed to tell the General?"

"Tell him Aoshi believes we've stolen his command, and he isn't happy about it," Ken'ichi replied wearily. "I can't even get past Ryuu to try and explain."

"Yuudai's going to lose it completely when he hears this," the courier fretted. "He's uneasy enough about the whole thing and under too much pressure."

"We're all under pressure. Believe me, I'd love to change places with him. Just tell him to keep up the offensive and you should break through in a few days. Then he'll be able to force the treaty on them."

"Won't that just lead to more dissent?"

"Yes and no. The rank and file won't object, it will be the

leaders. If Yuudai does his job they'll lose the support of their own troops. And without your men behind you leadership is pointless. That's the lesson Aoshi's forgotten. Hopefully this break will make the men realize how crucial his leadership is and make them appreciate him again, if not…" he trailed off, leaving unspoken the fact that the warlord would never return to power unless the men regained their trust in him. "Just tell Yuudai not to worry. I'll see him in a couple weeks, and I'll let him know where to contact me."

"You won't be here?"

"No, Ryuu asked us to leave because it's upsetting Aoshi. Kotone and I are heading out in the morning. I'll send word once we're settled. Is there anything else?"

"No." Akemi dreaded delivering this particular message. "I'll tell him."

"And Akemi," Ken'ichi called after him. "Don't let him do anything stupid."

Chapter Fifty-One

"I'm going to go talk to him," Yuudai declared as soon as Akemi delivered the news.

"That is exactly what you are not going to do," the courier replied. "General Fujii-san was very clear. You should stay here and let him handle it."

"Yeah, it's obvious he's handling it so well. Look, Aoshi will listen to me. He knows I'd never betray him."

"Oh, really? And what does sticking your dick in him without permission qualify as?" Akemi asked. "I'd like to see you survive this, and that means I'm not letting you go."

"I'd like to see you try and stop me."

"Just calm down for a minute and think. If you go there will be no one in command here. It would be the perfect opening for whoever is behind this plot to take over. The commander and General Fujii-san are counting on you to take care of things here. You can't let them down. We'll be home in a couple of weeks. You'll be more likely to get Aoshi to see you if you have a victory to regale him with." The courier paused thoughtfully before continuing. "Besides, the general said he couldn't get past Ryuu to talk to Fujiwara. He and Kotone are even moving out so as not to upset him. No matter what your relationship is with Aoshi, there's no love lost between you and Ryuu."

"This is all his fault," Yuudai groused. "Everything was fine before that damn scribe came along."

"I'd be careful if I were you," the courier cautioned. "you're sounding a lot like Benjirou."

"I thought you were on my side. It sounds to me like you've joined the Ryuu fan club."

"Jealousy doesn't suit you. Let me make this clear. Fujiwara told you he wasn't interested, Ryuu or no Ryuu. You need to let this go before you totally alienate him … and me," Akemi added under his breath.

Yuudai was so angry that the words just weren't processing. "Aoshi is my friend. It's my job to protect him, even from himself."

"That's it," Akemi bellowed, effectively derailing the general's thoughts. "I am fed up with doting on your every whim only to come in second to a man who's not even interested. You do whatever you want, but do it as far from me as possible. I do not want to see your sorry hide darkening my door ever again. I'm through with you." He grabbed his things and rushed out into the night.

What did I do? Yuudai shook his head. *I just don't get it.* He refocused on the problem at hand. *I need to go see Aoshi*, he decided. *I'll patch things up with Akemi when I get back. That'll give him time to cool down.* He hurriedly stuffed some things in a pack and saddled his horse, planning on riding through the night and arriving the next evening. *I'll only be gone a couple of days. That won't hurt anything.*

Several sets of eyes followed the general's movements as he rode out of camp, the looks they wore ranged from disappointed to amused to triumphant. Unaware of each other, yet almost in unison, the three watchers turned to go and act on what they had just observed.

Idiot, Akemi thought viciously. *I thought you had more brains.* He knew he should stick to his resolution and let Yuudai hang himself with his actions, but he just couldn't. So he wracked his brains trying to decide who he should let know about the general's departure.

* * *

Arashi smiled. *Interesting. It looks like Akemi and the general are on the outs.* He had been interested in the courier for a while, and the one time he'd come close Tanaka-san had interfered. Next time he'd get what he wanted with no interference.

* * *

Finally. I knew he couldn't stay away from Fujiwara-sama. Oki and his allies had been waiting for the general to leave so they could assume control. *Soon*, he thought as he rubbed his hands together. *Soon your balls will be mine, Aoshi.*

* * *

Akemi arrived at the tent he'd been seeking and stopped to collect his thoughts before calling to announce his presence.
"General, I have a message for you."
"Enter," a deep voice called.
The courier lifted the flap and slid into the tent. "I have a message from Fujiwara-sama," he lied, hoping that proof wouldn't be asked for. "He needs you to assume command while he meets with Tanaka-san and Fujii-san."
"Oh he does, does he? And I'm going to agree because?"
"Because you pledged your loyalty?" Akemi offered.
"Ha. To that pup? He's a good commander to be sure, but not half the man his father was," the general responded.
"Because otherwise he'll lose control completely," the courier admitted.
"Spill," the general demanded. "And don't leave anything out. I want to know what it is I'm getting myself into." The courier quickly ran through the recent events, touching briefly on the plot against Aoshi and Yuudai's rash actions, but leaving out the details of their fight or its reasons.
"So, I was the best choice in your mind?" he asked when the tale finally petered out.
"I thought you'd stay loyal to Fujiwara. I wasn't sure about anyone else. You need to assume power before anyone else realizes he's gone."
"I still don't know," the older man pondered. "What advantage is there for me?"
"You'll get in the warlord's good graces."
"I'm not so sure of that, based on what you've told me. Still, it would be better than the alternative. Alright kid, I'll do it. Now go away and let people know so I can get back to sleep. I'll take over at muster." With that he turned his back on the courier, heading back to his bed and the few hours of sleep he had remaining.
Akemi left the general's tent and headed for the mess. *I'll just let whoever's there know and then I'll grab some sleep*, he

reasoned. He walked inside and quickly talked to the few souls still awake. Turning to leave he ran into the solid wall of another man's chest. "Arashi, how are you?" He hadn't seen his friend since the day he'd gotten back together with Yuudai.

"I've missed you, Akemi," Arashi purred. "You've been keeping to yourself. Come to my tent for a drink and we'll catch up."

The courier thought for only a moment. He knew his friend was offering more than drinks. The question was if he was interested. He looked the tall man up and down. Arashi was handsome, attentive and wanted him. Yeah, he was interested. It had been too long since he'd had that kind of attention. "That sounds great. Let's go."

* * *

"It's time," Oki whispered, bringing the sleeping man instantly awake.

"Who else have you told?"

"You're the first, I'll be going now. I'll see you in a few hours at the usual place."

"I'll be there." The quiet response fell unremarked as Oki was already gone, leaving him to prepare for the events ahead.

Chapter Fifty-Two

Arashi quickly steered Akemi to his tent, lifting the flap and ushering him inside. "Have a seat while I grab some drinks." He disappeared for a moment, only to reappear with a bottle in hand. "Here, try some of this," he urged as he passed it over.

"Mmmm, that's nice," Akemi said with a smile after taking a drink and wiping his mouth with the back of his hand. "So, what have you been up to lately?"

"The usual. We've missed you at the dice games. Where have you been keeping yourself?" Arashi took another swig from the bottle.

"I've been wasting my time," the courier replied. "I thought things were going well, but I was just fooling myself."

"I can help you take your mind off your problems," Arashi offered. "No strings attached if that's what you want."

"I think that sounds like a wonderful idea." Akemi leaned in and captured the other man's mouth, hungrily lapping at his lips until they parted before thrusting his tongue inside. They continued to kiss deeply as their hands made short work of their clothes, fumbling with ties and buckles as they tumbled onto the bed.

The courier hovered over the taller man, aggressively controlling the kiss as he pinched and rolled perked nipples. "Gods, Akemi," Arashi muttered when he broke away to torment the tight nubs with his tongue. He let out a broken cry and arched off the bed when that same talented mouth closed around his aching erection.

Akemi lavished attention on the thick length, nibbling down the underside before licking it like a popsicle, finally sucking the head into his mouth while his tongue twirled and danced around the ridge and into the sensitive slit. He groaned around his mouthful, sliding slowly down to the base when Arashi grabbed his hand and began to suck and nibble at his fingers.

The courier began a slow up and down slide as he moved his hand to the other man's sensitive pucker, petting and stroking before gingerly pressing inside. Arashi bucked up hard into Akemi's mouth, making him growl and suck harder as he began to stretch the passage to make way for something much larger.

"Enough," Arashi decided. "Fuck me now." He pressed a vial into the courier's hands as he laid back and spread his legs, eyes avidly following every movement as Akemi fumbled open the vial and oiled his cock. "Gods that's so hot." The courier quickly positioned himself between long legs, lifting them to wrap around his waist as he slowly began to breech the tight ring, gasping when the head slid inside.

It's been too long since I've done this, Akemi decided as he reveled in the tight heat of the sheath he was slowly sinking into. Once he was seated he closed his eyes and panted, desperately trying to maintain his control. He slowly opened his eyes, studying the man beneath him, before leaning in for a slow, sensual kiss.

"Please move." Akemi slowly pulled out, only to slide immediately back in at the same measured pace, setting up a slow, gentle rhythm. "Mmm, I love the way your cock feels sliding into me."

Akemi took his words to heart, pulling out completely and flipping his friend over before grasping his hips and plunging back into his tight heat, drawing a strangled shriek and a full body shudder from Arashi. "Do that again," he pleaded. The courier was happy to comply, giving two or three sharp thrusts before withdrawing completely and slamming back inside.

Finally he could no longer stand the tease and he began to thrust in earnest, biting his lip to try and stave off his release as the man beneath him panted his name. The courier reached around and wrapped an oily hand around Arashi's cock, stroking it firmly in time with his thrusts, sending full body shivers coursing through the long frame. Eventually neither man could hold out any longer and Arashi came with a high pitched cry just before Akemi grunted and filled his ass with come.

The courier tried to stay upright, but gravity took its toll and he slumped on top of his friend, still buried deep in his ass, and panted as he recovered from his orgasm. "That was wonderful," Arashi gasped. "Please tell me we can do that again, soon."

"I think that depends on your definition of soon," the courier replied as his breath evened out. "I need sleep before I try that again."

"By all means, let's sleep." Arashi maneuvered them so they were spooned together on their sides, Akemi's cock still in his ass as they drifted into a sated slumber.

* * *

"Did you tell everyone?" The slender figure wrapped in an overly large black cloak struggled not to pout. "There's only ten people here."

"Apparently a lot of people are afraid to put their asses on the line and back up their words with actions. These are the only ones willing to take the risk."

"Still, with Fujiwara, Fujii and Tanaka out of camp there's no one in charge. This is our best chance to take control. Once we have it they'll come around," the young man replied confidently. "We'll make our move at muster. Once we're in control our allies will join us and we'll move south, reclaiming territory as our own as we go. Fujiwara won't know what hit him."

"He's mine," Oki hissed. "I owe him for what he did to me."

"Now, now pet," the man Ryuu knew as Kudo Seiya crooned. "Remember, if it wasn't for that we would never have met. I, for one, would regret that very much." He stroked Oki's tangled hair thoughtfully before placing a tender kiss on his lips. "Does everyone know what they're supposed to do?"

Pleased with the hearty response he smiled. "Meet back here before muster." He clasped Oki's hand and headed off for a few hours relaxation before their plans finally went into motion.

* * *

General Fusao rose early, his sleep uneasy after his talk with Akemi. Reluctant as he was to take command, he knew he had no choice. He splashed cold water on his face before dressing hastily and heading to the mess. When he arrived he was surprised to see how many men were up already. Something wasn't right. Not only were the men up, they were fully armed and highly alert. He decided backup would be a good idea and headed off to locate

Akemi.

He finally located the courier's tent, disappointed to find it empty. *Damn, time's wasting,* he realized, changing his mind and heading off rapidly to his new destination.

"Come in," the hearty voice boomed and Fusao shuddered. He steeled himself and stepped inside. *It's too early for this,* his mind offered as he was greeted by the sight of Kimura Jin clad in nothing but too much hair and a small towel.

"Put some clothes on, Jin. I need to talk to you."

"I am honored that you wish to converse with me," Jin boomed. "I will finish my morning preparations and be right back."

Maybe if I keep my eyes shut it won't be so bad, Fusao thought as he listened to the overly vibrant man as he finished dressing. *I'll definitely need a drink after this is over.* Once Jin returned the general quickly explained his position and headed off to the mess, leaving the other man to garner support. Hopefully he was wrong and when he made his announcement in the morning the men would accept it without question. Still, he'd feel better with some muscle on his side.

Chapter Fifty-Three

Yuudai leapt off his horse and banged on the door, desperate to explain his actions to the warlord and totally unfazed by the fact that it was the middle of the night. He pounded on the door and yelled again, finally relaxing when he heard footsteps approaching.

"Can I help…" Ryuu trailed off at the sight that met his eyes. "General Tanaka-san, what are you doing here? Shouldn't you be back in camp?"

"I have to see the commander. I need to explain what Ken'ichi and I were thinking…"

"No, you do not need to explain how going behind his back and stealing his command was good for him." Ryuu cut him off coldly. "It amazes me how you and General Fujii-san seem to think Aoshi's going to forgive and forget. He's the one who realized what you were up to, you know," he added with a decisive nod of his head. "You won't fool him twice."

"I'm not trying to fool him at all," Yuudai retorted. "Now get the hell out of my way."

"No, I'm not going to let you hurt him anymore."

"Look Ryuu, either move or I'll move you."

"I'd think twice about that if I were you." The deep voice caused both men to look up in surprise. "It's okay," Aoshi continued when the scribe opened his mouth to protest. "I'll take care of this."

"Aoshi, I had to come and see you…" Yuudai trailed off uncertainly at the disdainful look on the warlord's face.

"Just who, may I ask, is in charge if both you and Ken'ichi are here?" The warlord once again threw the general off balance.

"No one? I'll be back by tomorrow night."

"You expect me to believe you are worried about my enemies taking control. So worried, in fact, that you saw fit to relieve me of my command. Yet you aren't worried about leaving that same command with no one in charge?"

"Oh shit." The general paled."I didn't think about that. Akemi told me not to." He froze, a look of horror painted on his face as he realized his lover had left him, probably for good.

"Yuudai," Aoshi said, shaking him hard. "Snap out of it."

"I blew it. I've ruined everything."

"It appears that way," the warlord said cattily before turning and calling upstairs. "Ryuu, come here please."

The scribe appeared almost instantly from where he had been hovering just out of sight, monitoring the conversation to prevent anyone from hurting Aoshi further. "I need to get back to camp immediately. Are you coming?"

"Of course. As if I'd let you go anywhere alone."

The warlord smiled. "Thank you, Ryuu. It's good to know I at least have your support."

"You have my support too," Yuudai chimed in. "You always have."

The warlord ignored him, turning back inside and sliding the doot shut in his face. He took the steps two at a time, hurriedly dressing and grabbing his weapons before heading back downstairs. "Ryuu, are you…" The scribe was already dressed for travel and stowing some food in the pack he carried.

"I grabbed some things for you." The scribe gestured towards the second pack at his feet. "The horses are being harnessed. Are you sure you can manage? It wasn't that long ago you were unconscious."

"I'm sure I have to try. I have no intention of sitting here watching over my shoulder for assassins."

* * *

"Abe-san, what are you doing here?" General Fusao crossed his arms over his chest and glared in annoyance.

"I'm here to make sure the men know someone is in control. It appears all of our leaders have fled the coop like the chickens they are."

"I'd watch what you say," Fusao replied. "Fujiwara-sama left me in charge while he consults with his generals. I'd hate to have to tell him you were spreading rumors. You know his temper hasn't been the best of late."

"Listen, old man, get out of my way while I'm giving you the chance. If not, I'll go right through you to get what I want."

"That is most uncouth of you, Abe-san." Jin towered over the slight young man, dropping a heavy hand on his shoulder. "You should know our esteemed Commander Fujiwara-sama would never endanger us in such a way. He has always toiled ceaselessly for our well-being. My heart aches when I consider all he has suffered on our behalf."

Abe Hajime shuddered as the hand on his shoulder squeezed tightly in warning. Jin might appear to be a fool, but he was a powerful fool and much more cunning than he seemed. "I am only stating the truth. It seems suspicious that all three of them are missing at once," Hajime stated.

"Fujiwara-sama is still recovering, as is General Fujii-san," Fusao argued. "It's only natural that General Tanaka-san would want to get their advice on the campaign. He'll be back tomorrow." *I hope, I hope,* he added internally, not feeling nearly as confident as he sounded.

"Tomorrow then," Hajime spat. "If he's not back I'll assume this was all a ploy you cooked up for personal gain. Then we'll see which of us has the most support."

Fusao nodded brusquely in reply. He seriously hoped Tanaka got his ass back before muster tomorrow. Things like this were the reason he'd always avoided any sort of command responsibility.

* * *

"Why didn't you push harder?" Oki asked when Hajime related the events of the confrontation.

"Tomorrow will be soon enough, pet," he soothed. "Come now, let's go find something more enjoyable to do while we wait." He drew the reluctant man towards the bed, pulling off his clothes with rough hands as they moved.

"All you want me for is sex," Oki muttered as he was pushed back onto the bed.

"Not true," Hajime replied. "We have much in common. Our desire to destroy Fujiwara, for example. Now stop sulking and kiss me." He swooped down and captured less than willing lips.

Enjoy it now, Oki thought. *Because tomorrow everything's going to change.*

Chapter Fifty-Four

Aoshi was not in the kind of shape he needed to be for a forced ride. To be honest, he wasn't in shape for a walk around the garden. Ryuu kept a watchful eye on his lover as they rode, noticing how he sagged in the saddle after just a few hours. "We need to stop, he insisted. "What good will it do if we get there and you collapse?"

"There's too much at stake," the warlord replied wearily. "Everything I've spent the last ten years working for is about to go up in smoke. Even though it's unpopular, I still want to better the lot of the common man. I think what you do should be more important than who you are. Of course, that's what started all this mess."

"You mean it wasn't me?" the scribe asked, clearly unwilling to believe that Aoshi's problems had started long before his purchase.

"You made a convenient excuse, I'll admit that. But plots like this one take far longer than a few days to put into motion. As much as I hate to admit it, forces have been moving against me ever since I started pushing for a policy of equality."

"Well, I can understand how the nobles were angered by your actions. But I would think that your men would be in favor of a policy like that."

"So one would think," Aoshi said. "But the new policy also means you rise in the ranks based on what you do, not who you are or how long you've served. There were a lot of men who didn't advance the way they thought they should after I came to power."

"So this is all sour grapes?" Ryuu asked.

"Whatever you want to call it, I need to put a stop to it. Ken'ichi and Yuudai don't have the ability to keep all our allies loyal. Most of them pledged their loyalty to me personally. So, I have to get back to camp, even if it kills me."

"That's not an acceptable outcome. I refuse to risk your life over politics."

"My life isn't worth anything unless I regain control," Aoshi explained. "My rivals aren't going to risk my retaking power. If I don't fix this we'll both end up in front of an executioner."

Ryuu rubbed the back of his neck and sighed. He desperately wanted to find a solution to this dilemma, but he wasn't coming up with one. "I have a seat on the council," he remembered. "That should help."

"It might have once. But I stripped the council of most of its power. That's why your cousin was out to get me."

"So what you're saying is that we're walking into a trap."

"Probably," Aoshi admitted. "Unless Yuudai left someone in charge when he decided to come placate me. Judging from his appearance that's highly unlikely."

"Then it's even more important you rest while you can," Ryuu urged. "We'll have a bite to eat and rest for half an hour. It will do you good and we'll be able to ride a few more hours."

"We'll ride as long as we have to," the warlord declared through gritted teeth. "We won't be stopping, this is too important.

"And if you die?" the scribe asked. "Who takes control then? Is it worth the risk?"

"If I die it doesn't matter who takes over. No one else is going to be able to hold the alliance together, much less push through the reforms I have in mind. Like it or not, this is more important than one person. Even if it kills me, we have to go on."

"Fine. But once you get things settled I'm going to chain you to the bed until you finish your recovery."

"Promises, promises," the warlord replied teasingly, but his eyes were solemn and didn't meet his lover's.

* * *

"Ken'ichi, wake up and answer the damn door, this is an emergency." Yuudai pounded on the door.

"What the hell are you doing here?" the general asked blearily when he cracked open the door. "It's the middle of the damn night and you woke the baby. Kotone's gonna kill you."

"I fucked up big time." Yuudai slumped into a chair. "Akemi brought me your message and I was sure I could convince Aoshi that we were on his side. I blew off his warnings and came straight here."

"Who did you leave in charge?" Ken'ichi asked, not really wanting to hear the answer, but knowing he needed to deal with it.

"I didn't." Yuudai groaned as he clutched his head in his hands. "I completely messed things up with Akemi, then left without making sure someone on our side was in charge. To top it all off, I totally blew any and all chances that the commander will ever forgive me. He pretty much told me to drop dead."

"I'm sure he was just upset about everything that's happening." Ken'ichi tried to soothe the distraught general. "It wasn't personal."

"Oh yes it was. He shut the door in my face."

"Oh." Both men sat slumped in the entryway contemplating the problems they now had to deal with. They were so absorbed in their worries that neither man noticed Kotone coming in with baby Aoi.

"Yuudai, what are you doing here at this time of night?" she asked. "Did something happen?"

"He acted like a fool and an idiot," Ken'ichi replied. "I need to go talk to Fujiwara, middle of the night or not."

"He's gone," Yuudai muttered into his hands.

"What do you mean, he's gone?" Ken'ichi yelled, once again waking the baby and earning a glare from his wife.

"He and Ryuu headed back to camp as soon as he got rid of me. Even in his current condition you know he won't stop, not when it's this important. There's no way we can catch them."

"So what do you suggest?" Ken'ichi gratefully accepted the cup of tea his wife pushed into his hand.

"We leave now and get there as soon as we can. Hopefully we'll still be able to get Fujiwara alone and talk to him," Yuudai suggested.

"Honey." Ken'ichi turned to his wife. "We need to leave now. I'll have to explain later, trust me it's serious or I wouldn't be going." He stopped to consider his next words carefully. "It would probably be a good idea if you went to your mother's for a few days. I'll pick you girls up on my way back."

"Is it really so serious?" Kotone asked.

"It could be," Ken'ichi hedged. "I just don't know. Humor me and head for your mother's."

"Yes dear. Take care of yourself. We expect you back in a few days and in one piece."

"If I'm going to be gone longer than that I'll send word. Love you both," he murmured as he kissed his wife and daughter, hoping that this would not be the last time he'd get the chance.

Chapter Fifty-Five

By the time they reached camp Aoshi was barely able to stay upright in the saddle. Ryuu worriedly helped him down and into Yuudai's tent, deciding it was as good a place as any for the warlord to rest.

"I need to go find out what's happening," he rasped.

"I'll go find Akemi and see if he has any news. You need to rest until I get back. You're just about ready to collapse."

"Fine." Aoshi knew he was in no shape for a confrontation. As much as it rankled, Ryuu was right.

After making some inquiries around camp the scribe ended up outside a strange tent. "Akemi?" he called. "It's Ryuu. I need to talk to you."

"Hello," a strange voice responded. "I'm Arashi. Akemi will be out in just a minute, he's getting dressed."

"Oh," the scribe replied. "I'm sorry to disturb you so early. The commander and I just arrived. I need to verify some things."

"No problem. Although you might want to give him some coffee first. He had a good bit to drink last night."

"Hey, Ryuu." The courier slipped out of the tent. "See you later, 'shi."

"Come back whenever you finish with the commander and get some more sleep. You're always welcome."

"Thank you," Akemi replied. "I really appreciate it."

"As I appreciate you." Arashi pulled the courier in for a tender kiss before slipping back into the tent.

"So what's that all about?" Ryuu asked. "I thought you and General Tanaka were an item."

"Yuudai only has eyes for the commander," Akemi explained. "I tried, but it was too painful always coming in second. Arashi is just a friend, but at least he values my company."

"General Tanaka values you," the scribe assured him. "Once things get back to normal you'll see."

"I'm afraid it's too late for that. I'm not giving him any more opportunities to break my heart."

Ryuu nodded his head. "I understand. Although I'm sorry for both your sakes. Aoshi needs to talk to you. He's worried about who took command when the general left."

"I was worried about that too," the courier admitted. "So I got Fusao to play leader until someone got back. I was expecting one of the generals, not the commander. Is he really up to this?"

"No, not at all," the scribe replied. "Unfortunately he didn't feel like he had a choice. I left him in General Tanaka's tent while I came to find you. I didn't think having me drag him around camp would help his reputation."

"Let's get going." Akemi headed towards the one tent he thought he'd never enter again.

"Commander. How was the ride?"

"I don't envy you your job, that's for sure," Aoshi replied with a brittle laugh. "I don't think I'll be looking forward to riding for quite a while. What's happened since Yuudai left?"

The courier ran through the events of the last day, although he left out Fusao's confrontation with Abe-san since he'd slept through morning muster. "So now I have to deal with the old bear," the warlord muttered as he ran a hand through his hair. "When will things go easy for me?"

"Who's Fusao?" the scribe asked, never having heard of the man before.

"He was a good friend of my father's. Although, to be honest, I'm a bit surprised he supported me. He's stayed clear of politics his entire career."

"I'm sure it's because he knows you're a better choice than the men who would overthrow you."

"More likely it was just to get Akemi out of his face," Aoshi said with a weary chuckle. "I'm sure he'll be more than happy to go back to sleeping through muster." He turned to the courier. "Thank you for your loyalty and quick thinking, Akemi. If you hadn't acted as you did we would surely have a disaster on our hands. I think you've earned a jump in rank. I need trustworthy men close to me."

"Thank you, commander. I appreciate it."

"See, Ryuu," the warlord said as he turned to his lover. "That's why my policies work. Akemi, do you think you could persuade Fusao to come here and meet with me?"

"I can certainly try, sir." The courier headed out to locate the man in question.

"Okay, until he gets back you rest." Ryuu pushed the shaky figure towards the bed.

"But, Ryuu," the warlord protested. "I can't sleep in Yuudai's bed, it's just not right."

The scribe smiled at the childlike response. "I'm sorry. I know it's not the best choice, but better than the hard ground. If it makes you feel better, I'm sure he wouldn't like it either."

"Yes, he would," Aoshi muttered. "That's the whole problem. He can't seem to let go of his feelings for me. I should never have let what he did slide. I just didn't know how to handle it."

"If it helps, I think you did the right thing. After all, he did it because he cares about you. He just snapped when he caught us together. He might have wanted to hurt me, but I guarantee he'd never willingly hurt you. He's crazy about you."

"I just thought I'd get more comfortable around him," the warlord explained. "Instead I find myself avoiding him more and more. I just can't work with him anymore. One of us is going to have to go, and it's not going to be me."

"We should talk about that," Ryuu said. "I have some ideas that might work for both of you. Right now, though, it's bedtime for you." He settled Aoshi in the general's bed before perching on the edge, gently carding his fingers through tousled strands. "Sleep, I'll wake you when Akemi gets back."

The warlord closed his eyes with a sigh, instantly falling into a deep sleep. The scribe kept an uneasy watch while he tried to figure out which of his ideas might allow things to go back to the way they were. Eventually he, too, drifted off to sleep, his head dropping onto Aoshi's chest as his breathing slowed and he entered the realm of dreams.

Chapter Fifty-Six

"Sleeping on the job, eh pup?" a loud voice boomed, startling both men from their doze.

"Ah, Fusao. Ever the silver tongued bastard," Aoshi remarked drily.

"You look like shit, boy. You shouldn't be here."

"Aaaaa," the warlord replied. "There's lots of things I shouldn't have to do, like waste time bantering with you. What happened at muster?"

"Apparently Abe-san believes he's the best man for your job," Fusao said. "He plans on grabbing control tomorrow. He seems to feel he has the support."

"Well, isn't that interesting," Aoshi mused. "Any idea who's thrown in with him?"

"Didn't ask and don't really want to know. Politics isn't my cup of tea," the older man replied. "Now can I go? I have things to attend to."

"Yeah, get out of here," the warlord muttered. "Selfish bastard. I expect to see you at muster. I need to publicly thank you for taking over."

"That's okay," Fusao said, shaking his head and waving his arms. "Thanks anyway."

"You will be there," Aoshi insisted. "Jin too."

"Yeah, yeah," the older man muttered. "I liked your father better."

"Don't talk to him like that," Ryuu protested. "What a horrible thing to say."

"It's okay, Ryuu. He has his reasons."

"I don't care," the scribe said petulantly, lower lip sticking out in a pout. "I'm not going to let him talk to you that way."

"And how did you intend on stopping me, runt?" Fusao countered, taking a step towards the scribe.

"Touch him and I take your hand," Aoshi said coldly, freezing both men in place. "Get out of here, old man, before I change my mind," he growled, sending the white-maned general scurrying out of the tent, leaving the scribe to gape at his lover.

"What was that all about?" he demanded, hands on his hips.

"No one will ever lay a hand on you in my presence. It's my duty to protect you."

"I'm not some china doll you have to wrap in cotton wool," the scribe stubbornly retorted. "I was a slave for most of my life. I was abused and beaten. I've been raped and drugged, and I survived all of it. Don't worry so much." He wrapped his arms around the warlord and gave him a chaste kiss.

"I care about you," Aoshi said. "I don't want you to be hurt ever again."

The two sat in silence for a long moment before the scribe finally asked the question that he'd been pondering. "Who's this Abe-san?"

"Abe Hajime. His family has always been influential. He's a lot like me, an orphan who thrives on battle. The difference is he doesn't care about anything but his own desires. He'd drive his troops into the ground if it suited him. If he was in power it would be a disaster. He'd be a tyrant. It's crucial he doesn't assume command," the warlord explained, voice rising with his anger.

"Calm down, Aoshi. There's no point getting upset over it now. You're here and everything will be okay. Right now what you need is sleep," the scribe urged, worried about the warlord's physical and emotional state. "In the morning everything will look clearer."

Aoshi grumbled and tried to protest, but soon gave in to Ryuu's pleas and lay down on the bed, eyes wide open and staring sightlessly at the ceiling. "It won't do any good if you just lay there and fret," the scribe reminded him. "What do I need to do to get you to relax?"

"I can think of a few things," the warlord replied, although the pain etched across his face belied the suggestive tone.

"Why don't you turn over and I'll rub your back. It will ease your muscles and make you more comfortable." Ryuu carefully helped the warlord roll onto his stomach before leaning over and pulling some oil out of his pack. He warmed some in his palms before placing both hand on tense shoulders and slowly beginning to stroke and press, adding oil as he needed to keep the motion frictionless.

Ever so slowly Aoshi began to relax, nimble fingers seeking out and carefully working every knot, moving carefully down long legs to tense feet, and along the pale arms to ease tight fingers until he lay limp and motionless. The scribe wiped his hands on a towel and moved his attentions to the shaggy mop of hair, rubbing soothing circles on the scalp until the warlord finally gave in and slipped into sleep.

I should go hunt down Akemi and see what else I can find out, Ryuu thought as he quietly slipped out of bed. He pulled his clothes on and checked the warlord again, glad to see he was sleeping peacefully. The scribe headed toward the mess, hoping he'd find the courier there and not have to return to Arashi's. The last thing he wanted to do was interrupt them. *Although, that might give Yuudai a chance,* he mused.

"Psssttt, Ryuu. Over here." The scribe was startled out of his thoughts by a whispered call of his name. He looked around and saw a hand beckoning from between two tents.

"Oki. I thought you were dead." Ryuu's mind was whirling; he didn't want his old master to figure out he was on Aoshi's side. If, of course, he hadn't already. Hopefully his lie would be believed.

"My lover will be in charge after tomorrow. Throw in with us and reap the benefits," the slave trader entreated.

"Your lover … Kudo Seiya?" Ryuu asked, finally remembering the name of the man he had met who was so enthralled with Oki.

"His real name is Abe Hajime. He's stronger than even Fujiwara. With the old fool in charge it will be easy for my lover to seize control. Once he has it they won't be able to take it back."

"When is this supposed to happen?" the scribe asked.

"At muster," Oki mistook Ryuu's anxiety for impatience. "So, we'll see you there then?"

"Yes, at muster," the scribe assured him. "Good night." He hurried towards the mess, needing to speak with Akemi more than ever.

Chapter Fifty-Seven

Yuudai stumbled into his tent dirty and exhausted, only to stop dead at the sight of a naked Aoshi sprawled out in his bed. He dropped to his knees next to the futon and grasped a calloused hand. "Aoshi. Aoshi, wake up."

"Hey, Ryuu, come to bed." The warlord tugged sleepily on the hand holding his. "I'm lonely."

Yuudai didn't stop for a second thought about what he was doing. Truth be told, he didn't give it a first thought. He slid into the bed, molding himself smoothly up against the warlord's side and wrapping a burly arm around him before drifting into sleep.

* * *

Akemi wasn't in the mess, so the scribe reluctantly headed for Arashi's tent. "Hey, Akemi. It's Ryuu. I need to talk to you." When there was no answer he hesitantly stuck his head through the flap, gasping in shock when his eyes were met by the sight of the courier wantonly thrusting into his friend. "Sorry," he finally stuttered when he regained his composure and turned away.

"Ryuu?" he heard the courier's voice call as he dropped the flap.

"I'm so sorry. I just needed to talk to you. I didn't mean to intrude." The scribe blushed violently. "Never mind."

"No, that's okay. Just hang on a minute." Ryuu could hear soft whispers from inside the tent and sounds of fabric rustling before the flap pulled back and Akemi ushered him inside.

"I'm so sorry to bother you. I didn't know who else to talk to. Aoshi's asleep. He needs all the rest he can get."

"Of course, any time," the courier replied. "Would you like a drink?"

"No, I'll make it quick and get out of your way. I'm really sorry for disturbing you, Arashi." The scribe dropped his gaze in embarrassment.

"You can disturb me anytime. You're always welcome." Arashi stroked long fingers up the scribe's chest before settling on his shoulder and squeezing firmly. "You're downright edible," he purred, continuing to stroke and knead the tense shoulders, hoping to soothe the panic he seemed to have induced.

"Stop it." The courier pulled his friend's hands off the shocked scribe. "Ryuu is Fujiwara's. No touching, unless you fancy losing one of your hands."

The tall man pouted, eyes never leaving the scribe's face. "Fine. I'm going back to bed then." He yawned, leaning over and capturing Akemi's mouth in a deep hard kiss. He broke away, pulling back slightly before turning and placing a tender kiss on Ryuu's lips. He took advantage of the scribe's shock to slip his tongue inside, pulling the startled man close and wrapping him in strong arms.

"What the fuck is wrong with you?" the courier demanded angrily as he wrenched him away from Ryuu. "Hell, what the fuck is wrong with me? Why does every man I get involved with have the hots for someone else?" He steered the scribe out of the tent, deftly avoiding Arashi's attempts to embrace him.

"Wait, I didn't mean it that way. Give me a chance to explain at least."

"I don't think so. I seem to keep making the same mistakes, and it's time for a change." Akemi shuffled dejectedly outside before turning to a worried Ryuu. "What did you need to talk about?"

"Are you okay?" the scribe asked. "I didn't mean for this to happen. I just didn't know who to go to."

"It's fine. I can't blame you because I wasn't what he wanted. Apparently I'm everyone's favorite substitute, first Yuudai, now Arashi. I wish I knew what I was doing wrong."

"You aren't doing anything wrong," Ryuu assured him. "I don't know about Arashi, but I know that General Tanaka cares about you, even if he does act like an idiot. I know he was worried about how he left the other day." He went on to fill the courier in on his encounter with Oki. When he finished he pinned Akemi with worried eyes. "What should I do?"

"You need to tell Fujiwara," the courier decided. "I'll go with you." The two headed toward Yuudai's tent, hoping the information might improve Aoshi's position.

When they reached the tent they didn't bother announcing themselves, lifting the flap and slipping inside. Ryuu hurried to the bed, only to stop short at the sight of his peacefully slumbering lover cradled in the general's arms. "Aoshi?" he said, fighting back the tears that were threatening to overflow.

"Ryuu?" The warlord rolled to face the man embracing him. "Is it morning already?" he asked with a yawn, cracking open his eyes only to stare in horror at the man in his bed. "What the hell are you doing here?" His words shocked the slumbering general awake.

"Hey, Aoshi," he said sleepily. "I can explain."

"There is no explanation for your being in my bed."

"It's my bed," Yuudai retorted. "Why are you in it?"

"Because I had to come here and fix your mistake," Aoshi replied just as nastily, wrapping both hands around the general's throat and squeezing hard. "Why didn't you wake me up?"

"Aoshi, stop." Ryuu rushed forward to pry his hands from Yuudai's throat. "He's your friend."

"Not anymore," the warlord replied. "This is the last straw. Get the fuck out of my sight and stay there, Tanaka. I don't want you within ten feet of me."

"I'm sorry. I didn't do anything. I was tired and you pulled me into the bed."

"I most certainly did not," Aoshi insisted. "I would never do that." He turned imploring eyes on the tearful scribe. "Ryuu, I would never do that. I never want to hurt you. You have to believe me."

"You don't need me here anymore," Akemi interjected in a tight voice. "I'm gonna go home and get some sleep."

"Wait." Yuudai reached out to snag the courier's arm. "I'm sorry for the way I left."

"Sure," he replied bitterly. "Seems like you spend a lot of your time being sorry. See you around." He turned and strode out into the night, leaving the general gaping after him.

"I have news for you." Ryuu perched on the edge of the bed and stroked the warlord's arm, comforting them both with the touch. "I ran into Oki. He's involved with Abe-san." Before he could continue the tent flap was thrown back and Ken'ichi came storming in.

"Thanks for waiting for me, dick head," he hissed to Yuudai before addressing the warlord. "I came to offer my support." He bowed his head and waited for Aoshi's response.

"No, thank you," the warlord replied. "Go home to your wife. I have everything under control."

"Aoshi," Ryuu began, but he was cut off.

"I will handle this." With that Aoshi turned his back on them all and pretended to go back to sleep, refusing to extend what was, to him, a pointless argument.

Ryuu quickly hustled the generals out of the tent. "I'm sorry, Yuudai," he said apologetically. "I wasn't expecting you back. I feel terrible turning you out of your tent."

"It's okay. It's not your fault." The scribe hurriedly filled them in on what he had learned from Fusao and Oki.

"So, you'll be there in the morning?" he asked.

"Whatever he may believe, we are loyal to Fujiwara," Ken'ichi replied. "We'll be there."

"Thank you. He doesn't seem to realize how weak he really is," Ryuu said.

"Everything will be fine," Ken'ichi soothed. "We'll see you in the morning."

Chapter Fifty-Eight

"Aoshi, are you awake?"

"Are they gone?"

"Yes, it's just us." Ryuu stripped and slid into bed next to the warlord, wrapping his arms around him and resting his head on the broad chest. "What was all that about?" he finally asked, unsure if he wanted an answer.

"I don't know. I need to talk to you about some things…" The warlord trailed off uncertainly. Despite his prowess on the battlefield he was unsure when it came to his emotions. "I think I love you. You hold my heart."

"I love you too. Never doubt that."

"It's just," Aoshi hesitated, unable to find a way to say what he needed to without upsetting the scribe. "I don't know what's going to happen in the morning. Maybe it would be best if you headed back with Ken'ichi. I'll come when I can."

Ryuu studied his lover carefully. There was something he wasn't saying. "I know you're hiding something, so spit it out. I'm not leaving you. You might as well tell me."

"I'm weaker than I thought. I don't know if I can go up against Abe successfully." Aoshi looked down, refusing to meet the scribe's eyes.

"Which means?" Ryuu was afraid he already knew the answer.

"I could die," the warlord said. "I could die and there will be no one to protect you. That's why you need to leave."

"I'm not leaving," the scribe whispered through a suddenly tight throat. "Now more than ever. No matter what happens. I said I'd never leave you again and I meant it." Ryuu leaned over and kissed the solemn face, nipping at the warlord's lips until they parted before diving hungrily inside, devouring his lover's mouth. "I need you," he moaned when the kiss finally broke.

The scribe grabbed for the oil on the bed table and slicked the warlord's erection, kneeling over him and slowly lowering himself. He reveled in the feel of the thick cock slowly spreading his passage, finally releasing the breath he'd unconsciously held when he was flush with Aoshi's body. Ryuu let out a groan as he slowly relaxed, tossing his head back so his hair tickled the warlord's thighs and brushed teasingly over his tightening sac.

"Gods, so deep, so close," the warlord mumbled as he stroked his thumbs over the sensitive skin beside the scribe's hipbones. "I wish I could climb right inside of you."

"You are a part of me." The scribe bent to rain kisses over his lover's face. "You will always be a part of me." He slowly bent his legs, lifting himself before slowly sliding back down, arching his back and whimpering when his prostate was struck.

They kept up the slow rhythm for a very long time, languidly thrusting against each other as their mouths met and melded. It was an apology and a promise, both sweet and sad, and it couldn't last. Eventually the pace increased, the scribe thrusting down on the warlord's cock with abandon as a calloused hand circled his weeping erection, thumb dipping into the slit and making Ryuu cry out in pleasure.

When the pleasure became too great the scribe came with a strangled grunt, clamping down on the hard length still pistoning inside him as he shuddered and shook. Aoshi gave in with a howl and rammed into his lover, shooting streams of hot seed into his prostate, sending him into another paroxysm of shivers.

The warlord clutched the scribe to his chest, unwilling to separate from the warmth he so desperately desired. "Stay. Please, don't leave," he whispered as he stroked sweat dampened locks.

"I'm right here," the scribe husked. "Sleep now. I'll hold you, just rest with me." He continued to murmur soothing words as onyx eyes fluttered before closing completely. Ryuu lay awake long after the warlord had drifted off, worry about the coming morning chasing all possibility of sleep away. Still, he kept his word and remained where he was, tenderly nuzzling the column of his lover's neck until the sun began to peek over the horizon.

"Aoshi," he said as he shook a broad shoulder. "It's time to go."

"Okay." The warlord sat up and rubbed a hand over his weary face. He dressed and pulled the scribe into a tight embrace. "Stay here where it's safe, please? I'll be back soon." With that Aoshi stood, emotion draining from his face as he strode toward the confrontation that awaited him.

As soon as Aoshi left, Ryuu began to dress, running to meet the generals and support his lover. The three men were soon headed to the parade grounds, Yuudai and Ken'ichi looking as tired and haunted as the warlord.

They arrived just as Aoshi was moving to take his place before the assembled troops, startling Hajime who had been opening his mouth to address them. "Thank you Abe-san, but I'll take it from here."

"I don't think so, Fujiwara." Hajime's eyes swept down the lanky form as he tried to assess the state of the warlord's health. "You're in no shape to fight me about it."

"Oh no? Let's just see about that." With a roar Aoshi spun away, pulling his sword as Hajime drew his. The first clash of their blades acted like some prearranged signal, fighting breaking out between the two sides all over the assembly. Ryuu slipped between fighters as he maneuvered toward the front, desperate to get to his lover. Behind him Ken'ichi and Yuudai were fighting their way forward, blades rising and falling as they moved inexorably towards the warlord. On the other side, Fusao and Jin were holding back a surge of Hajime's supporters.

Ryuu finally reached the open area where Hajime and his lover were locked in heated combat. The warlord pressed forward confidently, driving the smaller man back. The scribe cheered inwardly, though he worried about the exhaustion evident on Aoshi's face. *He won't be able to keep this up for long*, Ryuu fretted. *I have to find some way to distract Hajime.*

He darted towards the pair, eyes searching for an opening. Seeing the warlord fall back a few steps he knew he had to hurry, so he boldly hooked one of Hajime's legs, pulling him off balance. The usurper turned and drove his blade through the person who had dared to interfere with his fight.

"Aoshi," the scribe managed to choke out, eyes going wide as he felt himself falling, unable to work his limbs. The warlord let out a primal shriek as he watched Hajime stab his lover. Sanity left him and he surged forward, slamming his blade to the hilt in the usurper's chest, consumed by the pain of failing to protect his most precious person.

Chapter Fifty-Nine

"You worthless piece of shit," the warlord hissed at the man impaled on his blade. "You never were anything but a waste of air." Aoshi growled ferally as he twisted the sword, ripping flesh and sending gouts of blood gushing over his hands. "I hope you're suffering. I want your death to be slow."

The generals redoubled their efforts, appalled at the carnage and at Aoshi's apparent descent into madness. "Is that Ryuu?" Ken'ichi panted as he directed Yuudai's attention towards the warlord's position, indicating the small figure crumpled by his feet.

"Oh kami." Yuudai surged forward with a roar, slashing and hacking at the men in his way in a desperate effort to reach his friend.

Oki watched in horror as Ryuu unbalanced his lover and was run through. He started moving toward them, the world around him slowing to a near halt as the warlord's blade thrust through Hajime's chest. He pulled a tanto from his belt, burying it in the warlord's back to the hilt. "Stupid fuck," he muttered, kicking the taller man as he fell. "That's for Hajime." He raised his leg and stamped down hard on the sprawled figure's crotch, grinding Aoshi's testicles under his heel until he felt them rupture. "And that's for me."

Yuudai couldn't believe his eyes when the warlord toppled to the ground. Rage fueled his actions as he watched Oki stomp down on his friend's crotch. With a mighty yell he slashed at Narita-san's neck, watching with detachment as the head rolled away to point sightless eyes in his direction. "What a cluster fuck." He scrambled to Aoshi's side, shocked to find him still conscious despite the blood pouring from his wound.

"Ryuu," the warlord rasped breathlessly as he stretched out his arm to try and touch the smaller man. "Please."

Yuudai wrapped an arm around Aoshi's shoulders, carefully shifting him to lie next to the fallen scribe. "Ryuu," the warlord tried again, fingers feathering hesitantly over his lover's face. "Love you."

"'m so tired," the scribe mumbled. "Love you. Kiss me? 'm sleepy. Kiss me to sleep."

The warlord gently pressed his lips to Ryuu's, trying to taste his love one last time through the thick coppery taint flooding his mouth. The scribe gave a slight shudder and lay still, too still. Aoshi's mind broke at the thought of life without him. *I think I'll just rest here*, he decided, exhaling one last time before the light left his eyes.

Things settled quickly once most of the members of the revolt had fallen. Ken'ichi limped over to join Yuudai, covering his eyes and choking back a sob at the sight of the fallen warlord and his love, tenderly embracing even in death. *How am I going to tell Kotone*, he wondered absently. *She'll be so upset*. He glanced over at Yuudai, shocked to see tears pouring down his face.

"I guess this means you're in charge," Fusao said, turning Yuudai to face him. "Buck up and get this under control. Then we'll care for him properly."

"I can't," the general whispered. "He wouldn't want that."

"You were his second in command, Tanaka-san," Fusao pressed. "You are the only logical choice. Unless you want all his sacrifices to be for nothing. Get the rest of the opposition locked up and the wounded treated. Then we'll have time to care for the dead."

"I will be honored to guard the commander's body," Jin offered. "I will allow no one to disturb their rest."

Ken'ichi grasped Yuudai's arm and propelled him forward, whispering quiet instructions in his ear until he gradually regained his control. "Can you do this?" he queried one last time before the general began to speak, seeing the short nod of reply as a step forward from the blankness of moments before.

Jin stood silently, watching as healers carried the injured off the field, horrified at the number who still lay sprawled as they had fallen. "I'm sorry, commander." He spoke to the spirit of the one whose body he now protected. "I wish I could have stopped this." He pulled back and took a hard look at the entwined figures. "Rest well, may you find each other again." With that he turned his eyes away, feeling like a voyeur peeping at something intensely personal.

Akemi skidded onto the field, slipping and sliding in the churned bloody earth. He frantically searched from side to side, looking for Yuudai's large form. He pulled up when he reached Jin's side, letting out a shocked gasp when he realized what he was guarding. His frenzy increased, fear fueled by the hitherto unimaginable sight of the mighty warlord Fujiwara felled on the field of battle. *Ryuu too*, he thought hysterically. *Yuudai must be nearby.* "Have you seen General Tanaka?" he screamed as he grabbed Jin's shoulders.

"He, General Fujii and Fusao have gone to see to the wounded. They will be back once the situation is under control."

Akemi didn't hear the end of his answer, feet propelling him toward the healer's tents as soon as he knew where to go. He skidded through the door, flying across the room and launching himself into the general's arms. He rained kisses over his lover's face as he murmured thanks to all the gods for saving Yuudai when so many others had lost their lives. "I'm sorry, I'm so sorry. Are you alright?" He pulled back to check the general for wounds.

"I'm fine. At least, I'm uninjured. I don't know if I'll ever be fine again." The general watched the light fade from Akemi's eyes as he listened to his response. "I'm glad you're here, safe," he whispered, pulling the courier close. "It would kill me to lose you. I'm just sorry it took all this for me to realize it. Can you ever forgive me for being such an ass?"

"Forgiven and forgotten," Akemi replied. Everything was starting to seem a bit surreal to him but he was shocked back into reality at Yuudai's next words.

"We need to go take care of their bodies. Will you please come and help me? I don't know if I can do it."

"Of course," the courier replied with a gulp, finding it hard to move on suddenly leaden feet.

It was midday before the quartet finally left the healer's. They spent hours grimly taking reports on deaths, injuries and arrests before heading to the site of the conflict, intent on laying their fallen comrade to rest.

They carefully lifted the entwined pair, settling them gently on a stretcher before heading to the edge of camp. A large pyre had already been constructed and the mourners placed their burden on top, stepping back and bowing their heads before sending up a silent prayer. "You both shall be missed. Go and suffer no more," Ken'ichi rasped before thrusting a torch into the dry wood.

All over camp eyes turned to the pillar of smoke now rising on the outskirts. Men bowed their heads and wished their commander god speed on his journey, even as they thanked the gods they had survived another day.

The five watchers stood unmoving until the fire had burned out. When nothing but ash remained they headed back to camp, beset with thoughts of their own mortality as their hearts sagged under the burden of the loss of their friends.

Chapter Sixty

Once the details of the transition were worked out Ken'ichi headed back to town to let Kotone know what had happened. *At least she'll be happy I'm staying*, he mused as he traveled, anxious to hold his wife and daughter. After the events of the last couple of days he appreciated them more than ever.

As Ken'ichi disappeared from sight Yuudai turned to the courier and pulled him into his arms, needing the contact to soothe his shattered heart. "Are you ready, Marc?"

"No, but that doesn't change anything," the former courier grumbled as the pair headed across camp to talk strategy with Fusao and Jin. "Are you sure I'm a good choice?" he finally blurted out, nervous about his soon to be promotion.

"There's no one I'd trust more to back me up," the general assured him. "I need you by my side."

"Well then, that's where I'll be." Akemi turned haunted eyes on his lover. "I don't want you ending up like Fujiwara."

"It was my fault," Yuudai insisted. "I lost his trust and couldn't protect him. I don't think I'll ever forgive myself for failing him when he needed me most."

"You need to stop beating yourself up about it. Yes, you made mistakes, but so did he. Remember he pushed you away, not the other way around. There's only so much blame you can lay on yourself. Of course you miss him. You were best friends for most of your life. Now you have to move on and leave him behind. It's very hard. Eventually it will hurt less. One day maybe you'll be able to smile when you remember him."

"I'd like that." They walked in silence the rest of the way, pondering all the problems and uncertainties that lay ahead.

* * *

Ken'ichi threw the door open. "Kotone, I'm home, where are you?" he called, sighing in relief when she appeared carrying baby Aoi.

"Sweetheart, what's wrong?" she gasped, immediately frightened by the look on his face.

The general didn't answer, merely sweeping her into his arms and holding her tightly, murmuring words of devotion into her hair as he breathed in its comforting familiar scent.

"I adore you Kotone, you and Aoi. I don't know what I'd do without you."

"Honey, you're scaring me. What's going on? Are we in danger?"

"No, no danger, not anymore." He pulled back and looked into his wife's eyes, steeling himself to deliver the sad news. "It went badly ... hell, worse than badly," he finally muttered. "I don't know any easy way to say this. The battle was violent, we lost almost a third of the men."

"Oh, Ken'ichi." Kotone caressed his face with her hand. "I'm so sorry."

"That's not the worst of it," he continued. "Ryuu and Aoshi…" he trailed off, unable to force the words out of his suddenly tight throat.

"What about them, were they injured?" she exclaimed. "I need to go take care of them. Ryuu's done so much for us, and Aoshi's like family."

"Sweetheart," the general husked, grabbing her hands and squeezing them tightly. "They didn't make it."

"No," she cried. "Oh, Ken'ichi, no." Her eyes filled with tears as she searched his face, hoping against hope that this was some juvenile joke they'd cooked up.

"I'm so sorry, honey." He pulled her tight against him, wrapping strong arms around her and stroking a soothing hand up and down her back. "If it makes you feel better, they died in each other's arms and we sent them on together."

The thought broke the barrier holding back her tears and Kotone clung to her husband as she wailed her grief. Baby Aoi took up the cry until it seemed that the whole world was grieving.

Eventually her sobs slowed and finally faded to gasping

hiccups. "What happens now?"

"Yuudai and I have split the command. No one but Fujiwara could handle it all by himself. I'm going to stay here, with you, and handle civilian affairs. I've changed my mind about a lot of things. I have no desire to leave your side," Ken'ichi whispered as he cradled her in his arms. "We're going to push through the reforms Aoshi wanted. It's the least we can do."

"What will happen with the troops?" Kotone asked, concerned that her husband appeared to be willing to abandon his life as it had been up until now.

"Yuudai is in charge of military affairs. Fusao, Jin and Akemi are helping him. He'd already wrapped up the Northern campaign and was involved in treaty negotiations so it seemed a logical choice. Besides," he continued wryly, "it's not like I'm up to it at the moment. Hell, I may never be up to it. This is for the best."

"I'm not so sure I agree with you." Kotone studied him closely. "But I certainly won't argue with having you here. Now come on." She tugged on his arm. "You need a bath, food and sleep, in that order."

"Yes, dear." The general gratefully followed her to the bath. He thoroughly enjoyed the fuss she made, filling the tub and laying out towels. He gave a thankful hiss when she helped him awkwardly clamber into the furo, leg hanging over the side, and began to rub his back. "I love you, sweetheart," he said suddenly, turning to capture her lips in a sweet kiss.

"I love you too. I feel really selfish, but I'm glad it was Aoshi and not you." He stroked her arm and nuzzled her chin, finally drawing out a tiny smile.

"It's alright to be happy, Kotone. It's what they both would want."

* * *

Yuudai looked at the other three men in shock; doing the job was one thing, but this crossed a boundary he wasn't ready to breech. "I refuse," he said almost hysterically. "Don't you dare call me that."

"But, commander," Fusao replied, emphasizing the title. "The men need to know who's in charge. It's just a word."

"No. It's just what he accused me of." Yuudai moaned,

dropping his head on the table.

"Give me a minute with him." Akemi moved to stroke his lover's back when the other men had gone. "You're getting upset over nothing."

"It's not nothing. I lost my best friend because he thought I wanted to take his place. I can't actually do it."

"Listen to me. Deep down Fujiwara knew how you felt. He loved you like a brother. I'm sure he forgives you."

"I wish I could believe that." Yuudai put his head on his arms and began to cry for what he had lost. Akemi could only sit and stroke his hair tenderly, waiting for him to let go of the past so they could make their future.

Chapter Sixty-One

Ever so slowly things began to settle back into their familiar pattern. The Northern campaign finally wrapped up, Akemi acting as Commander Tanaka's representative for the treaty negotiations. The troops headed toward the capital for some much deserved down time.

As the ranks passed through the gates of the city they were greeted by crowds of grateful citizens, as well as the revitalized governing council. Ken'ichi and, of course, Kotone with baby Aoi, were out in front. After what seemed like an eternity the column finally came to an end and Yuudai and Akemi came into view, trailing behind at a slow walk as they talked quietly.

"Oi, Yuudai." Ken'ichi limped determinedly towards the stragglers. "Took you long enough," he continued when he finally came abreast of them. "Come to the house, there's plenty of room. You can clean up and we'll talk over dinner."

The pair quickly dismounted, Yuudai and Ken'ichi clasping forearms before pulling each other into a rough hug. Akemi swept baby Aoi out of her mother's arms, making her crow with glee as she tugged on his dangling locks. "Ouch," he grumbled, rubbing his nose against the tiny girl's to distract her while he rescued his hair. "It's a good thing you're so cute."

"Sorry, Akemi," Kotone hurried to apologize as she reached for the baby.

"It's fine, Kotone. She can't help it if I'm irresistible. You have a beautiful daughter, Ken'ichi," he commented, in between blowing raspberries on a tiny tummy. "Good thing she takes after her mother. Oh wait," he continued through giggles as he took a lock of his hair and held it up to her tiny chin. "I'm wrong, she looks just like you."

"Ha, ha, very funny," the bearded general growled in mock anger. "Don't listen to him Aoi, he's just an…"

"Idiot," Yuudai threw in affectionately.

"Yeah, but I'm your idiot." Akemi smiled, wrapping an arm around Yuudai's waist and planting a kiss on his cheek.

"Give me my daughter before you smash her," Ken'ichi demanded, breaking into snickers at the affronted look both men sent his way.

"Men are just hopeless, aren't they sweetheart?" Kotone artfully plucked her daughter from Akemi's arms. "All big and grumbly." Aoi let out a delighted coo, clapping her pudgy hands together in glee.

"See, she agrees." Kotone gave the generals a pointed look before turning and heading for home. The three soldiers trailed behind her, already deep in debate about the new treaty and the plans Ken'ichi had for the civilian population.

Dinner was a relaxed affair. Little Aoi had been put to bed and the four adults lounged around the table laughing and joking. "This is delicious, Kotone," Akemi mumbled around a mouthful.

"I'm glad you like it. Ryuu gave me the recipe, it was one of Aoshi's favorites," she replied wistfully.

"Excuse me." Yuudai rose and left the room without a backward glance.

"What was that all about?" Ken'ichi fixed Akemi with a pointed glare.

"Aoshi is still a very sore subject for him. I'm sorry I didn't think to warn you. I'd hoped, here, with you, he might let go a bit." The former courier stared absently into the flickering hearth. "Guess I was wrong about that, too."

"Do you want to talk about it?" Kotone asked, laying a gentle hand on Akemi's shoulder.

"I left him before the battle, you know. I was fed up with his obsession with Fujiwara. But then I was so grateful he hadn't been killed, and I thought with Aoshi gone we could work things out. Only it's worse than ever. I don't think I can take much more." He dropped his head in his hands, pulling on his hair as if it would somehow provide him the answer.

"It will all work out," Kotone said firmly. "Honey, go talk to him."

"Yes, dear," the general replied despondently, not wanting to get involved. He did as his wife bid, however, rising awkwardly before limping determinedly after his friend.

"Ken'ichi will talk some sense into him," Kotone soothed, rubbing gentle circles on the slumped courier's back. "He can't mourn forever."

"It's not mourning," Akemi whispered. "He refuses to face the fact that Aoshi's gone and he's never coming back. He won't move on and it's killing me. Look, it's late and I'm exhausted. I think I'll just hit the sack. I'll see you in the morning. Thanks again for dinner, it was wonderful."

Kotone studied him as he rose and headed upstairs. *He's aged ten years*, she thought in horror. *This can't go on or we'll lose Akemi too.*

"Oi, Yuudai," Ken'ichi called when he stepped out into the courtyard, spotting the general leaning against the wall, swallowed in shadows. "What was that all about?"

"Nothing. Mind your own business, Fujii-san."

"If it affects you like that it is my business. You're in command, remember? Seriously, what's bothering you?"

"I miss Aoshi," Yuudai declared despondently. "Are you happy now? I destroyed our friendship and he hated me when he died. I can't help thinking that it's all my fault. If I hadn't been such an ass, maybe I could have prevented all this." He ran a large hand down his face, letting out a bark of what could have been tears or laughter. "I'm sure if he's watching me he's laughing like a loon. I'd give anything to trade places with him."

"Don't say that," Ken'ichi replied angrily. "You need to snap out of this. I have an idea that might help; I think we should have a memorial service for Aoshi. I know Kotone would appreciate the chance to say goodbye. Maybe it will make it more real for all of us. That day was … it all seems like a bad dream."

"I don't know." Yuudai sighed. "I'm not sure I could deal with reliving the whole thing all over again."

"You're not dealing with it at all," Ken'ichi pointed out. "And if you think Aoshi hated you, just imagine how angry he'd be if we let everything collapse back into chaos."

"I'll consider it. Just not right now. I'm going to turn in. I'll talk to you in the morning. Tell Kotone thanks for dinner."

* * *

"Well?" Kotone asked when her husband returned. "What did you find out?"

"He's upset about Aoshi. I thought maybe a memorial service would help." Ken'ichi tugged her around to face him, wrapping burly arms around her waist and nuzzling her neck. "It would give us all a push to move on. Besides, Aoshi certainly deserves it."

"What a wonderful idea, sweetheart," she replied in delight. "That is so thoughtful of you. You really have changed. And here I thought I couldn't love you any more than I already did."

"Well then, I'd best get you upstairs and take advantage of that." Ken'ichi scooped her up and kissed her breathless as he headed up to their rooms.

Chapter Sixty-Two

The next day everything continued on as normal, or so it seemed. Kotone noticed how quiet both Yuudai and Akemi were at breakfast, but decided not to interfere. *At least not yet,* she told herself. *Give them a chance to work this out on their own.*

Several hours later Akemi slipped out with his pack, heading for the encampment on the outskirts of town and the safe familiarity of his own tent. *Maybe I should tell him I'm leaving.* He studied Yuudai's familiar profile through the window. *Not worth the effort,* he concluded, knowing it would just cause him more hurt if, as he feared, his lover didn't care enough to stop him.

Even if he did, it wouldn't change anything, came the reluctant acknowledgment. Mind now set, Akemi squared his shoulders and headed toward camp, anxious to put some distance between himself and Yuudai.

When dinner rolled around again the general finally decided to show his face, creeping down the stairs and joining Kotone and Ken'ichi at the table. "Where's Akemi?" he asked absently as he pushed the food around on his plate.

"He headed back to camp this morning," Kotone retorted. "Didn't you even notice when he said good-bye?"

"I haven't seen him since breakfast," the general shot back. "So I guess he didn't bother."

"Stop it," Ken'ichi commanded, stepping between them with arms outstretched. "Kotone, it is none of your business. And you need to watch how you talk to my wife, Tanaka."

"Maybe I should just go," Yuudai decided, rising unsteadily from his chair. "I'm obviously intruding. Kotone, my apologies. I've been insufferably rude, please forgive me." He turned his attention to the bristling man across the table. "I'll see you in a few days."

The couple listened in silence as he trudged upstairs and gathered his belongings. When they heard him heading back down Kotone started to rise, but was stopped by her husband's hand on her arm. Ken'ichi shook his head no, motioning for her to sit back down, only speaking when they heard the door click shut.

"It's for the best, sweetheart. I'll go check on him in the morning."

Yuudai wandered toward camp, in no hurry to reach his vacant tent. He knew his actions were hurting his lover, had been since long before Aoshi's death, but he couldn't let go. He was too afraid to face the hard truth. Aoshi and he had parted as enemies and he would never get the chance to make it right.

* * *

The next several weeks passed quickly enough; there was plenty to be done reestablishing the encampment. Yuudai and Ken'ichi met almost daily to hammer out changes with the council, both men finding the dry work of governing to be much more exhausting than battle. Of Akemi, however, little was seen. He quietly performed his duties and disappeared back into the solace of his tent, shunning all companionship.

"Enough is enough," Ken'ichi suddenly declared, banging his hand on the dinner table and startling his wife and daughter. "I'm not waiting any longer."

"What are you babbling about?" Kotone scrubbed at the fresh stain blooming on the tatami as a result of his outburst.

"The monument's been done for a week and I've been tiptoeing around Yuudai about the memorial service, but he's completely avoiding the issue. I think we need to just get on with it. If he doesn't show, it's his loss. I'll make the announcement tomorrow. How does Friday morning sound?"

"I think that will be fine. Do you think Yuudai will show up?" Kotone wondered."And what about Akemi? Has anyone been in touch with him? Do you think he'll come?"

"I haven't seen him," Ken'ichi replied after a thoughtful pause. "And I'm not sure if he'll come. I'm fairly sure he's trying to avoid Yuudai; that's why he's been out of circulation."

"I'm just afraid it's more than that. He didn't look well the last time I saw him. I know he left, but I could see how much he cared for Yuudai. I worry, about both of them. I don't think the general could take another loss."

"I take it you have a plan?"

"Not yet. I really need to know what happened between Aoshi and Yuudai before he died."

"I can't help you with that. Whatever it was started before Aoi was born, right after Aoshi bought…"

"What? What?" Kotone demanded, swatting her husband's arm to get his attention.

"He was jealous," Ken'ichi whispered in a tone of awed realization. "I don't know why I didn't see it before. Yuudai was in love with Aoshi. They must have fought about Ryuu. That's why they were avoiding each other. That last night, when we followed the commander back to camp. I got there after Yuudai, of course. Stupid leg. Anyway, when I got there I saw Akemi storm out of the tent, and Aoshi and Yuudai were glaring daggers at each other. Something must have happened to set the commander off, because he was cold as ice."

Kotone gasped. "No wonder Yuudai can't move on."

"He watched Aoshi die. If that's not hard enough, the last thing the commander did was kiss Ryuu one last time, not his love-sick, former best friend." The general put his head in his hands. "I don't know what to do now. I wish I'd never figured it out."

"Let me think about it tonight," Kotone entreated. "Tomorrow I'm going to track down Akemi. After that we'll have a better idea of what you can do."

"But what about the memorial?" Ken'ichi croaked.

"Go ahead and schedule it," Kotone said. "It's not just about Yuudai. Are you planning on announcing the civilian reforms at the service?"

"It seems fitting. The details should be worked out by then. That will be Aoshi's real memorial, a new era of peace and prosperity for all citizens," the general said with a smile. "At least that's something to celebrate."

"We have plenty to celebrate," Kotone reminded him. "You're safe. We're together. We have Aoi. No wonder Yuudai and Akemi are avoiding us. It can't be easy to see us so happy when their worlds are falling apart."

"That may be true, sweetheart." Ken'ichi nibbled the column of his wife's neck. "But I wouldn't change it for anything, no matter how it hurts anyone else."

"I love you too, honey," Kotone whispered as he folded her in his arms, both of them basking in the simple pleasure of being together against all odds.

Chapter Sixty-Three

Kotone set out for camp bright and early the next morning, making her way to Akemi's tent. "Hello. May I come in?" she called from just outside.

"Kotone?" came the baffled response. "What are you doing here?"

"I came to see how you're doing." She swept past him and into the tent. Akemi immediately ducked in after her, quickly snatching up and hiding his personal papers before offering her a seat.

"Not much for housekeeping?" she asked with a smirk. "How have you been? Ken'ichi and I were concerned. We haven't seen you since you moved back to camp."

"I've just had a lot on my mind. It's nothing personal."

"You look terrible," Kotone retorted. "When was the last time you ate? You're nothing but skin and bones."

"I haven't been very hungry lately."

"Or have you been avoiding the mess?" she asked. "You need to let go of your pride and talk to him, Akemi."

"There isn't any point." He slumped into a chair and buried his head in his hands. "He didn't even notice I'd left, did he?"

"Well then, we'll just have to make him notice." Kotone neatly avoided the question in favor of a more positive response. "Come to dinner tonight. Yuudai won't be there, I promise. We'll figure something out. The important thing is not to give up." She patted him on the back before hurrying home to begin setting her plans in motion.

"Ken'ichi, where are you?" she called as soon as she walked through the door.

"We're in here, sweetheart," he called from the kitchen.

She hurried into the room, mouth open to speak, and stopped

dead at the sight that met her eyes. Every visible surface, including her sheepish husband and happily babbling daughter, was covered in a thick coating of flour. "What exactly are you attempting to do?" she finally managed between snorts of laughter.

"Ha, ha." Little puffs of flour blew off Ken'ichi's beard as he spoke, sending his wife into further gales of nearly hysterical laughter.

When she finally recovered, Kotone wiped her eyes and moved forward to hug her surprised husband tightly, heedless of the floury mess. "Thank you, I needed that. After you get this mess cleaned up, I'll fill you in on my talk with Akemi."

"We were trying to surprise you and make a cake," Ken'ichi said. "But Aoi decided it would be fun to grab the bag of flour out of my hands and toss it in the air instead."

"Blaming it on an infant? Really, sweetheart, is that the best excuse a big bad general can come up with?"

"Don't push me, woman," he roared, pulling her into a tight hug and kissing her soundly, then just as suddenly pushing her away to drop Aoi in her arms. "Take her and let me get to work."

By the time she had the baby clean and down for a nap Kotone had assimilated all she had learned. She wandered into the nearly clean kitchen and took a seat out of the way. "I invited Akemi to dinner tonight. He's been skipping meals because he's worried about running into Yuudai at the mess. I know you don't like it when I meddle, but this isn't resolving itself. I think we need to get them together at the memorial service. Yuudai will need someone after."

"Yeah, but for how long?" Ken'ichi retorted. "It isn't fair to Akemi to push him back into the same unhappy situation."

"Well, I'm hoping that it won't be the same. We need to know what Yuudai did to turn Aoshi against him, that's sure to be the key to getting him to let go."

"He won't talk about it, I've already tried," her husband responded automatically. "Although if anyone else knows what happened, it would be Akemi. We can ask him tonight at dinner."

"Great," Kotone cried with a clap of her hands. "Now let's finish getting rid of this mess. I have a dinner to cook."

* * *

Akemi reluctantly bathed and dressed, heading into town just after dusk. *This is such a bad idea*, he thought, nearly turning and heading back to the safety of his tent. *But Kotone's such a good cook*, a tiny voice in his head piped up, and his stomach was quick to rumble its agreement.

Only when he was sitting at the table did the former courier realize how nice it was to spend time in the company of others. "Thank you so much for inviting me, Kotone. The food is delicious, and I'm really enjoying the company."

"It's wonderful to have you," she replied sincerely. "We don't see enough of each other."

"So," Ken'ichi cut in. "Friday is Aoshi's memorial service. I hope you're planning to be there."

"The commander was always very good to me," Akemi muttered. "Of course I'll honor his memory."

"We were hoping," Kotone continued where her husband left off, "that it would help Yuudai let go. But we realized in order to ensure that result we need to know what happened between them."

"It's not my place to tell."

"I realize that," Ken'ichi said. "And normally I wouldn't ask. But with Aoshi gone there's no way for them to resolve their issues. If we can help Yuudai move past whatever it was, well, that would be good for both of you."

"We're not going to say anything to him," Kotone chimed in. "We'll be very discrete. It will help us decide what to say at the memorial that will put his mind at ease."

"You swear never to speak of it again?" Akemi asked suspiciously, only continuing when they both nodded their assent. "Yuudai walked in on Aoshi and Ryuu when they were, you know." He blushed brightly at discussing such things in front of Kotone. "And, well, he went a little bit crazy and knocked Ryuu down and raped Aoshi."

"Oh my god," Kotone hissed, hand to her mouth in shock. "I'm amazed Aoshi didn't kill him."

"I'm sure it was only because they were so close," Akemi continued. "After that, though, they were never alone together, not that they were obvious about it. They were just starting to act normally around each other when you two took control. Then just before you showed up that last night Ryuu and I found Yuudai had gotten into bed with Aoshi while he was sleeping. Nothing happened," he hastened to assure them. "But it was the commander's last straw. He said he never wanted to set eyes on Yuudai again. A few hours later, Aoshi was dead and Yuudai might as well be."

"Don't worry, it will be alright," Kotone assured him. "Just be there for him at the memorial."

"If you insist," Akemi muttered, hoping that this wouldn't turn into yet another disaster.

Chapter Sixty-Four

Friday dawned clear and crisp, and the townspeople began gathering in the square early, jockeying for choice spots for viewing the ceremony. Once muster ended the troops also began streaming into the confined space, until the viewing area was tightly packed with bodies, spilling between buildings and down the streets.

With less than an hour until the ceremony was to start, the last place Ken'ichi wanted to be was back in camp, arguing with Yuudai. Unfortunately, his wife had threatened him with a month of exile if he didn't deliver the reluctant general, so he raised his voice and began to press his point more forcefully.

"If you don't go it will be an insult to Aoshi and everything he worked for. It will prove he was right thinking you betrayed him, you know," Ken'ichi insisted.

"How dare you." Yuudai shoved Ken'ichi hard. "You don't understand anything about how I feel."

"I know you loved him. It has to hurt that he didn't feel the same."

"I never had a chance. I didn't admit how I felt, even to myself, until after he'd already met Ryuu. All I ever seemed to do was make things worse."

"Please, come to the memorial service. You two were always so close. I used to be so jealous of your friendship when we were younger, before I met Kotone," Ken'ichi admitted. "Don't throw away all those years."

"I don't know if I can face it," Yuudai reluctantly let slip. "I'm afraid I'll break down."

"Then we'll put you somewhere you can't be seen."

"Let's go then," Yuudai decided. "We'll be late."

By the time they arrived in the square, Kotone was pacing

restlessly behind the small platform erected next to the draped monument. "Finally," she exclaimed when the pair came into range. "I was wondering if I'd have to send out a search party."

"Sorry, Kotone," Yuudai mumbled, thoroughly chastised. "It's my fault."

"You're here now, that's all that matters." She gave him a peck on the cheek. "It's good to see you, Yuudai. You've been a stranger lately."

She turned to examine her husband with a critical eye. "What have you been doing, wrestling bears?" She brushed the dust off his tunic and moistened a corner of her sleeve to wipe a smudge from his face.

"Stop fussing, Kotone." Ken'ichi pushed her hands away. "We need to get started." He climbed onto the platform, holding up his arms and gesturing for people to be quiet.

"We are here today," he began in a voice that easily carried over the hushed crowd, "to celebrate the life of Fujiwara Aoshi. Whether or not you knew the commander, he had a profound effect on your life. He brought peace and prosperity where there had only ever been discord and despair. Every one of your lives was precious to him and he died to preserve and expand your rights."

"To that end, the council and I have followed through with his wishes for you. From this day onward the enslavement of human beings is prohibited. All existing slaves shall be given the option of freedom. If they choose to remain in their master's service they are required to be given food, clothing, shelter and medical care. Any slave who has been purchased in the last six months shall be required to continue to serve his master until the six month period has expired, during which time they will also be accorded basic rights."

Ken'ichi took a sip of water, eyeing the crowd to judge its reaction. "The other change we wish to announce is that, as of today, all children are guaranteed the opportunity to learn to read and write. Aoshi became a soldier almost as soon as he could walk, and he always felt hampered by his lack of education. It was his belief that the status you were born into shouldn't put limitations on who you could become. It is our hope that by enacting these reforms the people of Japan will become stronger, wiser, and more powerful than ever before in our history."

"Aoshi was more than just an amazing warrior, or a wise and

fair leader, however," the general continued when the applause and cheers that met his announcement died down. "He was, first and foremost, a surprising and intriguing man and I am privileged to have had the honor of being his friend. He strove always to see the good in people and to treat them accordingly. He was generous, loyal, and above all, forgiving. He will be remembered for his victories in battle, but his true worth was in the strength of his will and the purity of his heart."

Akemi shifted slightly to get a better view of the man he'd been silently observing, watching with morbid fascination as silent tears rolled down his cheeks. *Not yet, not yet,* he cautioned himself when the desire to give comfort grew nearly unbearable. *Kotone's smart, stick to her plan.* He ghosted closer to Yuudai, careful to remain hidden as he approached.

"This statue," Ken'ichi continued, "was commissioned to commemorate the anniversary of Aoshi's ascension to power. It is with both sadness and gratitude that I dedicate it to his memory, in the hope we will never forget his sacrifices, and as a promise to always strive to live up to his legacy." At that the general pulled off the large cloth draping the statue, revealing it for the first time. It showed Aoshi in full battle regalia but he was smiling broadly, and his right hand was held out in a gesture of peace.

When the statue was revealed the crowd went wild, cheering and applauding. The mood on the stage was very different; those closest to the warlord wiping tears from their eyes as they remembered the man they missed so badly.

Now, Akemi decided, and he slid behind Yuudai, wrapping his arms around his waist and leaning in close to whisper in his ear. "He forgave you for the worst betrayal imaginable. How could you possibly think he wouldn't have forgiven you again? He loved you too, you know. Even if it wasn't in the way you wanted. Aoshi wouldn't have wished this for you. Give both of you some peace, please."

The general's face twisted at Akemi's words. "I love you," he whispered, causing the courier's mouth to drop open in shock. "I love you and I pushed you away because it felt like I was betraying Aoshi. I felt responsible for his death. I thought if I was happy then I couldn't have really loved him and he would have suffered for nothing," Yuudai gasped between sobs. "I miss you so much. Please, come back. I'll never mention Aoshi again, I swear."

"Ssshhh, ssshhh," Akemi hummed soothingly. "Of course I'll come back, I love you too. I was jealous. I didn't understand, and I don't mind if you talk about the commander now that I know you care about me, too."

Kotone watched in satisfaction as the two men murmured comfortingly to each other before embracing and sharing a tender, lingering kiss. "My work here is done," she declared with satisfaction, causing Ken'ichi to roll his eyes exaggeratedly.

"Then let's go home." He took his wife's hand and headed off, anxious to see his daughter and newly appreciative of how lucky he really was.

Finally the square was empty, save for the towering figure of the warlord who continued his eternal vigil, silently keeping watch over his people.

Epilogue

Shinosuke finished his story and looked back up at the man he had so recently met.

"Aoshi's lover was a man?" Arthur asked in surprise.

"Hai. I'm sorry," Shinosuke replied in a disappointed tone. "I didn't realize it would offend you."

"Oh, no, no," the artist replied, waving his hands in front of his face. "It's nothing like that, not at all, I just never thought…"

"That men loved men in ancient times?" Ryuu asked with a chuckle.

"Well, yeah. It's not like we learned about it in any history class I ever took. It would have made class a lot more interesting."

"So, you're broad-minded?"

"I like men myself," Arthur admitted. "It would be hard for me not to be accepting, wouldn't it?"

"That is excellent news," Shinosuke replied. "Because you are a very handsome man. I would love to have dinner with you and tell you more about our beautiful city."

"Are you making a pass at me?" Arthur asked.

"Let's see how dinner goes first."

The pair set off, side by side, shoulders brushing provocatively. After several minutes of comfortable silence, Arthur finally spoke up. "Hey, Ryuu, did the warlord's slave die before he did?"

"The legend says they died together, but there's no way of knowing. We wouldn't even know Fujiwara-sama existed if it wasn't for that statue. Maybe it's all just a legend. The romantic in me wants to believe it's true, though."

"So, you're a romantic then?" the artist asked.

"Not usually," came the honest reply. "There's just something about that story that's always struck a chord in me. When I was a child I used to pretend I was Ryuu's reincarnation waiting for my Aoshi to come carry me away. My father did not approve."

"I know how that is," Arthur muttered. "I haven't spoken to my father in three years."

"When I was older," the dark-haired man continued almost dreamily, "I realized just how sad it would be forever looking for your lost love ... looking for love in general." He let out a sarcastic bark of laughter.

"I believe in love," Arthur heard himself say. *Although I don't have any reason to*, he reminded himself.

"Really?" Shinosuke said.

Dinner was a comfortable affair, the two men sprawled out across from each other at a low table, sipping sake and chatting as if they had known each other for years.

"So Arthur, may I walk you home?" Shinosuke asked with a sunny smile when they finally stood to leave.

"I hope so. I'm going to need help to find the inn. Hopefully they'll still have some rooms available."

"You don't already have a room?" Ryuu inquired hopefully.

"Not yet, I went exploring as soon as I arrived," Arthur admitted. "I know it was a bad idea."

"Not necessarily." Shinosuke moved closer, until he could feel the heat radiating from the artist's lean form. He eased forward and bought their lips together in a chaste kiss, letting out a loud groan when Arthur wrapped wiry arms around him and deepened it.

When they broke for air, Shinosuke husked, "Come home with me then. We'll talk more of love."

"I'd like that." Arthur wrapped an arm around his waist and tugged him close as they headed off into the night together.

~~~~

ABOUT THE AUTHOR

Sessha turned to writing full time after a twenty year stint in video production editing, scripting and creating motion graphics. Her short story *Wintersong* is included in *In Dreams*. Her Celtic fairy tale *Amadan na Briona* is part of eightcuts gallery's *Once Upon a Time in a Gallery* exhibit and is also included in *In Dreams*. Her short story *The Poetry Game* is included in *New Sun Rising:Stories for Japan*, an anthology for tsumani relief. Originally from Belfast, she lives in the States with her husband, son, a very old cat and too many swords.

More from This Author

SHADOW WOLF

Will love be sacrificed when duty and honor rule all?

The life of a shinobi is, at its best, a selfless devotion to duty. In modern day Japan, the ninja legends live on in a grim saga of political maneuverings, betrayal, sexual abuse, torture and dark homoeroticism.

The Shinobi clans lurk in the shadows, performing services that not even the hardened Yakuza will touch. Takahashi Yoshi fulfills his duty with soul-stripping resolve, each assignment driving a nail into a coffin of lost faith. After years of sexual abuse and torture in the name of clan honor, Yoshi must learn to trust, but the man who offers him hope is himself flawed. Sasaki Makoto has spent a career in torture and interrogation, exploring not only the dark secrets of his clan's enemies, but also the darkness within his own heart.

How far must Yoshi run to escape his shame and torment? And what price freedom when fear and self-loathing threaten to upend the hard fought struggle to find meaning and safety in a world fraught with danger.

Yoshi seeks time and space, only to find himself once more at the mercy of power mongers and despots. When Makoto finds him, Yoshi is broken in more than body. Near death, his spirit recedes to find safety within, locking out all who care.

They say time will heal but the path to acceptance is never easy, the roadblocks many and none will emerge unscathed as Yoshi embarks on a struggle for balance.

Short Stories from Sessha Batto

PERFECT MATCH

They are slaves to tough, dangerous, demanding jobs.
Both are desperate for companionship.
Neither believes himself worthy.
The matchmaker disagrees.

IN DREAMS

Sometimes the great divide between love and lust is not clear…

Wintersong

A chance meeting where one is bold enough to take the first steps and overcome the fear… But in the winter of their love, all Armand wants is to reconnect with Peter. In the end, some obstacles are too big to overcome.

Amandan na Briona: A Celtic Fairytale

Storms call them forth, riding the sky … or so it is said. But for Sean danger is nearer, his pursuer relentless, the vision inexplicable. When the unseleighe Court takes notice, more than evil rides the forests.

GEISHA

Duty and honor-bound, Yoshi draws on years of training to fulfill his clan's expectations and obligations, suppressing emotions to safeguard and protect both himself and those he's sworn to serve.

His current assignment is to the Shuhan of Mochizuki who deems that training unsuitable and launches Yoshi into the world of women, of the fabled Geisha, to learn the grace and skills his master desires. Pain Yoshi understood, humiliation was something else entirely.

And his keeper, Zenshiro, decides that while Geisha training is all well and good, the matter of seduction would be handled in a different fashion.

Keeping up the masquerade might be the biggest challenge Yoshi has ever faced

CPSIA information can be obtained
at www.ICGtesting.com
Printed in the USA
LVOW04s1932250916
506142LV00016B/575/P